WEDDING DAY DEAD

A MURDER ON MAUI MYSTERY

ROBERT W. STEPHENS

For Felicia Dames

1

THE MADNESS

THE MADNESS WAS TEMPORARY, AT LEAST I HOPED IT WAS. I DON'T EVEN know what caused it in the first place. I assumed it was greed. After all, most of us tell ourselves that some money is better than no money, but I've come to the conclusion that controlling one's sanity and blood pressure can be infinitely more valuable than having a few extra dollars in one's pockets.

The madness that overcame me was my decision to have a garage sale, or yard sale if you prefer that term. I think Dante referred to garage sales as the innermost circle of hell. If you're one of those people who fanatically visit garage sales on the weekend to search for that priceless gem, like an original copy of the U.S. Constitution hidden behind a worthless painting, or maybe one of those Hummel figurines that some people like to put on their mantels, I mean no disrespect, and I'm truly sorry if I have, in fact, offended you. But it's my humble opinion, after having hosted a few of these events, that garage sales bring out the worst in humanity. I can only imagine this is how the apocalypse might go - everyone for him or herself. All is fair in love, war, and garage sales.

I listed my garage sale as starting at 8 a.m. on a Saturday. I moved most of my items into the garage the night before, so I could easily take them into the yard the next morning. It took me hours to price everything, but I figured that was better than answering "How much is this?" a million times. I had a few fold-out tables on which to display the smaller items, and I went to the bank so I would have plenty of change for that person who would hand me a twenty dollar bill for an item that I had priced at twenty cents. I recruited my retired neighbor, Mrs. Coyer, to help me. She would handle the money, while I did the negotiations with the customers. Let's face it, no one ever pays the sticker price at a garage sale. Even if you list the item for free, someone will try to negotiate with you simply out of time-honored tradition.

I opened my garage door around 6 a.m. I thought two hours would be plenty of time to get everything staged. Imagine my surprise when I saw several people already standing in my driveway. They swarmed my belongings like a pack of vultures on a rotting carcass. I considered immediately slamming the door in their faces and running into my house to hide behind my sofa. In hindsight, I should have done that. However, at that moment, the madness still had me in its tight grip, and I saw the upcoming struggle as a battle to be won. I was convinced, naively as it turned out, that I would be declaring victory at the end of the day.

Mrs. Coyer must have been watching my plight from her kitchen window because she came out about fifteen minutes later to help control the herd. It was a fruitless effort. There was a steady stream of new customers over the next two hours, and by eight, the official start of my garage sale, most of the good items were gone. This caused the people who followed the guidelines of my ad to yell at me for selling items before the allotted time. How did I respond to that? I didn't. I just walked away and tried to obscure myself behind my yard tools and lawnmower.

Those few hours were some of the worst of my life. I had to contend with the thieves who didn't think I saw them shoving my belongings into their coat pockets, and there were liars who would tell Mrs. Coyer I quoted them a price substantially less than what I actually did. Do you think asking five dollars for a toaster that actually works is unreasonable? Apparently someone did because she was enraged that she would have to pay more than twenty-five cents for it.

Probably the most egregious act of the day came from an old guy who showed interest in my candle-making kit. I had a cardboard box filled with small metal molds and pots that I used years ago to make candles for Christmas gifts with an old girlfriend. The box stayed in the back of the closet ever since then and had collected a substantial amount of dust. I hoped to unload it for three dollars. This guy proceeded to walk around the yard and pick up everything made of metal. He then tossed those items into the box with the candle supplies and handed me three dollars. I informed him that the candle supplies were three dollars, but he still owed me for all the other stuff he tossed into the box. He reminded me that the box had a sign on it that said three dollars. I really didn't know how to respond to his logic, so I told the guy that the three dollars was for the supplies in the box. It wasn't designed to be an "everything you can fit in the box" price. The conversation after that comment went something like this.

"Well, I'm not interested in paying more than three dollars," the old guy said.

"Are you serious?" I asked.

"The box says three dollars."

"Yeah, but that's like going to Target, opening up an appliance box, and then cramming whatever else you can fit inside. You can't do that. Everyone knows the price refers to what's inside the box, not the box itself."

"Listen, man, you're going to lose a sale if you don't give me this stuff for three bucks."

"I can't believe we're actually having this conversation. What's wrong with you?"

"I'm walking if you don't give me this price."

"So walk. Get the hell out of here."

He shoved the three dollars back in his front pocket and stormed off.

Dear God, why did I do this to myself?

If a garage sale is the equivalent of enhanced interrogation, then Craigslist is not far behind. I decided to sell most of my large items, like furniture, on that website. Here's how that experience generally went. People would see my sofa on the site, and they would email me to set a time to come see it. They would then not show up and wouldn't bother to call or text to say they couldn't make it. Next, they would write me the following day and set a new time to see the sofa. No apology or reason for not showing the day before was ever offered. Again, they would not show. They would then write me a third time - still no apology - and my response would be to ignore them. I understand that we're all ultimately self-absorbed people. Let's face it, we all care infinitely more about our own issues than we do other people, but isn't there something called self-awareness? Why does it seem like most people have no clue how they come across to other people?

Forgive me for ranting. Like I said, the madness overcame me, and I'm clearly still struggling with the after-effects.

Allow me to introduce myself before I continue with the rest of my story. My name is Edgar Allan Rutherford. Yes, my parents were huge fans of the mystery writer Edgar Allan Poe. The name Edgar was not an easy name to grow up with, but by the time I reached high school, my friends took to calling me Poe. The nickname stuck, but you may call me Edgar if you wish. I'm no longer bothered by my birth name.

About a year ago, at the tender age of thirty-five, I was laid off from my job as an architect during the recession. I did nothing but watch Star Trek on Netflix and sit on my butt for the first six months of unemployment. I had the good fortune to be able to do that because my parents left me a sizable inheritance. I eventually got off the sofa when I finally decided to accept my best friend's long-standing invitation to visit him at his new home on Maui.

Foxx and I have been friends since we were children, and he wanted me to meet his girlfriend Lauren and see the sights on the island. I was as shocked as anyone who truly knows Foxx when he told me he was in a serious, committed relationship with Lauren.

Foxx is a huge guy. He once played professional football for the Washington Redskins until a knee injury ended his career. He's always had incredible success with women, but I never knew him to date one for longer than a week or two.

Lauren was different for some reason. She kept his interest, and apparently, she didn't take any of his garbage. Lauren was a world-famous artist by the way. I say "was" because she's unfortunately no longer with us. On my first evening in Maui, Lauren was brutally murdered - at an art show of all places. Foxx was arrested for the crime, and he looked guilty as hell. I would be lying to say I didn't have my doubts as to his innocence, but he is my best friend, so I set about starting my own investigation of the crime.

This brought me face-to-face with Detective Alana Hu, who arrested Foxx and had no suspicions that he might not be the guilty party. Alana is a stunning woman, easily the most beautiful person I've ever met. I was instantly captivated by her, but there was that tiny thing called a murder investigation standing between us. I eventually wore her down with my charm, though, and we've been dating for the last few months. For those of you who read *Aloha Means Goodbye*, you'll realize I'm over simplifying my relationship with Alana. It was quite up and down at the beginning, and my so-called "charm" is not exactly difficult to resist.

Eventually I discovered the identity of Lauren's real killer, and that person is now rotting behind prison bars. Don't worry, though, I wouldn't dream of ruining the surprise for you new readers by spilling the proverbial beans and telling you the name, or even the gender, of the guilty party.

After I decided to stay on Maui, I had to figure out what to do with my house and belongings in Virginia. I thought briefly about renting the house, but I had heard too many horror stories from friends about their brief and unpleasant experiences as landlords. Almost all of them had eventually gotten stiffed on the rent and ended up having to pay two mortgages at the same time while some freeloader stayed in their places. They also invariably returned to their rental properties to find holes in the walls, stained carpets, and in one case, a master bedroom and bathroom that was painted in polka dots.

I decided to spare myself the headaches. I flew back to Virginia to prep the house for sale. Most of the houses in my neighborhood were underwater. I was a little more fortunate because I had paid a sizeable down payment on the house and was also one of the early people to move into that particular housing development. I guess you could say I was on the front edge of the housing bubble.

I met with a real estate salesperson, and we agreed on a price that would hopefully sell the house quickly. This, unfortunately, caused one of my neighbors to confront me on my morning jog. He was also trying to sell his house, but he listed his for over $200,000 more than mine. He bought at the height of the bubble and didn't put any money down. Apparently he got one of those interest-only loans.

For a second there, I thought he might pull out a gun and shoot me. His face was blood red, and I thought he was going to give himself a heart attack while he blamed me for bringing down the prices in the neighborhood. I didn't try to reason with the guy, or explain to him that I wasn't the one that overpaid for a house. I also wasn't the one who wrecked the economy, but I did feel bad for him and realized how horrible it feels to have your back against the wall with no good options. I just listened to him rant, and he walked away after he tired himself out. I still can't believe those Wall Street thieves got away with it all.

I had my garage sale nightmare about a week after that encounter with the angry neighbor. The only items I decided to take with me to Maui were my camera, laptop, a box of my favorite books, and one suitcase of clothing. I didn't bother to pack my winter clothes, and most of my summer clothes were old and needed to be replaced.

About a month after the garage sale, I sold my house. I never met the couple who bought it, but my agent said they were a young military couple who got transferred into the area.

I scheduled my flight back to Maui for the day after my house closing. It was a risky schedule since I knew house closings are often postponed for one reason or another, but I was anxious to get back to the sunshine of Maui and even more anxious to get back to Alana.

The house closing went smoothly, and I was able to keep my scheduled flight. Somehow, the airline forgot to put me in the middle seat of the last row just in front of the bathroom. The flight was over-sold as usual, and everyone was fighting for overhead space for their overstuffed carry-on bags.

I saw something on that flight that I didn't think I'd ever see. One man - let's call him Man A - walked down the aisle and pulled a large bag behind him. He was clearly frustrated to see there was no space for the bag in the overhead compartments.

He stopped right beside me, reached up into the overhead compartment and removed another person's bag. He then placed his bag in the compartment and sat down in the aisle seat across from me. He completely left the other person's bag sitting in the aisle.

That bag belonged to Man B, who happened to be sitting in the aisle seat directly behind Man A. Man B proceeded to yell at Man A for what he had just done. Man A looked at Man B like he was completely crazy. He then accused Man B of being rude and said he couldn't understand why he was yelling at him. This only proceeded to make Man B even angrier.

Two flight attendants walked by, and neither of them said a word. Like your typical DMV or post office worker, they refused to make eye contact with either guy. I think there's a theory that if you don't look at the person or the problem, then you can't be accused of not doing anything to fix it. Oh, the little mind games we play with ourselves.

I was a bit concerned that if a fight actually broke out, I was going to be stuck right in the middle of it. Sure enough, Man B got out of his seat and started pointing his finger in Man A's face. This caused Man A to stand up, and I assumed a fight was inevitable.

One of the flight attendants finally appeared and threatened to kick them both off the plane. She listened to both their stories and decided to check both of their bags. This thoroughly pissed off men, especially Man B. I don't blame him, but I also understand the flight attendant's predicament. I managed to stay out of the whole thing. Thank God, she didn't ask me for my opinion of what happened. Both guys eventually sat down, and the plane finally pulled back from the gate.

The rest of the flight went by without incident. The couple who sat beside me were going back to Oahu to celebrate their twenty-fifth wedding anniversary. They had not been to the islands since their honeymoon. I found them to be a nice and charming couple, and it was a rare pleasure to spend those cramped hours talking to them. The experience came close to wiping out all of the negative energy I experienced during the boarding process.

We landed in Honolulu. I said goodbye to my new friends and wished them a wonderful anniversary trip. I walked the short distance to my new gate. It was only about an hour before my flight to Maui.

I called Alana to confirm my flight was on time. She was waiting for me in baggage claim at the Kahului airport. She was dressed in business attire, so I assumed she had driven directly from work. As usual, she looked fantastic. Alana is half Hawaiian and half Japanese. Her long black hair perfectly frames her face. Her body is slender and graceful. Her dark eyes are undoubtedly her best feature, at least as far as I'm concerned. She has a way of looking at me that leaves me utterly defenseless. She can get me to do anything in these moments. I hope that she doesn't realize that vulnerability of mine, but she's a woman, so I'm sure she is well aware of the power she holds over me. As I walked toward her, I remembered the first time I laid eyes on her. It was during a Halloween parade. She was the Little Mermaid, and I played the role of the captivated and enchanted man.

It had been a couple of months since I saw her last. Although we spoke every day by phone, I was surprised by how much I missed her. I guess that sounds harsh, and I don't mean it to, but the feeling was a bit overwhelming and a little disconcerting. I had not given myself over to someone so freely in such a long time.

I think as we get older, and we experience the pains and heart-breaks that every relationship has, we instinctively start to hold a part of ourselves back. Maybe it's a form of self-protection - sort of a feeling that if we hold that small portion back from the other person, then that's something that can never be hurt. However, it was different with Alana. I held back nothing. I don't believe it was a conscious decision on my part. It just happened, and I wasn't even aware that it happened until that moment at the airport. I wasn't sure if that was ultimately self-destructive on my part or whether I would come to regret it later. I hoped it wasn't and that I wouldn't. But no one can predict the future, least of all me.

I kissed Alana hello, and we told each other how much we missed the other and how great it was to be reunited. Being with her was more than worth the hassle of the garage sale, the house closing, and the long flight back to the island with psychopathic guys fighting over bags.

Alana and I didn't have to wait long for my belongings to start coming down the baggage ramp. I grabbed one of those airport carts and put my suitcase, box of books, and laptop bag on it. We pushed the cart out to her car and drove to Alana's favorite sushi restaurant, which was not far from the police station where she worked.

I had my usual rainbow and California rolls, while Alana had the sashimi. We each had a large hot sake, and she was gracious enough not to laugh too hard when I told her my tale of sorrow and pain regarding the garage sale.

After dinner, we drove back to her house, and a few minutes after arriving, we were in her bed. We made love and collapsed on our backs, completely worn out and content. How did I get so lucky?

2

MAUI THE DOG

AFTER MOVING TO MAUI, I STARTED SEARCHING FOR AN APARTMENT, but Foxx convinced me to stay with him. He argued there was no reason to rush into finding a place when I really didn't know the island that well. It was a sound argument, but I thought it was more about Foxx not wanting to be alone. After all, his girlfriend had been murdered, and he had just gotten out of jail. That would shake the strongest of us.

In addition to being company for Foxx, the location of the house added another benefit. Lauren had been quite wealthy from the success of her art, and she had purchased one of the most beautiful homes in Ka'anapali, one of the most exclusive parts of Maui. The home sits on a gorgeous piece of property that overlooks the Pacific Ocean.

I loved spending the morning jumping in the pool and the evening watching the sun set into the water. It's quite a life, but there's always a part of me that feels guilty for being here and enjoying the place so much. This house belonged to Lauren. I didn't know her well at all. I only met her briefly before her life was tragically cut short. I discovered that a lot of people didn't like her. Many accused her of stealing their ideas and their work, but she was still a human being. She deserved better than what she got.

Lauren's death caused her already-expensive art to skyrocket in price. She left her fortune to Foxx and all of the sales of her remaining art also went to him. He was set for life, but his time in jail had left him questioning everything about his life and what he wanted out of it. Like me, I don't think he had a clue what he should do next. He was a retired professional football player with no need to work ever again. I was an ex-architect with no desire to design anything ever again, and although I wasn't as wealthy as Foxx, my parents' hard work and careful financial planning left me wanting for nothing. I guess he and I were both sort of lost when it came to deciding what path we wanted our futures to take, but neither of us seemed in a hurry to figure it out. I realize these are amazing problems to have.

So how did I spend my carefree days? Most of my time was spent photographing the island and spending as much time as I could, usually at night, with Alana. She worked a lot of hours as a detective, especially for an island as small and slow as Maui, but somehow that made our time together even more valuable. We talked briefly about moving in together, but ultimately decided we didn't want to rush things. It was kind of silly, though, because we practically lived together anyway. I spent a few nights a week at her house, and she spent at least one or two nights with me at Foxx's place. Life was good, and even though I didn't know what direction my life should go, I was content to stay on cruise control and not overthink things.

Just when you think things are going beyond great, the universe comes along and punches you upside your head.

The tale started on a Saturday. I remember this because it was exactly one week from the surprise wedding. I started my day as I usually did by climbing out of bed and making my way out to the swimming pool. I dove in and felt the cool water instantly wake me up. I dried myself off and walked to the kitchen to make myself a breakfast of cereal and soy milk.

I turned on the tiny television on the kitchen counter to listen to the news. I still don't know why I insist on watching the news. It usually just leaves me depressed, as do many of the commercials and public service announcements. Am I the only one who frantically searches for the TV remote so I can quickly turn the channel every time that Sarah McLachlan commercial for animal adoption comes on? It's depressing and manipulative, which I realize is completely the point. Unfortunately, or fortunately depending on how you look at it, it wore me down after about the tenth time I saw it.

It had been about twenty years since I last owned a dog. I was so devastated by his death that I swore I would never have a dog again. Maybe you think I'm being overly sentimental for getting so upset over the loss of an animal, but for those of you who have had the pleasure of owning a furry companion, you know the pain I speak of when they pass to the great beyond.

I had been thinking about buying a dog for a few weeks now. Sarah's latest blatant manipulation of my heartstrings pushed me over the edge, and I decided to spend my morning in search of a hound.

I pointed my car in the direction of the nearest dog pound. Actually, it was Lauren's BMW Z3 convertible. Foxx offered to sell it to me, and I initially declined. I actually declined several times. I just felt like it was yet another way I was profiting from Lauren's death. Foxx convinced me, though, that he was going to sell it to someone, and it may as well be me. So I bought the little silver car. I loved driving it, even though it was without a doubt the most impractical vehicle on the road.

I drove the several miles to the dog pound and pulled into the parking lot. The building looked like two trailers put together. The walls were paper thin, and I could hear the dogs barking from out in the parking lot. I entered the building and told the attendant of my intentions to adopt a dog. She enthusiastically showed me around as I silently cursed Miss McLachlan. All the dogs had that helpless and pitiful look while they sat in their tiny cages. I wanted to adopt them all but knew that would be insanity. I made my way from cage to cage, and then I saw him. He looked like he weighed about ten pounds. He had a silver face and legs, and a black body and tail.

"What's this little guy?" I asked.

"He's one of those new breeds."

"New breed?"

"He's a mix between a Maltese and a Yorkie."

"So he's a mutt?" I asked.

"You could say that, but the breed is actually called a Morkie."

"How old is he?"

"He's about a year. His owner moved back to the mainland and couldn't take him with her."

How could anyone leave this little guy behind? I thought.

"What's his name?" I asked.

"George."

I cringed. George was the name of a guy I met during Lauren's murder investigation. He lied to me repeatedly and eventually tried to kill me. The dog's name would have to change.

"Is he full grown yet?" I asked.

"He may gain another pound or two as he matures."

I leaned toward the cage.

"Well, little guy, what do you say?"

The dog barked once, and I took that to mean he was cool with going home with me.

I turned to the attendant.

"I'll take him."

The attendant sold me a small bag of dog food and gave me George's vet records. I carried the dog outside and put him down on the ground and hoped he would use the bathroom before I put him in the car. He lifted his leg and peed on the front steps of the dog shelter. Then he kicked his back legs several times, as if to wash the dirt of the shelter off his tiny paws. He took one last look at the building, and then turned and walked toward my car. I'm not sure how he knew which was the right car, but this little guy was already starting to impress me.

I put the dog in the front passenger seat and popped the roof back so he'd enjoy the wind through his fur. Yes, I know. I was spoiling him already.

I drove straight for Alana's house, anxious to show her my new friend. I usually pull into her driveway, but there was already another car there when I arrived, so I parked on the street. The dog stood up in the seat of the car and balanced himself by placing his front paws on the top of the car door. He looked toward her house, and I wondered if he thought I was taking him to his old home. Poor guy. I assumed he missed his original owner badly.

I picked up the dog and carried him to the front door. I would need to buy a leash soon. I rang the bell and after several long seconds, Alana swung the door open. It was obvious from the sour look on her face that something wasn't right.

"You okay?" I asked.

"Fine," she said.

She looked at the dog in my arms.

"So that commercial finally broke you down."

"Yeah, what can I say?"

Alana scratched the dog behind his ears, and that little gesture seemed to make them both feel better, not that the dog was feeling bad to begin with. She stepped aside, and I walked into the house. I put the dog down, and he dashed into the back room.

"Looks like he already knows his way around," Alana said. "Is he house trained?"

"I hope so," I said.

"Hey there, cutie. Who are you?" I heard an unfamiliar female voice say from the other room.

"Who's that?" I asked.

Alana didn't say anything. She simply turned and walked toward the direction of the voice. I followed her, thoroughly confused as to what was going on.

To say I was floored when I got to the back room would be the understatement of the year. There, standing side by side with Alana, was her identical twin.

"Hello there," the twin said.

"Hi," I said.

"Poe, this is my sister, Hani," Alana said.

"Her younger sister," Hani said.

So they weren't twins. But you caught the reference to "younger" sister, I'm sure. Alana certainly wasn't old by any means, unless you consider thirty old. It didn't take a genius to pick up the tension between the siblings.

"This is my boyfriend, Poe," Alana said.

"Boyfriend? Why haven't I heard anything about him?" Hani asked.

I'm sure you're assuming my feelings would be hurt since Alana apparently hadn't mentioned me to her sister. But they weren't. I was too confused by the situation. Before I could comment, though, the dog ran up to Alana and put his front paws on her lower legs.

"What's his name?" Hani asked.

"Maui. Maui the dog," I said.

I'm not entirely sure why I said Maui. I certainly didn't think up the name on the drive over. It just came out of my mouth and was as big a surprise to me as to you.

"Hello, Maui the dog," Hani said.

Hani bent over to pat him, but he backed away from her. He didn't growl or anything. He just didn't want to be touched by her. Was he picking up something that I wasn't?

I looked at Alana and saw a smile on her face. She noticed the dog's slight too.

Hani stood back up and did her best to ignore the fact Maui the dog just dissed her.

"So, how did you and my sister meet?" Hani asked.

"On a murder investigation," I said.

"Was it the one involving the artist Lauren Rogers?"

"The one and the same."

Hani turned to Alana.

"I read about it. You certainly made everyone proud when you solved the case."

"Actually," Alana said, "it was Poe who solved the mystery."

"Really?" Hani turned back to me. "So you're showing up my sister? I'm surprised she continued to date you after that."

"Actually I couldn't have solved it without her. I thought we made a great team," I said.

"A gentleman too, refusing to take all the credit," Hani said.

"Have you been on Maui all this time, and I just haven't seen you?" I asked.

"I grew up here with Alana, but for the last year, I've been living in L.A. I'm a model."

I just nodded. I really didn't know how to respond to that, so I kept my mouth shut. Who tells people within the first few minutes of meeting them that they're a model? She certainly had the looks to be a model. She was downright gorgeous, but why brag about it?

"So you just came back here to visit family?" I asked after several long moments of uncomfortable silence between the three of us, four if you count the dog.

"I'm getting married next Saturday," Hani said.

Alana looked away. I had no idea why her sister's wedding would piss her off so much. I was sure she would tell me later.

"Congratulations," I said.

Hani smiled at me, and I smiled back.

Maui the dog barked once. I looked down at him. He was standing by my feet and looking straight up at me. I wasn't sure exactly what he meant by the bark, but if I had to guess, I think he was saying things were about to get weird.

3

WHAT ARE FRIENDS FOR IF NOT TO MAKE YOU FEEL UNCOMFORTABLE?

THE NEXT MORNING PROVED TO BE ALMOST AS STRANGE AND unexpected as meeting Alana's sister. The night before I put a towel down on the floor beside my bed for Maui to sleep on, but he preferred to sleep on my dirty clothes instead. He must have been waiting for me to wake up because he leaped to his feet the moment mine touched the floor. He followed me to the back door. I slid the door open. Maui barked once and then raced outside. That's when I saw them.

"What the hell?" Foxx asked.

I looked up and saw Maui the dog standing at the edge of the pool. He barked once more at Foxx who was in the pool with a very attractive and naked young woman. It was obvious from this short distance that Maui and I had caught them in the act. Foxx is a big man, just over six foot four and weighing around two hundred and forty pounds. He easily dwarfed the woman with him in the pool.

"Sorry," I said.

"Who the hell is that?" Foxx grumbled.

"Your new roommate," I said and walked back inside the house. I turned to the dog, who continued to watch Foxx.

"Maui, come."

The dog turned and ran into the house. I slid the door shut and tried to erase the image of what I had just seen from my brain. I fed the dog and gave him water. He seemed content in his new home.

An hour later, Alana picked me up, and we drove toward our surfing spot. She had been giving me surfing lessons for the last few weeks. Although I still wasn't very good, I had shown some small improvement. Unfortunately she was still in a bad mood. I wasn't sure if I should ask questions or just wait for her to talk when she was ready.

We pulled up to the beach, and there was no one there. We took the surfboards off the roof and carried them down to the water. Alana walked into the ocean without even saying anything to me. It was definitely going to be a tense morning.

I followed Alana into the water. We both paddled to our usual spot and waited for a wave to come. The first wave approached, and I didn't make a move because I assumed Alana would take it. She didn't. The next wave came and then another. Neither of us moved. I wasn't wearing a watch, but I could have sworn a good ten minutes went by with neither of us saying a word. Finally, Alana broke the silence.

"She wants us to have dinner with them tonight."

"Hani and her fiancé?" I asked.

"Yes."

"Is that something you want to do?"

"No, and I've been trying all morning to come up with a good excuse to get out of it."

"Just say you have to work," I suggested.

"I thought about that. But sooner or later, I'm going to have to see them both."

"Have you met her fiancé before?" I asked.

"Yes, he used to live here on the island."

"Nice guy?"

"Depends who you ask," she said.

"Well," I said, "I thought I was asking you."

"Then, no, he's not a nice guy."

"The dinner is up to you. It doesn't matter one way or the other to me," I said.

"I don't even want to go to that damn wedding, but I don't see how I can get out of it. She wants me to be her maid of honor."

"Makes sense. You seem the logical choice."

"Not really. We can't stand each other," she said.

"Sorry to hear that."

"Don't be. Sometimes that's just the way it is."

"So let's not go to dinner. No reason for you to do something you don't want to do."

Alana said nothing, and it was quite obvious she was struggling to make up her mind. Finally, she spoke.

"Let's just do it and get it over with."

A wave rolled in, and Alana took it. Her form was graceful, as usual. Another perfect wave appeared a few seconds later, but I ignored it. I couldn't stop wondering what it was that had her so upset. I'd never seen Alana like that before. There's nothing like family to really piss you off.

Alana didn't feel like surfing anymore, so she drove me back to the house. She promised to call me later in the day and give me the time for dinner. I kissed her goodbye, and she sped off. I saw Foxx's car was still in the driveway as I walked to the house. I wondered if he and the mystery lady were still at it in the pool. I didn't see them there, nor did I see them in the house. His bedroom door was closed though, so it wasn't hard to imagine what they were up to.

I really didn't have anything to do that day, so I just hung out at the pool with Maui the dog. He sat under my chair to give himself some shade. A couple of hours later, Foxx emerged from the house. His hair was a mess, and he looked exhausted. He walked over to me.

"How's it going, buddy?" he asked.

"Fine. How are you? You look a little hungover."

"Yeah. Probably had a few too many."

Foxx's nickname is Five Beers. As you can imagine, it centered on his ability to consume a large amount of alcohol in a short amount of time. It was a name he'd grown to hate, so I tended not to use it unless I really wanted to give him a hard time.

Foxx looked around the yard.

"You know, I could have sworn I saw a dog here earlier."

Maui the dog must have known that was his cue. He barked once.

"What the hell was that?" Foxx asked.

"He's under my chair," I said.

Foxx kneeled and looked at the dog.

"What the hell is he?"

"He's a Morkie. His name's Maui the dog."

Maui appeared from under the chair. He walked up to Foxx and rolled onto his back.

"Manipulative little bastard, isn't he?" Foxx said.

"Sorry. I should have consulted you first," I said.

"It's no big deal. As long as I don't step in his shit, we'll be good."

"Who was the girl?" I asked.

Foxx smiled.

"Michelle. Met her at Harry's two nights ago."

Harry's was a bar in Lahaina that Foxx and I had been frequenting. It had a laidback, locals' feel to it, and it was a few blocks away from Front Street, which tends to draw the most tourists because of its heavy dose of clothing shops, art galleries, and ice cream parlors.

"Here on vacation?" I asked.

"No, she just moved here with a friend. She asked me to show her around the island."

"And you thought the best place to start was at your house," I said.

"Naturally. The thing is, I wasn't even trying to get her. It just sort of happened. We spent all day and night together."

"You have a way about you, Foxx. I'm envious."

"You? This from the guy dating Alana," he said.

"Speaking of Alana, did you know she had a younger sister?"

"I think I heard that, but I never met her. Why do you ask?"

I told Foxx about meeting Hani the day before and her sudden appearance to announce her mystery wedding. I asked him if he had heard anything about the tension between Alana and Hani.

"Can't say I have, but I can ask around if you want," Foxx said.

"No, don't do that. I'll find out soon enough."

Unfortunately, I found out that night, and I wished I hadn't.

Alana called me later that day and told me to pick her up around seven o'clock. I drove over to her house in the convertible. The weather was perfect, and there wasn't a cloud in the sky. Alana was waiting for me on her front porch when I pulled up. I wondered if she was anxious to see me or just ready to get the night over. She was still in a rotten mood, but she looked terrific. She wore a pair of white shorts and a loose top. Her black hair was down.

She directed me to a steak house about twenty minutes away. It was in Lahaina, like Harry's Bar, but square in the middle of tourist land. I had driven by it before but had yet to try it out, mainly because of said tourists. I don't consider myself a local yet, but I have no desire to be around families on vacation with screaming kids while I try to enjoy dinner. Alana and I got there a few minutes before our reservation time, so we decided to wait outside for Hani and her fiancé. They arrived just a few minutes after we did.

They pulled up in a black Lamborghini Aventador. I assumed the guy was short in multiple ways and was obviously overcompensating. I'm six foot two, so I tend to be taller than most guys. It's my childish way of exerting some small amount of superiority. But when Hani's fiancé got out of the car, it was obvious he was taller than me. He looked about six-four, maybe even six-five. The guy was ripped, like he'd just jumped off the cover of a men's fitness magazine. I had been working out quite a lot since moving to the island, and I was now in pretty good shape. But I had to admit, I looked nothing like this guy. He had muscles on top of muscles. He also had movie star good looks. A young George Clooney had nothing on him.

Hani waved to us. Neither Alana nor I waved back. Hani was dressed a lot like Alana. She had on shorts and a tight tank top that showed off her figure. I had called it right earlier. The woman was gorgeous. The muscle-bound fiancé wore khaki pants and a silk shirt.

Hani walked up to Alana and hugged her. Alana hugged her back, but I could tell there was no affection in the gesture. Then the fiancé approached us.

"Hello, Alana," he said.

He smiled at her. Alana didn't smile back.

"Hello, Panos," she said.

At least I now knew the guy's name.

"Panos, this is Alana's boyfriend, Poe," Hani said.

Panos turned to me and offered a hand.

"Hello, Poe."

"Hello," I said.

We shook hands, and I was surprised he didn't try to crush mine.

We walked into the restaurant, but not before I noticed the sign above the door, which read "the View." Who the hell names their restaurant after that god-awful TV show? The lobby of the restaurant was walled in dark wood. White and red tropical flowers were artfully placed throughout. There was a small hostess stand in the center of the lobby with the name of the restaurant on the wall just behind it. Overall, the place had a very high-class feel.

I thought the hostess was going to break a speed record, though, when she ran from behind the stand to hug Panos. So much for classy.

"Shae!" Panos exclaimed.

He kissed her on the cheek, and they exchanged pleasantries. She told him how great it was to have him back on the island, and he told her how wonderful it was to see her and the restaurant again. I looked at Hani to see how she was dealing with this obvious display of affection between her guy and the hostess. Hani had a smile plastered on her face. I didn't know her well enough to know if it was genuine or one of those "I'm-going-to-kill-you-later" smiles women can do.

After a couple of minutes of listening to them talk and ignore the rest of us, we were shown to a table in the back corner that offered a terrific view of the ocean. I noticed on the way to the table that the restaurant was half full at best. Maybe the food wasn't that great, or maybe I was about to pay three hundred dollars for a steak dinner. Shae handed us our menus and made Panos promise to come see her again.

Our waitress appeared, and the same scene repeated itself. She ignored the three of us while she lavished all of her attention on Panos. I looked at Hani again. She still had that plastered smile. I turned to Alana. She seemed more annoyed than ever. I turned back to the waitress, and I wouldn't have been surprised if the waitress jumped on Panos' lap while she took our orders based on the way she giggled at everything he said.

I scanned through the menu and confirmed my original suspicion that I would have to rob a bank to cover the cost of an entrée and drink. I did notice, much to my surprise, that Panos was one of the owners of "the View." His photo, along with another man, was featured prominently on the back cover of the menu. There was an accompanying story detailing how Panos and Wes, his co-owner, opened the restaurant a few years ago and, of course, were dedicated to the usual tenets of quality food, attentive service, and fair prices. But you tell me, is sixty-five bucks a fair price for prime rib?

The waitress reluctantly left the table after I ordered last. I thought she might go into Panos withdrawal before she reached the computer where she input our orders for the kitchen staff.

Panos turned to me.

"So, Hani tells me you and Alana met on a murder investigation."

I nodded.

"Is that what you do? A private investigator?" he asked.

"No, it was more of a one-time thing," I said.

"So what do you do?" he asked.

"I just moved to the island. I'm still trying to figure out what I want to do," I said. I felt like a complete zero.

"Of course, of course," he replied. "Well, you're certainly one lucky man to end up with Alana."

He turned to Alana, but she didn't smile at his compliment.

"Yes, I am," I replied.

"I'm so glad you agreed to have dinner with us," Panos told Alana. "I was worried you wouldn't see me."

Alana said nothing. I was tempted to ask what the hell was going on, but I kept my mouth shut.

Panos turned to me.

"Sometimes things can be cold between former lovers," he said.

"Former lovers," I repeated more than asked.

"Yes, Alana and I were once an item. But it was not meant to be."

Hani reached over to Panos and held his hand. I wasn't sure if she was doing that female hand squeeze that says "Shut the hell up" or if it was a natural display of affection. Maybe she was trying to emphasize to Alana that Panos was now hers. Either way, I really didn't care.

"That's interesting to hear, Panos," I said.

Hani turned to me.

"You didn't know?" she asked.

I smiled. She turned to Alana.

"You didn't tell him?" she asked.

"No, I wanted more time, but you insisted on dinner tonight," Alana said.

We were saved when a man walked over to our table.

"I heard you were back in town," the man said.

Panos stood and hugged the man, but I could sense the tension between them.

Panos turned to us.

"This is Wes, my business partner," Panos said.

So he did own the restaurant. This was shaping up to be a shitstorm of an evening. Panos showed up in a Lamborghini, we're eating at a place he owns, and now I've found out he used to bang my girlfriend. How nice.

"I wish you had told me you were coming," Wes said to Panos.

"But then it wouldn't have been a surprise." Panos laughed.

"I really need to talk to you," Wes said.

"Some other time. Tonight is a time for celebration."

"Then when? Every time I call you, you say some other time."

"I promise. We'll get together this week before my wedding."

Panos sat down.

"I have your word?" Wes asked.

"Yes, yes, of course."

Wes nodded to us and walked away.

"So, you own this place," I said.

"Yes, Wes and I opened it a few years ago."

"It must be difficult running a restaurant from Los Angeles," I said.

"Wes is more of the general manager. I would just bring in the customers."

So that explained the lack of a crowd. Panos was the draw, but he was thousands of miles away.

Panos held up his glass of wine.

"I'd like to propose a toast - to sisters reuniting."

He turned to Hani.

"And to my beautiful bride-to-be."

Hani smiled.

We joined our glasses together. I was tempted to throw mine at Panos, but I just smiled and sipped my wine. This was going to be a long dinner.

The food was okay at best, but I really wasn't in the mood to enjoy it anyway. We spent most of the evening being interrupted by Panos' friends coming to our table. It didn't seem to bother Hani. She just smiled throughout the evening. I didn't look at Alana that much. I was royally upset with her for not telling me about her relationship with Panos. On my first date with Alana, I sensed she had come out of a bad relationship and was hesitant to date again. I spent the evening wondering if it was the relationship with Panos that had almost stood in the way of Alana and me. How could it not be? She was clearly in pain. I didn't know how much animosity there was between Alana and Hani and whether it was 100 percent over Panos. Part of me didn't really want to know. I just wanted this damn dinner to end.

Panos informed us the dinner was on the house. At least I had that going for me. We walked outside and said our goodbyes at the cars. Panos and Hani climbed in their car and drove away. Alana and

I just stood beside my car and watched them leave. Well, this is about to get worse, I thought. We got into my convertible and left. I expected Alana to immediately apologize now that we were alone, but she said nothing the entire drive back to her house. I pulled into her driveway. She didn't invite me in, which was fine since I didn't want this evening to last any longer. But she didn't say anything. No good night. No nothing. She climbed out of the car and started for the door.

"You have nothing to say?" I asked.

She stopped but didn't turn around to face me.

"What would you have me say?" she asked.

"I don't know. An explanation. Maybe a simple heads-up about your relationship with the guy before I went to dinner with him."

Alana turned to me.

"I'm sorry. I should have said something this morning. I intended to. I just didn't know what to say."

"What am I missing here? It's not like I thought you never dated anyone before me."

"We dated for about six months, and then he left me for my sister. Shortly after that, they moved to Los Angeles."

"How long ago was that?"

"Less than a year. She's tried to contact me a million times, but I haven't spoken or emailed either of them since they left the island."

"So your relationship with Panos ended just a few months before you met me?" I asked.

Alana nodded.

"You still could have told me," I said.

"I should have, and I'm sorry."

Alana turned and walked toward the house. I just stayed in the car and watched her the entire way. She pulled out a key and unlocked her front door. She entered her house and shut the door behind her. She didn't even wave goodbye.

I started the car and drove back to Foxx's. His car wasn't in the driveway. I assumed he was with Michelle or maybe another girl he'd met at Harry's Bar. I opened the front door and was greeted by Maui the dog racing toward me. At least someone was glad to see me.

I took him for a walk around the neighborhood, and he did his business. Then he and I went into the backyard and sat by the pool while I listened to the ocean waves. The dog walked to me and rolled onto his back. I scratched his belly.

How did everything go so horribly wrong tonight? I wondered.

I would call Alana in the morning. Maybe she would be in a better mood. Maybe things would improve.

But I was wrong. Things were about to get much, much worse.

4

THE SEA SERPENT

I GOT UP EARLY THE NEXT MORNING AND TOOK THE DOG FOR A WALK again. I took him around to the back yard and jumped into the pool to wake myself up. I climbed out of the pool and plopped down on one of the chairs. Within a few minutes, Foxx slid open the glass door.

"Hey, Poe, look who's here," Foxx said.

He walked outside. Alana was a few steps behind him. Maui the dog raced around the pool and ran up to her. The dog completely ignored Foxx.

"What? I don't get a hello? It's my house you're living in, dog," Foxx said.

But Maui the dog continued to ignore him as Alana rubbed him behind his ears.

"How did last night go?" Foxx asked.

Alana shot him a look.

"That good, huh?" he said.

"Were you showing Michelle the island last night?" I asked Foxx, trying to change the subject.

Foxx smiled.

"Who's Michelle?" Alana asked.

"A friend I met a few nights ago," Foxx said.

"A friend?" Alana asked.

"She's new to the island," I said. "Foxx has been kind enough to volunteer his services as a tour guide."

"I'm sure," Alana said.

"What are you two lovebirds up to today?" Foxx asked.

"That's actually why I'm here," Alana said, and she turned to me. "Hani has invited us out on their boat."

"You're actually thinking of going?" I asked.

"I don't want to."

"Then why do it?"

"Because I need to get over this. She's my sister. I can't spend the rest of my life avoiding her."

Alana turned back to Foxx.

"You're invited too. You can even bring your new friend."

"And Panos?" I asked.

"He's going to be my brother-in-law. I need to accept that."

Alana walked over to me.

"I'm sorry I didn't tell you about him. I was embarrassed. When Panos left me for my sister, I was humiliated. I didn't want to even think about it, and I was worried you'd get upset if you knew I dated him."

I didn't know how to respond, so I said nothing.

"Will you come with me today? I don't think I can get through it without you," she said.

I certainly didn't want to spend the day with my girlfriend's ex-boyfriend. Would you? I was stunned by her change in attitude. It didn't make sense to me, but I didn't know how to get out of it without creating even more tension with Alana.

"I'll go," I said, "on the one condition that Foxx goes with us. I need some kind of buffer between me and that guy."

"What's wrong with him?" Foxx asked.

"He drives a Lamborghini Aventador," I said.

"Huh, must be compensating," Foxx said. "Count me in. It's been a long time since I've been out on a boat. I'll give Michelle a call."

Foxx laughed and walked back into the house.

"Do you forgive me?" Alana asked.

"Sure," I said. "Just no more surprises."

Alana leaned down and kissed me. Maui the dog tapped her on her lower leg with one of his paws. She looked at him. He wagged his tail.

"Pushy little guy, isn't he?" Alana said.

A few hours later, Alana and I were on the dock where Panos kept his boat. It was a forty foot sailboat with a beautiful, sleek design that must have cost him a small fortune. We were the first to arrive, so we just sat down on the dock and let our legs hang over the side as we looked out to the ocean. The deep-blue sky matched the water perfectly, and it was difficult to tell where the two met on the horizon. It should be a fun day of sailing if I could keep myself from getting riled up by Panos.

"Do you know if they intend to go back to L.A. after the wedding?" I asked.

"I don't know," Alana said. "But I assume so."

"It would be nice if they did."

"Yeah," Alana said.

"Hey, you two," Foxx yelled.

Alana and I turned to see Foxx walking down the dock with Michelle. I had only seen her once before, and it was only a partial view at that. As was usually the case, though, Foxx had found another looker. Her hair was as black as Alana's, but her skin was pale. She was maybe a few inches taller than Alana. She had a small waist that seemed to accentuate her large breasts. I tried not to stare, but it was difficult. What did I tell you before? Foxx had a way with women.

"She's pretty," Alana said. She turned to me.

"She's okay, a solid five," I said.

"Really?" Alana replied.

"No real comparison to you," I said.

"Good boy," she said. She sounded like she was talking to Maui the dog. I halfway expected her to pat me on the head.

Alana and I stood as Foxx and Michelle walked up to us.

"This is his boat?" Foxx asked.

"We think so," Alana said.

Foxx looked over the boat's smooth lines.

He whistled. "Hell of a beauty."

"Hi, I'm Alana." Alana extended her hand to Michelle.

"I'm Michelle."

"Sorry," Fox said. "This is my best friend, Poe, and his girlfriend, Alana. This is Michelle. She just moved to Maui."

I shook hands with Michelle.

"How do you know the owner?" Michelle asked.

"Alana used to date the guy," Foxx blurted out.

I could have killed him, and Foxx caught the meaning of my glare.

"What? Better to get it all out in the open," Foxx said.

"It's okay. His name is Panos," Alana said.

As if on cue, Panos and Hani drove up.

"You weren't kidding about the Lamborghini," Foxx said. "Gorgeous car."

Panos and Hani made their way down to the dock, and we introduced them to Foxx and Michelle. Foxx and I helped Panos cast off the lines while Alana, Hani, and Michelle made their way to the bow of the boat. Within a few minutes, we pulled away from the dock.

We sailed for a couple of hours. The views were spectacular as expected. I did my best to avoid Panos, but it was difficult. The guy had a huge personality, and I couldn't help but constantly compare myself to him. It was easy to see why everyone liked him. He was funny, good-looking, and he had charm to spare. He was the type of person you just notice when he walked in the room. I didn't want to admit it, but I understood why Alana would want to date him. I also couldn't stop wondering what he and I had in common that would make Alana interested in us both. It wasn't that he made me feel bad about myself. We were just so different.

Alana seemed okay during the initial part of the trip. She spent most of the time speaking with Foxx and Michelle. Hani seemed to prefer not leaving Panos' side. It was almost like she expected us to try to steal the guy, even though we were on a boat.

We eventually made our way into a small, secluded cove. Panos dropped the anchor.

"My sister and I used to come here to swim," Panos said. "There's no way to get to this beach except by boat. We have the whole place to ourselves."

Panos walked to the bow where the women were sunbathing. He turned to Foxx and me.

"Poe, Foxx, join me for a swim?" he asked.

"I didn't bring my swimsuit," I said.

"Neither did I," Panos said.

Then he dropped his shorts in front of the women. I'm pretty sure I heard Michelle gasp. Foxx and I were wrong about the Lamborghini. Panos was not compensating for anything. He was hung like a porn star. Either that or he had a sea serpent trapped between his legs. Panos turned to the women.

"Anyone is welcome to join me," he said.

Then Panos dove overboard. He had the grace of an Olympic diver. I decided then and there that I hated him with every fiber in my body. I watched him swim to the shore. He actually had the arrogance to do the backstroke.

"What the hell," Foxx said. "Let's do it."

Foxx walked to the bow, tossed his pants near Panos', and dove overboard.

Alana looked at me. I wasn't sure if she wanted me to join Foxx and Panos. I'm not embarrassed about myself, and I want to make it abundantly clear that I am above average when it comes to that department, but there was no way I could compare my equipment to his Loch Ness Monster.

I looked back to the shore. Panos climbed out of the water and walked naked onto the beach. Foxx wasn't that far behind.

"Are you going to join them?" Hani asked.

She smiled at me, and I couldn't tell if she was making fun of me or not.

"You don't have to go if you don't feel like it," Alana said.

"Why wouldn't he?" Hani asked. "The water's spectacular."

Hani then took off her clothes and jumped into the water.

"Wait for me," Michelle said.

She removed her clothes too and leaped overboard. Alana and I were the only ones left on the boat. We were also the only ones with clothes on. Panos had beaten me again.

"Do you want to join them?" Alana whispered.

"No, what I want to do is fire up this boat's engine and leave their bare asses there on that beach. But I can't very well do that, can I?"

"Don't get snippy with me," Alana said.

"Sorry. You just failed to mention you dated a porn star."

"Now you're being vulgar," she said.

"If the shoe fits. Or in this case, if the dick fits..." I said.

I pulled off my shirt and started on my shorts.

"You're going in?" she asked.

"I can't stay on this boat," I said.

I tossed my shorts near the pile of discarded clothing and jumped overboard. I swam to the beach, walked onto the sand, and plopped down on my back. Within a few minutes, a naked Alana sat down beside me.

"You might want to lay on your stomach," she suggested.

"And why would I want to do that," I replied.

"I'm guessing there are parts of you that haven't seen the sunlight in years. You don't want to get burned."

"Nonsense. I'll be fine," I said.

But Alana was right as usual, and within thirty minutes, I was feeling rather toasty. I stood and walked back into the water to cool off my sensitive areas. Alana was already in, so I swam over to her. We looked back to the beach and saw Panos and Hani in a full make-out session on the sand. They got up and disappeared behind some trees, but not before I got another glimpse of Panos in all his glory. I waited for Michelle to let out another loud gasp, but she didn't, at least not one that I could hear.

"I guess they're going for it," I said.

"I guess so," Alana said. "I'm sorry about this. It's not how I imagined the day would go."

"Really? You didn't think we'd all end up naked on a beach?" I asked.

I don't know how long we stayed on that beach, maybe an hour, maybe two hours, but it felt like all day. Never in my wildest dreams had I seen this coming. We eventually returned to the boat and retrieved our clothing. Panos elected to use the boat's motor instead of the sails to get back to the dock. That was fine by me, whatever got us there the fastest.

"So where do you see your relationship with Alana going?" he asked me.

"Sorry, I don't see how that's your concern," I said.

"I don't mean to be forward. I was just curious. She's a great lady," he said.

"Yes, she is," I said.

"I'm glad I was able to talk her into coming out today," Panos said. "I didn't think she was going to accept my invitation when I visited her at her home last night."

"You went by her home?" I asked. I immediately regretted my question.

"She didn't tell you?" he asked.

I left Panos without answering him and joined Foxx near the bow.

"Don't let the guy get to you," Foxx said.

"He's not getting to me."

"Of course he is. How could he not?"

He must have noticed his words didn't help me much because he followed up with, "Alana's with you. Don't forget that."

We finally got back to the dock after what felt like an eternity. Foxx and I helped Panos with the boat lines even though I just wanted to walk straight to my car and leave everything behind. We all walked up the dock toward the parking lot together, and then went our separate ways. I was beyond grateful no one suggested we all do dinner.

I wish I could say Alana and I spent the evening on her sofa, watching an old Bogart film and eating a bag of barbeque potato chips. But we didn't. We said nothing to each other on the drive back to her house. It was just like the previous night on the return drive from the restaurant. The boat ride had been the disaster I thought it would be, but it didn't take a genius to predict that. I still wasn't sure why Alana agreed to do it in the first place.

I pulled into her driveway, and she got out of the car without saying a word.

"Panos said something interesting to me today," I said.

Alana stopped and turned to me.

"He said he was the one who invited you on the boat. He also said he did so in person at your house."

Alana said nothing.

"You told me Hani invited you. Why did you lie to me?"

"Because I assumed you would get upset if you knew he came by the house."

"Why would I be upset?" I asked.

"I should have told you," she said.

She took a few steps toward her house and then stopped.

"I'm sorry that Panos embarrassed you," she said.

"He didn't embarrass me," I said, but we both knew that was a lie.

Alana said nothing more and walked into her house. I didn't see her for the next few days because of her work schedule. I talked to her a few times each day by phone. Everything seemed to be okay between us, but I did find it rather odd that she didn't once bring up her sister or Panos. Part of me wanted to know what Alana was thinking. The other part of me was glad I didn't know. I couldn't stop thinking about Alana not telling me about dating Panos or him visiting her at her home. They weren't really huge lies, but don't some people refer to omissions as a form of lying? Maybe. Maybe not. In those few days after the boat ride, I reflected on my time with Alana. The truth was that we really hadn't been together that long. I thought I knew her well, but I probably didn't. The intensity of a new relationship can often give us a misperception of how well we really know someone, especially when physical intimacy is involved. It can sometimes give us a false sense of emotional intimacy too. Yes, we spent a lot of time together, but probably not a lot compared to someone who had known her for almost thirty years like Hani? I tried my best to push the doubts about us out of my mind, but this was really the first crisis of our relationship. I hoped we could weather it.

5

EVERYTHING CHANGES

THE WEEK WENT BY QUICKLY. ON THURSDAY EVENING, ALANA STOPPED by the house and told me she had to attend the wedding rehearsal on Friday. I assumed earlier in the week that she had agreed to be Hani's maid of honor, but she never officially told me. After the rehearsal, there was going to be a party at Panos' restaurant. Alana asked if I would meet her there. I told her I would and asked if I could invite Foxx and Michelle as well. Alana said she didn't think Hani would object since she and Michelle had really hit it off on the sailboat.

I went for a swim and a run on Friday morning. I don't think I realized how much I had upped my workouts since meeting Panos. In hindsight, it's easy to see I had. I spent the afternoon playing with Maui the dog. I was pleased to see he had really taken to his new home, and he had also finally made friends with Foxx. I found him a couple of times sleeping on Foxx's legs when Foxx had fallen asleep while watching television.

Alana told me she was getting a ride to the rehearsal with Hani and Panos. I wasn't sure how the three of them were going to all fit in the Lamborghini, but maybe they had another, larger car.

That night, I hopped in my convertible and drove to Lahaina to meet Alana at the restaurant. The party had already gotten started by the time I arrived. I was a little surprised to see Foxx and Michelle already there since he told me earlier in the day that he thought they would be late.

"We ended up going to the wedding rehearsal," Foxx said. "Hani asked Michelle to be in the wedding party."

"Really? They barely know each other."

"Yeah, I'm just as surprised as you. You'd think Hani would have plenty of friends or relatives on the island."

"Have you seen Alana?" I asked.

"I think I saw her in the back."

I told Foxx I'd catch up with him later, and I walked to the back of the restaurant to find Alana. I saw her talking to an attractive woman with dark hair. Alana smiled when she saw me approach. She had a martini in her hand, and she already appeared a bit tipsy.

"Poe, I want you to meet Daphne. She's Panos' sister."

Daphne extended her hand, and I shook it. She looked to be in her mid-thirties, about the same age as Panos. She was around the same height as Alana, and her frame was just as delicate. Good looks definitely ran in their family.

"It's a pleasure to meet you," I said.

"Alana was just telling me about you. She said the two of you met on a murder investigation."

"Something like that."

"She also told me that the first time she met you, you stepped on her toes at an art show," Daphne said.

"It wasn't one of my best moments," I admitted.

"But those always make for the most interesting stories. Much more fun than saying you met at work."

"Do you live here on the island or did you fly in from California?" I asked.

"I moved here with Panos several years ago. We share a house," she said.

I thought that was a bit odd considering they were both adults and would probably want their own space, but then I remembered I lived with my best friend. Chalk that snap judgment up to hypocrisy on my part.

"So you stayed here when Panos moved to Los Angeles?" I asked.

"Maui's my home now, and I couldn't see myself living in such a large city."

"Will Panos and Hani go back there after the wedding?" I asked, trying not to sound anxious for them to leave.

"I think so, but I wouldn't be surprised if they moved back soon. I think Hani wants to be back on Maui."

"That's surprising. She hasn't told me anything. Then again, she didn't tell me about the wedding until a week ago," Alana said.

"They didn't tell anyone. I still don't know if it was meant to be a surprise, or if they just decided at the last minute to do it."

"Knowing Panos, they probably decided at the last minute," Alana said, laughing.

I must admit it really bugged me that Alana used the phrase "knowing Panos." I couldn't stand the fact she had dated the guy, and my jealousy was getting out of control. I hated being at this rehearsal party, even though it was for Panos' wedding to Hani. I couldn't stop picturing Alana in Hani's position if things had gone a different way.

Alana finished her martini.

"Excuse me while I get another drink. Can I get you two anything?" Alana asked.

"No, thank you," Daphne said.

I shook my head and watched Alana disappear. Daphne turned to me.

"So, how do you like living on Maui?"

"I like it a lot. It's so different from Virginia, but I guess that's the point."

"Were you not happy there?" she asked.

"It's not that. It was just time for a change. Meeting Alana here sort of sealed the deal."

"She's a great person. I thought for a while she might be my sister-in-law," Daphne said.

Now that is surprising, I thought. Alana never mentioned she was that close to Panos. There's certainly a difference between dating someone for six months and someone's sister thinking you are well on your way to getting married. I guess the look on my face was obvious.

"Sorry. I don't mean to bring up a sore subject," she said.

"It's fine. Really."

"Panos can be difficult. Always the life of the party. It can be a bit much. Trust me. I know," she admitted.

"Yet you still live with him," I said, instantly wishing I'd kept my mouth shut.

"I know. But it can be equally difficult not to be around him. There's never a dull moment when he's near."

"Are you also in the wedding party?" I asked.

"No. I wasn't asked," she said.

There I went, sticking my foot in my mouth again, but you have to admit that I'd just discovered an interesting piece of information. His own sister wasn't a bridesmaid, but some lady Hani had met less than a week ago was. That couldn't sit well with Daphne. Part of me was now surprised that she was even here at the party.

"Well, I'm not in the wedding either, so maybe we can sit together at the ceremony," I said.

"Yes, let's do that."

"Are there other family members coming to the wedding?" I asked.

"No, just me. Most of our family is still on Santorini. Our mother is actually there now taking care of some business. There wasn't enough notice for them to get a flight. Maybe that was one of the reasons Panos planned a last-minute wedding," she said.

Daphne and I talked for several more minutes. Overall, I found her to be rather likable and easy to be around. It's strange how siblings can be so different from each other. Then again, I wasn't competing with her for Alana's affection.

Daphne and I drifted apart to talk to other people. I was going to look for Alana, but Wes, the guy who co-owned the restaurant with Panos, intercepted me.

"So how do you know Panos?" he asked.

"Alana is my girlfriend."

"You know she and Panos used to date," he said.

Of course I knew.

"How are things in the restaurant business?" I asked.

"A bit slow. This damn party isn't helping either. We're losing an entire Friday night's revenue."

"You've got a great location," I said, not sure what else I could say or how I could possibly comment on the party hurting his business.

"Yeah, but the rent is astronomical. That's always the trade-off. Good location or cheap rent."

"Why are things slow for you?" I asked.

"Things started going downhill once my chef quit. He and Panos didn't get along."

Surprise, surprise, I thought.

"Sorry to hear that," I said.

"I hoped he would come back once Panos moved to Los Angeles, but he landed another job in Kihei. I couldn't talk him out of it."

Just then we heard laughter, and we both turned to see Panos talking to several ladies. They all looked utterly entranced by him.

"A little piece of advice for you. Never go into business with someone else, especially if that person is a self-absorbed piece of shit," Wes said and stormed off.

Wow. I can't say I saw that comment coming. I have to admit it made me smile, though. It was good to know I wasn't the only one who didn't like Panos. I know that may seem small of me, and it probably is, but I want to be as honest with you as possible regarding how I felt at the party.

I rejoined Alana and was introduced to various friends and acquaintances. It was all typical party chatter. "What do you do?" "How did you two meet?" Stuff like that. Nothing at all inspiring or surprising, but it was refreshing when no one else found the need to point out Alana's past relationship with Panos. After a couple of hours of more drinking and talking, I found myself at the bar with Foxx.

"Where's Michelle?" I asked.

"Dancing," Foxx said, and he nodded toward a section of the restaurant someone had cleared to make space for an impromptu dance floor. I saw Alana and Hani there with Michelle. The three of them were dancing away to some 80s song I recognized but couldn't remember the name of. I was surprised to see how much Alana was enjoying herself. I didn't expect her to be miserable, and I certainly didn't want that either, but she'd made it seem like this was going to be one awkward event for her. Now she looked like she was having the time of her life. Maybe it was the martinis. I turned to Foxx.

"You and Michelle seem to be getting along great."

"Yeah."

"That didn't sound too enthusiastic."

"Sorry. She's a great girl. I really like her."

"Then what's the problem?"

"Nothing."

"Okay," I said and dropped it.

We both ordered more beers and sat in silence for another few minutes. The 80s song transitioned into another one, and the three ladies and their companions continued to dance.

"I just feel a little guilty," Foxx admitted.

"For what?"

"Over Lauren. I miss her. I still can't believe she's gone."

"Of course you do. Why wouldn't you miss her?" I asked.

"And that's why I feel guilty."

"You mean being with Michelle makes you feel guilty? Like you're somehow betraying Lauren," I said.

"Exactly."

"You shouldn't feel that way. Lauren would want you to be happy."

Foxx laughed.

"Come on, Poe. I guarantee you that Lauren is looking down on me right now and is royally pissed off I'm with this other chick."

It was my turn to laugh.

"Probably. But she'd still understand the situation," I said.

Foxx and I drank more of our beers.

"Have you always felt this way? You've been with other girls since Lauren passed," I said.

"Yeah, but none as serious as Michelle. It's only been a couple of weeks, but I'm surprised at how much I like her. She's done things to me in the bedroom that no one has ever done before."

If you knew Foxx like I did, you'd know that was really saying something.

"So that's why you like her so much?"

"No, of course not. Well, that's part of it. She's also so damn easy to talk to. I just enjoy being around her."

"I don't know what's gotten into you, Foxx. First you end up in a serious relationship with Lauren. Now you seem to be starting another one with Michelle. That's two in a year. Did some alien kidnap your body? Am I talking to your clone?"

Foxx smiled. He turned to the dance floor and watched Michelle for a few moments.

"Look at that body, Poe. Have you ever seen anything so incredible?"

But I wasn't looking at Michelle. My eyes were glued to Alana. And to answer Foxx's question, no, I had not seen anything as magnificent as Alana.

A few more hours passed, and the party was still going strong. Drinks were flowing and the conversations were getting louder. I assumed everyone was going to be hungover for the wedding the next day.

"Leave me alone!"

I turned to see Hani yank her arm out of the grip of some guy I didn't recognize. He was about her age, of average height and build. He looked like a native Hawaiian. I walked toward them, wondering if there was going to be a problem, but Panos beat me to the scene.

"What's going on?" Panos asked.

"This isn't your concern," the stranger said.

"You're hassling my fiancée. How is that not my concern?" Panos asked.

"No one is hassling anyone."

"You want her back. Is that the problem? You think Hani should be with you and not me?" Panos asked.

The stranger glared at Panos.

"It's fine," Hani said.

"It doesn't matter if she's with me or not. She just shouldn't be with you," the stranger said.

"And whose decision is that to make? Is it yours?" Panos asked.

The stranger said nothing. He looked away from Panos and Hani, and that was the first time I got a good look at his face. He looked embarrassed to me.

The music was still playing. By this point, though, everyone had stopped talking and was watching the argument unfold.

"It's time to move on. Get a life. You can't have mine," Panos said.

I studied Hani. Despite her earlier outburst, she seemed concerned for the stranger now. Panos laughed and further humiliated the guy.

"Get out of my restaurant before I have you thrown out, and don't let me see you at the wedding tomorrow."

The stranger didn't move.

"Are you going to test me now?" Panos asked.

"No, Panos. He'll leave," Hani said. She turned to the stranger. "Please leave. This is supposed to be a joyous event. I don't want it to turn ugly."

Too late for that, I thought, but Hani's soft words had the desired effect. The stranger turned and made his way through the crowd.

"Everyone, please, get back to the party. My wedding is tomorrow! Everyone have fun!" Panos yelled.

Alana walked up to me.

"Poor guy," she said.

"Who was that?" I asked.

"His name's Makani. He used to date Hani all through high school and college. Everyone thought they were going to get married. I thought so too, but she just broke up with him one day. Never gave him or anyone else a reason. He never got over it."

Poor guy was right, I thought. He looked utterly defeated, like the life had been drained from him.

"I guess he thought tonight was his last chance," Alana continued.

"I guess so," I said.

I looked around the restaurant. The party was back in full swing as if the argument between Panos and Hani's former boyfriend hadn't even occurred. I turned back to Alana.

"How are you enjoying the party?" I asked.

"I've had way too much to drink, but that's the point, isn't it."

I nodded, and then a song came on that Alana liked.

"Dance with me?" she asked.

"Maybe the next one," I said.

"You sure?"

"The next one. I promise."

Alana smiled and ran back to the dance floor. She found Foxx and Michelle and started dancing with them.

I went back to the bar for another beer. I drank it slowly while I watched the television behind the bar and thought about this past week. It had been surreal to say the least.

I finally finished my drink and went to find Alana. She wasn't on the dance floor anymore, and I didn't see her anywhere near the bar. I walked around the entire restaurant but still didn't find her. I walked outside, thinking she might be out there to get some fresh air. Instead, I found Hani. She was sitting on the curb in front of the parking lot.

"That's a hell of a party you guys are throwing," I said.

Hani smiled.

"I hope you're enjoying yourself," she said.

"Mind if I sit down?" I asked.

"Of course not."

I sat on the curb beside her.

"Sorry about that scene in there," she said.

"No problem. It wasn't your fault, and it seemed to resolve itself."

"Not really. He'll be back, either later tonight or tomorrow."

"Are you worried about him? Has he threatened you?" I asked.

"No, nothing like that. We were together a long time. Makani won't let it go."

I didn't know what to say, so I said nothing.

"I wish Panos hadn't made fun of him. He didn't deserve it," she continued.

"I'm sure he'll be okay. He looked like a tough guy." I knew that wasn't true. The guy looked like an injured puppy.

"He's not tough," Hani said. "That's the problem."

"Well, now's not the time to be thinking any more about that. You have a wedding to think about. You nervous about tomorrow?"

"Not really. I feel like I'm doing the right thing, so what's to be nervous about?"

"Marriage is a big deal. It's perfectly natural to have butterflies."

"What about you and my sister?" she asked.

"What about us?"

"Don't avoid the subject." She smiled. "When are you going to be walking down the aisle together?"

"We've only been together a few months," I said.

"Yeah, but I can see the way you two look at each other. Why waste time, Poe? Life is short."

I smiled. The truth was that I had thought of proposing to Alana. We had only been together a short while, but I knew I already loved her more than I'd ever loved another woman before. I couldn't imagine those feelings going away. I'd changed my entire life to be with her. I'd sold my house and moved thousands of miles away. Everything I knew, I left behind. What was I waiting for? Some arbitrary time to pass before it was acceptable to propose? Yes, I had thought about marrying her. Maybe Hani was right. Maybe I needed to give it more serious consideration and start thinking of a plan.

"I'm happy for you and Panos," I said. "I think it's great you found each other. I'm sure it's going to be an amazing wedding. And I'm sure you'll look gorgeous in your dress."

Hani smiled.

"I should go find Panos. If I don't get him to go to sleep soon, he may not be awake for the wedding."

Hani and I stood, and we both walked back inside the restaurant. I took another quick look around but still didn't see Alana. I checked the dance floor and the bar and all four corners of the place. Nothing.

I saw Hani again. She was walking toward the back offices. I decided to follow her. Maybe Alana had gotten tired after all that dancing and drinking and decided to lie down in the back for a few minutes. I hadn't quite caught up with Hani before she opened the door to the manager's office, but I was close enough to see inside. There was Alana, kissing Panos. When they heard the door open, Alana stepped away from him.

"You son of a bitch," Hani said.

I wasn't sure if she was talking to Panos or her sister, but she ran inside and started hitting Panos on the chest. He was so much bigger and stronger than her that the blows did nothing. I felt confident I could do far more damage to him, but I was too stunned to move. Panos laughed. I knew it was directed toward Hani, but I couldn't help but feel it pierce me instead.

"It meant nothing," he said.

Alana looked at me. Her eyes were glazed over. She didn't say anything. I didn't either. I just turned around and walked to the exit. Everything went a bit fuzzy after that. I'm pretty sure Foxx said something to me on the way out, but I don't remember what it was. I don't even remember if Michelle was with him or not. The DJ's music seemed to fade away, as did the sound of people talking and laughing. The crowd seemed to part for me, like they had all seen inside that office too and wanted to let me go without interference.

I went outside and fished my car keys out of my pocket. I jumped into the car and slammed it in reverse. I looked toward the restaurant. Alana wasn't at the doorway. She wasn't running out to stop me or explain herself. I put the car in drive and sped away.

I was home in no time. Maui the dog greeted me at the door. I grabbed his leash and took him outside. I had my phone with me and kept expecting it to ring. It would be Alana begging me to forgive her, telling me how sorry she was and how she didn't intend to hurt me. She just had too much to drink, and Panos had forced himself on her.

I knew that wasn't true, but part of me allowed myself to believe the lie. Alana didn't call.

I walked Maui for at least an hour. When we got back to the house, I saw that Foxx's car wasn't there, and I wondered if he had seen or heard what had happened between Panos and Alana.

I looked down at the dog. He was exhausted. I don't think anyone had ever walked him that far before. He collapsed on the cool tiles of the living room floor. I sat down on the sofa and turned on the television. A second later, I turned it off. I couldn't concentrate on anything. My mind was buzzing too hard.

I went into my bedroom and fell on the bed. I lay on my back and stared at the ceiling. I knew I couldn't go to sleep, despite how late it was, but I didn't know what else to do. I checked my cell phone again. I assumed I might have put the phone on silent mode and didn't feel it vibrate when Alana called. The display showed no calls. No text messages. Nothing.

I don't know how long I lay there. Eventually I heard the back door open. I climbed out of bed and saw Foxx scratching the dog behind his ears. He looked up at me.

"How are you doing?" he asked.

I could tell by his tone that he didn't expect me to be doing well.

I didn't answer him. I just watched him pat the dog.

"I gave Alana a ride home. She told me what happened," he continued.

I still said nothing.

"I'm sorry. It's really shitty."

I nodded.

"For what it's worth, she was crying the whole way to her house. She's devastated."

"She is?" I asked, my tone harsh and bitter.

"I'm guessing she didn't intend for it to happen. It was pretty obvious she had too much to drink," he said. "I had to help her into her house."

"That doesn't excuse anything," I said.

"I'm not saying it does."

"So why hasn't she called?" I asked.

"Maybe she doesn't know what to say. Maybe she doesn't want to hear how bad she's hurt you."

"She should call," I said, "even though I don't want to talk to her."

"I understand, buddy, but give her a chance. I'm sure she'll call you in the morning once her head has cleared. You two can get past this. I know you can."

Foxx walked up to me and patted me on my shoulder.

"It will be okay, man. It will be okay."

He walked into his bedroom. I sat down on the sofa. Maui the dog jumped onto my lap. I looked down at him. He wagged his tail. I couldn't tell if he knew I was hurting or if he just wanted some affection. Probably the latter. He was a pushy little thing after all.

I kept my phone by me the entire time, but Alana didn't call that night. She didn't call that morning either. No texts. No emails. No messages by carrier pigeon. Nothing.

I hung out by the pool all day and alternated between sitting in the sun and swimming underwater laps. Maui the dog stayed in the shade the entire time. Later that afternoon, Foxx came outside. He was wearing a nice pair of pants and a silk shirt. I looked awful by comparison. I hadn't showered that morning, and I was dressed in ratty swim trunks and no shirt.

"Off to the wedding?" I asked.

Foxx nodded.

"Give Alana my best," I said and tried not to hide the sarcasm in my voice.

Foxx walked over and sat down beside me.

"I take it she hasn't called," he said.

I shook my head.

"I'm a little surprised by that. Maybe she feels you don't want to talk to her. Hell, maybe she's too embarrassed to face you."

I said nothing.

"For what it's worth, I don't want to go to this damn thing. If Michelle wasn't in the wedding party, I'd blow it off," Foxx said.

"I'm sure it will be a nice wedding, provided Alana can keep herself from making out with the groom during the service," I said.

"I know you're really hurting, but don't let it consume you. Things have a way of working out. Hell, do you know how many girls have caught me in the act with other girls. They all forgave me."

"Yeah, but that was them catching you. What would you do if it was the other way around?"

"I see your point, but I think the principle is the same. It's about forgiveness."

"No, Foxx. It's about her humiliating me. It's about her being more interested in him than me. I thought we had something, and in one moment, she shit all over it."

"Yeah, she did, but that doesn't mean she can't make it up to you."

"Why are you on her side?" I asked.

"Look. I like Alana. I like her a lot. But make no mistake about it. I'm on your side ten times out of ten. I'd do anything for you, and I think you know that. That's why I'm defending her. I know what you two have. I've seen how she makes you feel, last night not included. She's changed your life for the better. I don't want to see you lose sight of that."

Foxx stood.

"It's cool for you to be angry. I don't mean to imply that you shouldn't be. You should be pissed off. And mad as hell at Alana and that asshole Panos, but when you calm down, I think you should see if there's something left that's salvageable."

Foxx looked at his watch.

"I'm already late. I better go get Michelle. I hope you feel better, buddy. I mean it."

I nodded. Foxx turned and walked toward the back gate. I looked down at Maui the dog. He was asleep on his back in the shade. I could have sworn I heard him snoring.

"Well, Maui, I guess it's just you and me."

6
—————

PANOS

I don't remember when I finally fell asleep on the sofa that night. I do remember watching some god-awful science fiction film on TV about aliens or crocodiles or aliens fighting crocodiles. I woke up when I heard the back door open.

"You feeling any better?" Foxx asked.

I didn't answer him.

Foxx walked over to the sofa and sat down beside me.

"How was the wedding?" I asked.

"What wedding?"

"Come on, Foxx."

"I mean it. What wedding? There actually has to be a wedding for me to tell you how it went," he said.

"What are you talking about?" I asked.

"Panos was a no-show. He left Hani standing at the altar. It was awful, man."

"He didn't show?" I asked. I wasn't really sure I heard him correctly.

"Everyone was in their seats. The harp was playing but no groom."

"What did Hani do?"

"What do you think she did? She hid in the back the entire time. She was too embarrassed to come out."

"Did you find out what happened to Panos?"

"No idea. Michelle took Hani back to her house. She said she's going to spend the night there to help console her. I left and went to Harry's for a few drinks."

"What about Alana?"

"She was a no-show too."

Dear God. You know what I was thinking at that moment because you're thinking it too as you read this. Things just went from bad to very bad.

"I know what's going on in that brain of yours, but she didn't run off with the guy. I saw her on my way home," Foxx said.

"Where?" I asked.

"It took me almost an hour to drive back from Harry's. There's some kind of incident at the marina. They had one of the two lanes blocked off in front of the entrance. There must have been at least ten police cars there with their lights flashing. I saw Alana talking to some cops when I drove by."

Foxx stood.

"I'm gonna hit the sack. I'm exhausted. Have a good night, buddy. Things will get better in the morning."

Foxx left for his bedroom. I lay back down on the sofa. I didn't have the energy to walk to my room. Maui the dog stayed with me.

I woke the next morning when the doorbell rang. I waited for Foxx to answer it. I looked like shit. I hadn't showered in two days, and my mouth felt like it had dirty socks in it. Foxx didn't come out of his room, and the doorbell rang again. I figured it was Michelle, and he'd want me to let her inside, so I dragged myself off the sofa and stumbled to the front door. I swung open the door without looking through the peephole. It was Alana. She was dressed in her work clothes, and her hair was much neater than mine, but she looked just as tired. I stood in the doorway and stared at her.

"May I come in?" she asked.

I stepped back from the door to let her pass. I didn't say anything.

We walked into the living room, and I sat back down on the sofa. Maui the dog ran up to Alana. She ignored him at first but then finally bent over to pat him on the head. Several long moments of silence went by. Neither of us knew what to say. Finally, Alana spoke.

"I do want to talk about us, but there's something else you need to know first. I wanted it to come from me before you heard it on the news. I really don't know how to say this, but Panos was murdered at the marina last night."

"What?"

"They found his body in the cabin of his boat. His throat had been cut."

"Who did it?" I asked.

"We don't know. I was one of the detectives who got the call."

"So you're the lead on the case?"

Alana shook her head.

"Not with my personal connection to him. Another detective named Glen Adcock got it. Unfortunately, he's a first-class asshole."

"Panos is dead," I said. I really couldn't believe it.

"Hani is going to move in with me for a while. She's as torn up as you'd expect her to be."

"How are you?" I asked.

"Not good."

I wasn't sure what to say or do at that point. All of a sudden my relationship problems didn't seem to matter.

Alana shoved her hands into her pockets.

"About us - I'm sorry. I really have nothing I can say to defend myself. I wanted to call yesterday. I dialed your number a million times only to hang up before it started ringing. I just didn't know what to say."

I said nothing.

"Panos came up to me on the dance floor. He said he wanted to talk to me in private. I didn't know what he wanted. I had way too much to drink, and honestly, I didn't care what he had to say, but he insisted that I come to the back office with him. He apologized for leaving me for Hani."

Alana looked away like she was reliving the conversation. I thought about saying something in response but thought better of it. She turned back to me.

"I can't tell you how long I waited for that apology, but when he finally gave it, it didn't really matter. He said he still loved me, but he loved Hani too. He was still going to marry her, but he wanted me to know how he felt about me. That's when he kissed me, and you and Hani walked in the room at the worst possible moment. If you had been one second later, you would have seen me push him away."

I wanted to tell her that it didn't look that way to me, but now definitely didn't seem like the time for a debate. Panos was dead.

"Yesterday morning I went by Hani's house and apologized to her, and I backed out of her wedding," she said.

"So you had time to apologize to her in person, but you couldn't even send me a text message?" I asked.

"I love Hani. She's my sister, but you mean more to me. I couldn't stand what I had done to you. I know it doesn't make any sense, but it was easier to face her than you."

"What now?" I asked.

"I don't know. I think I just need time."

"Time for what?"

"To figure out what to do," she said.

I wasn't sure what she meant. A million questions ran through my mind. Did she not want to be with me anymore? Did I want to be with her? Where do we go from here?

Alana said she needed to go and be with her sister. I walked her to the door. She turned to me once she got out on the porch. We just looked at each other for several seconds. I thought she wanted to tell me something else, but she said nothing. She finally nodded and walked to her car. I stood in the open doorway and watched her drive away.

Maui the dog ran between my legs and took off down the street. I called to him, but he completely ignored me. I spent the next five minutes chasing the little guy down and praying he wouldn't get hit by a car. I finally caught him when I cornered him between the neighbor's house and backyard fence. Maui rolled on his back. I couldn't believe the audacity of this guy. He expected a belly rub after making me run him down. I picked him up and carried him back into the house.

Foxx came out of the bedroom a few minutes later, and I told him about Panos. We both sat in stunned silence for what seemed like an hour. Foxx called Michelle. She'd just seen the news on television and was already on her way to see Hani. Bad news does travel fast.

The next few days were a complete blur. Panos' murder was all anyone talked about. I didn't know if the police were making any progress, and Alana didn't call to give me any updates on the case or Hani's condition. I wanted to call but was worried about intruding. Besides, Foxx kept me somewhat up-to-date. Michelle had been spending a lot of time with Hani. She said Alana wasn't there most of the time, and Hani didn't want to be alone. I assumed Alana was helping with the murder investigation despite her connection to the deceased. It was about five days after Alana's visit that Panos' sister, Daphne, called me.

"I'm so sorry about your brother," I said.

"Thank you," she said.

I wasn't about to ask her how she felt. It seemed like a stupid and obvious question.

"The reason I'm calling is that my mother is in town. She's requested to see you."

"Your mother wants to see me? I don't understand."

"I really would prefer not to get into it over the phone. Would it be possible for you to come by the house tonight around seven? Her flight arrives later this afternoon. I'd like to give her a few hours to rest before she meets with you."

"Of course. No problem," I said.

"Good. I'll text you my address."

I hung up the cell phone and slipped it back into my pocket. I didn't have the slightest clue why Panos' mother would want to see me. I'd certainly never met the lady. I didn't know why she would even know about my existence.

I went on a long run that afternoon to try to clear my head. I'd been doing that every day since the news of Panos' murder, but the runs didn't seem to make a difference, at least not in erasing the fog that was my brain. After the runs, I'd walk the dog for a cool-down and to get him some exercise too. I was glad for Maui's presence. He was the only positive thing in my life right now, even if he was always demanding attention.

I took a shower right before heading to Daphne's home. I put on nice clothes, a pair of pressed khaki pants and a linen shirt. I showed up at her house exactly on time. The house was two stories and had to easily be three thousand square feet. It also sat on an acre of ocean-front land. I had no idea what a piece of property like that cost, but it must have been in the millions.

The door opened before I could ring the bell. I was greeted by a Hawaiian woman who looked to be in her late sixties. She was on the short side, and I believe the polite term in referencing her size is "pleasantly plump."

"Good evening, Mr. Rutherford," she said.

"Good evening," I said.

I entered the house, and she closed the door behind me. The house was as impressive on the inside as it was on the outside. Dark, rich wood covered the floors. Large tropical plants and flowers were tastefully placed throughout. The decor reminded me a little bit of the lobby of the View, and I wondered which place inspired which.

"My name's Kalena. Mrs. Laskaris is waiting for you in the back."

She led me down the front hallway. We rounded the corner, and I saw Daphne. I walked up to her and hugged her. We weren't close by any means, but it seemed and felt like the appropriate thing to do. I told her again how sorry I was about Panos. She thanked me for coming over to see her and her mother.

"I'll see him to the sitting room," Daphne told Kalena.

"Yes, ma'am."

"It was nice meeting you, Kalena," I said.

"Nice meeting you, Mr. Rutherford."

Kalena left, and Daphne took over guiding me to the back of the house.

"One of the bedrooms here is for our mother. She visits at least once a year. Her sitting room is in the back."

"Kalena seems like a nice woman," I said.

"Yes, she's been with us since we moved to Maui. Panos hired her. She does a little bit of everything for us."

We entered the back room. There was a small book shelf on one wall. The other walls were covered with family photos. The entire back wall of the sitting room was glass and offered a magnificent view of the ocean. Someone had opened the sliding glass door, and a cool ocean breeze blew through the room. I could see why Daphne's mother would want to spend as much time here as possible.

"Can I get you anything to drink?" she asked.

"No, I'm fine. Thanks."

Daphne smiled.

"I'll go tell Mother you're here."

Daphne left. I walked over to the wall of photos. There were several shots of what I assumed was Panos as a boy. There were also photos of Panos and Daphne as teenagers, both smiling and laughing. I couldn't help but feel horrible for Panos and his life cut short.

"He was such a wonderful boy. Always running around. Always the center of attention."

I turned to see Panos' mother standing in the doorway. I guessed her to be in her late sixties to early seventies, but she still appeared strong and vibrant.

"Hello, Mrs. Laskaris," I said.

I expressed my condolences for the loss of her son, and she was gracious in her acceptance. She led me over to the two chairs by the back windows, and we sat down. The ocean breeze felt good. I expected Daphne to return, but she never did.

"Thank you for coming to see me on such short notice. I won't be in town very long, just long enough to claim my son's body and bring him home."

"So he's to be buried in California?" I asked.

She nodded.

"We have a family plot on our property. I intend to bury him beside his father. He and Panos loved each other so much. It seems only right they should be together now."

She paused, looked out the window, and then turned back to me.

"Panos said he built this room especially for me. I don't know if that's true, but I do love this view."

"It's quite remarkable. I never get tired of looking at the ocean," I said.

"I assume you wonder why I've asked you here," she continued.

I nodded.

"Have you met this Detective Glen Adcock?" she asked.

"No, Alana mentioned his name to me a few days ago, but I'm not part of the investigation in any way."

"I'd like to change that," she said. "My daughter is under the impression the detective is an idiot."

"I can't speak to that. Like I said, I've never met him."

"Panos' killer must be found, and I have no faith in the local police."

"I've had some interaction with them. I don't think you should feel that way."

"I'm a businesswoman, Mr. Rutherford. It's called 'limiting the risk.' I'd like to have a second team working the case. That's why I asked for you."

"I'm afraid I don't understand," I said.

"I had a long conversation with Daphne about you. She told me how you solved that case involving the murdered artist. She said the police you speak so highly about falsely imprisoned your friend, and you were the only one who believed in his innocence. She said you seemed like a very smart man."

She was really laying it on thick, I thought. Part of me was flattered. Part of me was annoyed by the obvious manipulation.

"I want to hire you to find my son's killer," she continued.

"I appreciate your confidence in me, Mrs. Laskaris, but that's not something I do. It was sort of a one-time thing."

"Panos was my only son. You must do this for me. I'll pay you for your efforts."

"I'm sorry, but I'm not for hire."

"Nonsense. Everyone is for hire."

The woman was persistent. I'll give her that.

"Daphne will be your assistant. She'll report to me each night on your progress."

"I don't like having to refuse you, but this isn't something I can do."

"Did you like my son?" she asked.

It would be beyond rude of me to tell her the truth, but my hesitation told her everything.

"I didn't think so," she continued. "Is that why you won't do this for me?"

"I didn't know Panos well. We spent very little time together. The simple fact is I wouldn't have the slightest idea where to begin an investigation regarding your son. I don't know any of his connections, and I have no idea who might have wanted to harm him."

"Daphne knew him better than anyone. She'll help you with those details."

"I'm not a professional. I only took on Foxx's case out of desperation because no one else believed in him."

"I'll pay you half your fee upfront. The other half will be paid when you deliver me the name of his killer."

I turned from Mrs. Laskaris and looked out the window. It was another beautiful day on the island. The sky and ocean were as blue as they'd been that day I sat on the dock with Alana before our sailing trip with Panos. Alana was probably doing whatever she could to help with Panos' case, even if she'd been forbidden to by her department. I thought back to my flight to Maui. I was so anxious to arrive because I knew Alana would be waiting for me at the airport. I wasn't sure exactly what changed my mind to help Mrs. Laskaris in that minute of staring out at the ocean. Maybe I thought I had something to prove to Alana. Maybe I had something to prove to myself. I turned back to her.

"Very well. I'll get started first thing in the morning," I said.

"How much is your fee? I'll write you a check now before you leave."

I stood.

"My fee is zero. I'm doing this to find a killer, not to profit from the dead. Again, I'm sorry for your tremendous loss."

Mrs. Laskaris nodded, and I left the room. I headed to the front door and saw Daphne waiting for me.

"Is it safe to assume you've agreed to her request?" she asked.

"So you knew what this was all about?"

"I'm sorry I didn't mention it on the phone. She asked me not to."

"I understand. Please write a list tonight of who you think may have wanted to harm your brother. We'll start interviewing them in the morning. I'll be back at nine o'clock."

I left the house and drove to the marina where Foxx said he'd seen Alana the other night. I parked and walked down to the dock. There was crime-scene tape blocking the entrance to the stern of Panos' boat. I looked down on the spot Alana and I had sat just a couple of weeks ago. I remembered us dangling our legs over the side as we looked out to the ocean. I wondered if I should call her and tell her about my new agreement with Panos' mother, but I decided not to. She would be against it, and I had no desire to have another argument with her. I still didn't know where we stood regarding our relationship. I wasn't even sure we had a relationship anymore. I couldn't believe the terrible turn my life had taken in such a short time, and I felt guilty for even complaining about it. At least I was still alive. I had a second chance to make things right. Panos didn't. I decided at that moment to stop feeling sorry for myself. It wasn't helping anyone, least of all me. It certainly wasn't going to help me solve the murder of Panos.

I drove back to the house and went for another run despite having done one that morning. When I got back to the house, I found Foxx and Michelle sitting by the pool.

"You're gonna run those legs of yours right off," Foxx said. "What have you done? Three marathons this week?"

I smiled.

"How are you, Michelle?" I asked.

"I'm okay. I've spent most of the week at Alana's. Hani's been living there."

"How is she doing?"

"Like you'd expect. The police have been coming and going and always asking her the same questions."

That didn't make any sense, but I decided to let it go.

"I'm sure she's glad you're there for her. It's really nice of you," I said.

"It's not a problem."

"How is Alana? I assume she's been at work the majority of the time."

"Yeah, she hasn't been home that much, and when she's there, we can't get much out of her. Hani keeps asking her about the case, but all Alana says is that they're still working on it. Between you and me, I don't think they have any idea who killed Panos," she said.

"Well, she has to keep everything to herself. It's just police policy. She can't even tell family members."

"I understand, but it's more than that. She's just really frustrated with that detective. Alana seems to make sure she's at the house when he comes by to interview Hani. I don't know Alana as well as you guys do, but it doesn't take a mind reader to see she's really annoyed with him."

"Alana will set him straight. She's one tough cookie," Foxx said.

Michelle looked up at me and smiled.

"You know she talks about you all the time."

"Who?" I asked.

"Alana, of course. All she says is 'Poe this' and 'Poe that.' She really thinks the world of you."

"Have you two had a chance to talk?" Foxx asked me.

I shook my head.

"Not since the day after they found Panos."

"Maybe you should give her a call," he suggested.

"I think she needs more time."

I told Foxx and Michelle about my conversation with Panos' mother and how I intended to start on the case the next morning.

"Please don't say anything to Hani and especially not to Alana," I said to Michelle. "I know she wouldn't want me interfering with a police investigation."

"But you're going to do it anyway," Foxx said.

I nodded.

"Good for you. It will get you off that damn sofa." Foxx smiled.

"Do you know where you're going to start?" Michelle asked.

I told her how I'd asked Daphne to write up a list of people she thought didn't like Panos. I had no idea how long that list might be. I knew Wes, the co-owner of the restaurant, was certainly mad at Panos, but was he angry enough to cut his throat? Then there was Makani, Hani's old boyfriend. Panos thoroughly humiliated him at the rehearsal party. Had Makani gotten his revenge later that night? Those were just two people I accidentally found out about in only a week of being around Panos. Logic said there were probably many more, maybe even dozens more. The man was a force of nature who had to have attracted as many detractors as admirers. Finding his killer would not be easy, that's if I could even identify him or her at all.

7

DETECTIVE ADCOCK

I GOT UP EARLY THE NEXT MORNING AND TRIED TO REMEMBER ALL THE little tricks I had learned while interviewing people during Lauren's murder investigation. I was about to leave for Daphne's house when the doorbell rang. I was hoping it might be Alana, but it was some guy I'd never met.

"Hello, can I help you?" I asked.

"Yes, I'm looking for Mr. Rutherford."

"That's me."

"I'm Detective Glen Adcock. May I come in and ask you a few questions?"

The detective was in his late fifties. He was average height and a little heavy - even for his age. He had salt-and-pepper hair. His most distinguishing feature was easily a pair of fuzzy black eyebrows. They were so long and thick that they threatened to migrate across his forehead and join the hair on top of his head. I found it difficult not to stare at those caterpillars. Since they were obviously right above his eyes, I could only hope he thought I was making solid eye contact with him instead of gawking at those beasts.

Alana described the man as an idiot, so I was tempted to shut the door in his face. I knew Daphne had no faith in him either, but I stepped back and allowed him to enter. He followed me into the living room. Maui the dog was lying on the floor near the sofa. He opened one eye when he heard us enter. He growled at the detective, which made three negative opinions against the guy. I didn't offer him anything to drink. I just wanted to get whatever this conversation was going to be over with as quickly as possible. I gestured to the sofa, and he sat down, while I took a chair off to the side.

"What can I do for you, Detective?"

"You may or may not know this, but I'm heading up the investigation into the death of Panos Laskaris."

"Alana told me you were the lead on the case."

"So you still talk to Detective Hu?"

"I'm not sure I know what you mean."

"Word is that you two are on the outs."

"Excuse me, Detective, but I'm not sure what business that is of yours."

"So you're denying it?" he asked.

"I'm not denying or confirming. I'm simply saying it's none of your business."

"Oh, but it is very much my business. I've been told by multiple witnesses that you and the deceased had a disagreement at the rehearsal party the night he was killed."

"I really don't know why anyone would say that. There was no disagreement."

"So you were okay with him kissing your ex-girlfriend?" he asked.

I knew what he was trying to do. Despite knowing this rather obvious interrogation tactic, I still found myself highly annoyed by the guy.

"I'm not sure I understand what you're getting at. Why don't you make things a lot easier for both of us and just tell me what you want to know. I have somewhere I need to be."

"And where is that?"

"Again, it's none of your business."

Pissing off a police detective probably wasn't the best course of action, but I didn't see what good it would do to tell him I was going to see Daphne and start a second investigation that would be competing with his. I also didn't want to lie to him and have it come back on me at a later date.

"Why are you being hostile with me?" he asked.

"I apologize, Detective, but please, tell me what you would like to know."

"Very well. Where were you the night Panos was killed?"

"I was here. I left the party and came directly back here."

"And was there someone here who can vouch for you?"

"Just the dog."

"You think this is cute, Mr. Rutherford?"

"No, I don't think it's cute. A man has been murdered, and judging from your presence here, you've made zero progress on the case."

"Why do you say that?"

"Because if you're questioning me as a potential killer, then you don't have the slightest idea who murdered Panos. I would never hurt anyone. I've certainly never killed anyone. This lead is a complete dead end for you."

"So you wouldn't want to hurt Mr. Laskaris even if he was banging your girlfriend?"

Detective Adcock smiled. I smiled right back.

"Is there anything else, Detective?" I asked.

"Not at the moment, but I'll probably be back in the near future."

"Of course. But please call first and make an appointment to waste my time. I have a very busy schedule and most likely won't be here."

"Of course."

We both stood, and I walked him to the door. He turned to me before he left the house.

"Shame about you and Alana. She's quite beautiful," he said.

"Yes, but 'stunning' is the more appropriate word to describe her."

He turned and exited the house. I watched him all the way to his car, and then I shut the door as calmly as I could.

His last comment gave it all away. He wanted Alana for himself, and he resented me for dating her, or having dated her, whatever the status of our relationship was at that moment.

Alana was right. The guy was a first-class asshole. This was his case, so I had no doubt I'd eventually run into him again, especially since I was about to start my own investigation. He would tell me to back off, maybe even threaten me. I didn't care. I was even more determined at that moment to find the killer myself just so I could shove it in his face.

8

PETER BELL

I DROVE OVER TO DAPHNE'S HOUSE AND RANG THE DOORBELL. I WAS greeted by Kalena again.

"Hello," I said. "I have an appointment with Daphne."

"Yes, she told me you'd be coming by this morning. She's in her mother's sitting room."

Kalena escorted me to the back of the house even though I remembered the way from my previous visit. When we entered the room, I saw Daphne standing by the window and looking out at the ocean.

"May I get either of you something to drink?" Kalena asked.

"No, thank you," I said.

"Ms. Laskaris?" Kalena asked.

Daphne shook her head. Kalena smiled and left the room.

Daphne motioned to one of the chairs, and I sat down. She sat opposite me in the same seat her mother had been in before.

"How's your mother this morning?" I asked.

"She's already left for California."

"Already?"

"She just came here to get Panos' body. His funeral will be in a few days."

"Have you made the list for us?" I asked.

Daphne picked up a small piece of paper on the table beside her chair and handed it to me. There were several names on the list, two of which I immediately recognized, Wes and Makani, the co-owner of the overpriced restaurant and the ex-boyfriend of Hani who wanted her back. There were a few other names I didn't know, but the last name on the list was the most intriguing one of all. Mine. I guess she could tell by the look on my face that I'd read to the bottom of the list.

"You asked me to write down everyone I thought might want to harm Panos," she said.

"Yes, you were right to put my name down, so let's get this out of the way before we proceed with our investigation."

I laid the list down on my lap.

"Ask me any question you want to," I said.

She said nothing, but I already knew what her questions were.

"I left the party after I saw your brother kissing Alana. I didn't leave the house for a few days because I couldn't stop feeling sorry for myself."

"I want you to know I was against my mother's decision to hire you for this job."

"Then why did you mention my involvement in a murder investigation?" I asked. "It sounds to me like you encouraged your mother to hire me. I didn't ask for this assignment. I did everything I could to talk her out of it."

"As you know, my mother can be very insistent. She kept asking me to find her the name of someone who could do an independent investigation. I think it should be left up to the police, though," she said.

"Your mother told me you didn't have confidence in Detective Adcock," I said.

"I don't, but I don't see how we can do much better. We don't have the authority to investigate anyone."

"That's exactly why we may succeed. They'll never see us coming. The badge is bound to make people nervous, whereas you're the grieving sister. There's a good chance people will let their guards down around you. Our job is to pay attention closely and listen for inconsistencies in their stories. Sooner or later, the lies will be revealed."

Daphne said nothing. I could sense the wheels in her head turning. She wasn't sure if she could trust me. I understood. We didn't know each other well at all, but at the same time, I knew she'd probably rather be out there trying to solve her brother's murder than sitting in this house waiting for an incompetent detective to catch a lucky break. That was the only way Adcock would be able to solve this thing. The killer would have to walk into the police station, confess to Adcock directly, and then lock him or herself up because the detective would probably still not comprehend what was going on.

"I don't mind working alone, if you'd prefer not to come with me," I said.

"No, I'll be fine. Who would you like to interview first?"

I looked at her list again. I read the first name on the list.

"Peter Bell works at the marina. Is that correct?" I asked.

"Yes, he's the one who found Panos' body."

"Then he's our first interview."

Daphne and I left her house and took my convertible to the marina in Lahaina where Panos' boat was docked. Fortunately, the traffic was light, and we made good time. We entered the marina manager's office and asked the young woman behind the counter for Peter Bell, only to be informed that he was touring the marina with a customer. We were told we could wait for him, so we decided to walk the docks until he returned.

"What made you add Peter to the list?" I asked.

"Panos' boat used to belong to Peter. He has a gambling problem and came to Panos, asking for a loan. Panos took advantage of the situation and instead made him an offer on his boat."

"Let me guess. He got it for substantially less than it was worth," I said.

"Peter was understandably reluctant to sell it to him for that price. Panos told him he could buy it back for the same price once he got back on his feet, but when he tried to buy it back a year later, Panos refused to sell it to him."

Great guy, I thought.

"I assume Peter was pretty upset."

"He was furious. He threatened Panos, but Panos only laughed."

"What exactly do you mean when you say 'threatened him?' Did Peter tell Panos he would hurt him?"

"No, nothing like that. I was there when it happened. He came by the house and demanded the boat back. When Panos refused, Peter told him he would tell all of our friends that Panos had taken advantage of him. Panos told him to go ahead. Panos said that Peter would only be exposing himself as a gambler. Peter dropped it. Maybe he was worried that he would lose his job if the truth about his finances came out."

Daphne looked past me toward the gate near the front of the dock.

"There he is now," she said.

I turned and saw a tall, blond man about the same age as Panos talking to an older gentleman. The two shook hands, and then the blond guy turned and walked toward us. I could see his expression change once he noticed Daphne. His wide smile vanished and was replaced by a decidedly depressed look. I couldn't tell if he was upset because he didn't like Daphne or if he just didn't want to be reminded of Panos again.

"Hello, Peter," Daphne said.

"Hello," he responded.

Peter looked at me suspiciously.

"This is my friend, Poe," Daphne said.

"Hello," I said, extending my hand.

He hesitated a moment and then shook my hand.

"We wanted to ask you a few questions," she said.

"Actually, I'm late for my next appointment."

"It will just take a couple of minutes," I said.

"It would really help us out," Daphne said.

"Okay."

"Where did you first meet Panos?" I asked.

"At his restaurant in Lahaina. I would go there a few times a month, and we'd talk at the bar. One day I invited him out on the boat."

"How did you find Panos' body?" I asked.

"I already went over this with the police," he said.

"I'm sure, but it would help us if you could go over it again."

"Why? Are you a private investigator or something?"

"Or something," I said.

"Maybe I should call my lawyer."

"We don't think you had anything to do with this, Peter. We're just trying to get some information that might help us," Daphne said.

Peter looked past us, perhaps searching for his next client. Finally, he turned back to us.

"I was walking on the dock that night when I saw blood. It was on the walkway right below his boat. I thought someone might have been hurt, so I climbed aboard."

"What were you doing on the dock that night?" I asked.

"I have a friend who lets me use his boat sometimes. I planned to take it out the next morning, and I was taking some supplies down to it."

"And it's docked near Panos' boat?"

"That's right. Just a few slips down from his."

"It must get pretty dark down there. How did you notice the blood?"

"There's a dock light just a few feet from Panos' boat. The blood wasn't hard to see."

I looked around the marina for security cameras.

"What about a security system? Are there cameras placed throughout?"

"Like I told the police, we have a security system, but it was down. It should have been fixed before that night, but the repair guy from the security company was on vacation."

"Did anyone know that other than the staff here?" I asked.

"No, just us and the security company. We wanted to keep it quiet.

Figured the boat owners might get upset if they knew the system was down."

So the killer either somehow knew the system was down, I thought, or they just got incredibly lucky.

"Daphne says the boat used to belong to you and that you sold it to Panos," I said.

"That's right."

"She also said that he refused to sell it back as promised."

"What's your point?" he asked.

"It seems like a pretty shitty thing to do to a guy," I said. "I'm just wondering who else he screwed over."

Peter glanced at Daphne. I assumed he wondered what her reaction would be to my comment regarding Panos' character.

"I'm not suggesting you had anything to do with his death, but you must have been pretty mad at how he took advantage of you," I continued.

Peter shrugged.

"It's my own damn fault. I never should have allowed myself to get into that situation in the first place."

"Sounds like you took it pretty well," I said.

"What else was I supposed to do?"

"That's not true, Peter. I was there when you confronted Panos. You were screaming at him," Daphne said. "You threatened him."

"What do you want me to say, Daphne? Panos ripped me off when I was at my lowest. That boat was worth four times what he paid for it. I've done my best to get my life back on track. Do you know how hard it's been to come here every day and see the boat that should have been mine? I worked for years to buy that thing. He paid extra each month for us to maintain it while he was in California. I had to clean and maintain my own boat for him. Now who's going to want it after what happened inside? I don't."

"That's what you're worried about? A damn boat? Panos is dead," Daphne said.

Peter looked away. He turned back to Daphne.

"You're right. I'm sorry. It's just a boat."

"You're not sorry. You didn't give a damn about him. I know that wasn't the only money he loaned you. Why don't you tell Poe about that?"

Daphne stormed off. Both Peter and I watched her as she headed back to my car. I turned back to Peter.

"Is that right? Panos loaned you money before?"

Peter nodded.

"A hundred bucks, here and there. Certainly nothing that covered the cost of that boat."

"Yeah, but you have to admit that was decent of him. How many other people gave you money?"

"Look, man, Panos could spare the money. He was some rich, trust fund baby. He had no idea how good he had it. He could have easily paid me what that boat was worth, and then we wouldn't have had a problem."

"Daphne's gone. Now you can tell me what you saw."

Peter hesitated again.

"Don't worry," I said. "I won't repeat what you say."

"I saw the blood on the dock. It led onto the boat. I should have just called nine one one. Maybe if it was any other boat, I would have done that, but I went aboard. The door to the cabin was open. It's always locked at night, so I went inside. There were more blood tracks on the carpet in the main cabin. They led all the way to the steps. I went down into the bedroom and saw him there. He was lying on the bed on his back. There was blood everywhere, on the carpet, all over the sheets. Everywhere. I threw up, man. I'm not ashamed to admit it. After that I ran out and called the cops. Look, I didn't want anything bad to happen to Panos. I certainly didn't want him dead. But I didn't see anything that night that could help you find the killer. I don't have the slightest idea who did it."

"You must know someone who didn't like him."

Peter laughed.

"How much time do you have? As many people hated Panos as loved him. He was a cool guy to be around at first, but after a while, you saw him for who he really was. The guy didn't care about anyone other than himself, and he wouldn't think twice about screwing you over. He did it to me. I'm sure he did it to countless others."

I tried to think of other questions but didn't really have anything.

"I appreciate your time," I said.

"I saw you out on his boat the other day. You were with Alana and two other people."

He waited for a reaction from me. He didn't get one.

"How long did you know him?" Peter asked.

"Not long," I said.

"Be glad. He was bad news, man. He would have done you wrong too."

What is that phrase of not speaking ill of the dead? I guessed Peter had never heard it. He didn't say goodbye, and I didn't either. He just turned from me and walked back toward the marina office. I looked up to the parking lot and saw Daphne leaning against my car. She wasn't facing me, so she didn't see me looking at her.

I walked back down the dock to Panos' boat. The blood had been washed off the dock. I looked past the crime-scene tape on the boat and saw the traces of blood that stood out against the white surface of the boat deck. It was easy to spot in the daylight, but I had no idea how hard it would be to see at night, even with a dock light nearby. I wasn't sure I believed Peter when he said he didn't have anything to do with the murder. I'm sure his anger would have grown every time he washed and cleaned that boat for the guy who had practically stolen it from him. It might have been too much to take once Panos returned to the island. I wondered if maybe Panos had said something to Peter the day he took us sailing. Peter said he saw us at the marina, so he and Panos were at the same place, at the same time. Panos took multiple shots at me. It wouldn't be a stretch of the imagination to assume he took a shot at Peter that day too. But did Peter respond by slitting Panos' throat? How did he even know Panos was on the boat that night to begin with? Why was Panos even there?

I didn't understand why Panos would leave the rehearsal party at his restaurant to spend the night on his boat when he had a beautiful house nearby. I considered for a moment that the murder of Panos took place somewhere else, and then his body was transported to the boat cabin, but I quickly dismissed that theory. Panos was a big guy. It would be too much effort to drag his body down to the dock. It would also be far too risky. For some reason, Panos decided to come to the boat himself, and the killer either knew he was coming or followed him there.

I walked back to my car and found Daphne still leaning against it.

"Are you okay?" I asked.

"Fine. I just figured he might be more open if I wasn't there."

"That's very observant of you."

"Not really. It was pretty obvious he was holding back. Did you learn anything?"

"The main thing is I'm just not sure he would have been able to spot those blood stains on the dock or the boat at night. That dock light is several feet from the boat. I'm not sure it would have cast enough light to tell it was blood versus an ordinary shadow."

"So you think he's lying?"

"I don't know," I admitted.

"Where to next?" she asked.

"The restaurant. Let's hit up Wes."

We climbed in the car and drove away.

9

WES AND THE VIEW

IT TOOK US LESS THAN FIVE MINUTES TO GET TO THE RESTAURANT, AND the parking lot was mostly empty. I guessed the only cars there belonged to the employees. I parked close to the front entrance, and we went inside.

We saw Shae, the hostess, along with a few of the waiters, placing glasses and silverware on the tables. Shae looked at us when she heard the door open. Even from a distance, I could recognize the look of sorrow on her face. Shae put one of the glasses down and hurried over to Daphne.

"I'm so sorry, Daphne."

Shae hugged her. I wasn't sure Daphne wanted one based on her reaction. She seemed reluctant to hug Shae back. She eventually did, but I'm not sure Shae noticed the initial hesitation on Daphne's part.

"I'm so sorry," Shae repeated.

"Thank you," Daphne said.

Shae turned to me.

"It's nice to see you again," I said. "I'm not sure we were ever formally introduced the other night. I'm Poe."

"Nice to meet you," she said while wiping a few tears out of her eyes.

We didn't shake hands.

"We were wondering if Wes was here," Daphne said.

"He's in his office."

"Do you mind if we go back there?" I asked.

"Of course not."

Shae turned to Daphne.

"Please let me know if there's anything I can do," she said.

"Thank you," Daphne said.

Daphne and I walked to the back of the restaurant. The office door was open, and we saw Wes sitting behind a desk. He had a stack of receipts in front of him. I felt weird being back here. The last time I stood in this doorway, I saw Alana kissing Panos.

Wes looked up from his receipts. His expression was neutral.

"Hello, Wes," Daphne said. "May we come in?"

Wes stood, and, to his credit, walked around the desk to greet Daphne with a hug.

"I'm very sorry about Panos," he said.

"Thank you."

I knew everyone meant well, but I wondered how many times Daphne had heard that phrase in the last week. I'm sure she was getting tired of it.

"We were hoping we could ask you a few questions about the night of the rehearsal party," Daphne said.

"Sure," Wes said. He looked somewhat confused.

He walked back around his desk and sat down. We sat in two chairs in front of the desk.

"Do you know what time Panos left the party?" I asked.

"No idea. I closed up around four in the morning. I asked Panos to see me before he left, but he ducked out before talking to me."

"What were you going to talk about?" I asked.

"The restaurant operations."

"Was the rehearsal party the best time for that discussion?" I asked.

"Who are you again?" Wes asked.

"My name's Poe. I'm a friend of Daphne's."

"The answer to your question is 'no.' The party was not the best time to talk about the restaurant's problems, but Panos had been ignoring me for months. I called and emailed him dozens of times, only to be completely ignored. I thought he would want to know we were on the verge of bankruptcy. Apparently, he couldn't have cared less."

I couldn't blame Wes for being mad at Panos or even pissed off at me for sticking my nose into his money problems. But that was the point of these little interrogations. Get people angry at you and expose their true feelings.

"You mentioned the other night that you were having business issues. How did you think Panos could help?"

"By giving a damn. I wanted him to help me get Jim back."

"Who's Jim again?" I asked.

"My ex-chef. The guy Panos drove away."

"You couldn't get him back on your own?"

"I tried. God knows, I tried. But Jim wouldn't come back without a personal apology from Panos. Who knows if he would have come back even then."

"You said Panos drove him away. Why?"

"Nobody likes to be micromanaged, especially a chef. Panos argued with Jim about everything - the menu, the quality of the food, the service, everything. But Jim is the best chef on the island. He didn't need to put up with Panos, so he left."

"How did you and Panos end up in business together?" I asked.

"I owned a small place in Paia that Panos came to a few times. He heard me talking to a customer about wanting to open a bigger restaurant here in Lahaina. I just wasn't getting the traction I needed in Paia. Panos approached me about being his partner. He said he would put up the money, and I would run the business. It sounded like a dream deal."

"But it wasn't," I guessed.

Wes shook his head.

"It was a nightmare from the start. We clashed constantly. Panos had to get his way. He felt the need to remind me a hundred times a day that he was the one with the cash. Like I needed to be reminded of that. Of course, my twenty-five years of experience in the restaurant business counted for nothing. But I was desperate to get to this area, so I agreed to everything."

"What were some of the things you argued about?" I asked.

"The food, the prices, you name it. I wanted to go middle-of-the-road, appeal to the broadest group of tourists, but Panos wanted to go high end."

"So your business didn't do well from the very beginning?" I asked.

"No, things did go well. We were making good money. We had great reviews. It proved to Panos that he had been right on every call, and I was wrong about everything. He threw it in my face every day. He gave no credit to Jim or me. I was in charge of the restaurant operations, the hiring and training of the waiters and bartenders, the ordering of food and supplies, but if you asked Panos, he did everything, including slaving over the stove and carrying the food out to the tables."

"He must have done something," Daphne suggested, trying to salvage something of her brother's reputation.

"Yeah, he brought in the crowds. I'll give him that. He was a magnet. You know that. People loved Panos. When he fired Jim and left for California, I couldn't recover."

"I don't believe Panos would completely ignore you. I know he was away, but Panos never wanted this place to fail. He had too much invested in it," Daphne said. "He was proud of this place."

"Would you like me to show you the emails? All of them went unreturned. Then there's this building. Panos bought it and rented it back to the restaurant. The rent's astronomical. Once we started having troubles, I asked him to lower the rent, but he wouldn't do it."

"What are you going to do now?" I asked.

"I don't know. Maybe try to sell the business."

"You can't sell without my family's permission," Daphne said.

"Is that right? I guess Panos never showed you the operating agreement."

Wes opened the top drawer of his desk and pulled out a document. He shoved it across the desk toward Daphne, but she didn't pick it up.

"I now own one hundred percent of this business," Wes said.

I picked up the operating agreement and began to flip through it.

"That's impossible. Panos would have left his shares to his family."

"The operating agreement says that in the event of a general partner dying, the shares revert back to the other partner. Panos' shares went to me."

"That's crazy. He never would have agreed to that."

"Agreed to it? He insisted on it. I wanted to leave my shares to my wife, but Panos said he didn't want to get stuck in business with someone he might not be able to work with. That was our biggest point of contention, but I gave in, like I always did. Now it's come back to bite him in the ass."

I found the section of the agreement that detailed what happened if one of the owners should die. Wes was right. All of the shares went to the surviving member. I put the document back on his desk.

"I'm afraid he's right, Daphne. Wes now owns all of the restaurant."

"This was all your plan," Daphne said.

"My plan? How was this my plan?"

Wes suddenly realized why we were there.

"You think I had something to do with Panos' death, don't you?"

I said nothing.

"Well, I didn't. What did I have to gain? I now own one hundred percent of a bankrupt business. I'll be lucky to get pennies on the dollar for this place."

Daphne stood up.

"I still expect the rent on time," she said.

She turned and left before Wes could respond.

"I didn't want him to die. I just wanted him to help me," he said.

I believed Wes, at least I thought he sounded sincere. But I'd been fooled before.

"How did you hear about Panos' death?" I asked.

"The same as everyone else, I guess, on the news. Panos was well known around town."

"It must have been somewhat of a relief for you, to know you could now make all of the decisions by yourself."

"It was. And I feel terrible admitting that to you. He just didn't give a damn about anything or anyone other than himself."

"Yet people were still attracted to him," I said.

"I fell under his spell in the beginning too. The guy had so much confidence. You just got the impression he could do anything."

"Have you considered just closing the doors and cutting your losses?"

"I can't. My wife and I sunk every penny we have into this place. We'll be ruined if it doesn't work out."

"I'm sorry," I said. "I wish you the best. For what it's worth, I do think things will turn around for you."

I stood. Wes said nothing nor did he stand to walk me to the door. I didn't really expect him to. He didn't know me, so why would my opinion mean anything to him? I left him sitting behind the desk with his receipts, staring off into space.

I exited Wes' office and looked for Daphne. She was nowhere in the restaurant, so I figured she had gone outside to my car. I caught a glimpse of Shae behind the bar as I walked toward the front door. She looked worried.

"Is everything all right?" I asked.

"It's fine," she said.

"You don't sound very confident of that. Is there anything I can help you with?"

"I just feel terrible for what happened to Panos."

I nodded.

"We all do," I said.

"Have you talked to Hani?" she asked.

"Not yet."

"I was just wondering how she was."

"I'm sure she's as torn up as you'd expect her to be."

"I don't know what I would do if I'd just lost my fiancé."

I looked back toward Wes' office. He was still inside, and I hoped far enough away that he couldn't hear my conversation with Shae.

"Why do you think things didn't work out between Panos and Wes? Did Panos really just disappear from this place?"

"He lost interest, like he usually does. He can make you feel like you're the most important person in the world. Then he's just gone."

"So that's what he did here? This restaurant was important to him until it wasn't?"

"Once he moved to California, nothing on this island meant anything anymore."

"Do you remember what time Panos left the party? Did he leave with Hani or Alana?

"I don't know. I left around two in the morning. He was still here."

"Who was he talking to?"

"He was outside when I left. He and Hani were arguing. She was screaming at him about something."

I had a pretty good idea what the fight was about.

"I tried to steer clear of them. I don't think they saw me," she said.

"Where was Alana?" I asked, and I felt bad that I was now inserting my own personal drama into the questioning.

"I don't know. I didn't see her."

I picked up a cocktail napkin off the bar and wrote my phone number down.

"If you remember anything else, please call me," I said.

I handed her the napkin.

"Do you think Hani will be okay?" she asked.

"I think so. But it will take time."

I said goodbye to Shae and walked outside. Daphne was on the phone, listening to the person on the other line. She looked up at me as I approached.

"Thank you," she said into her phone.

Then she pressed the end button.

"Wes is two months behind on the rent," she said.

"Who was that on the phone?"

"I called the accountant for my family's businesses. He collects the rent for this restaurant. Wes is two months behind."

I didn't think it necessary to remind her that technically Wes and Panos were behind on the rent.

"Once he hits three months, I can start the process of kicking him out," she continued.

"Are you sure you don't want to give him a chance to turn the business around?"

"Why should I?"

"If you kick him out now, you'll get nothing."

"I don't give a damn about the money. I don't appreciate him trashing Panos like that."

"We didn't expect him to be a fan. That's why we came here. Remember? We need to determine if he had anything to do with Panos' death."

"I don't know if I can keep doing this. It's too hard."

"I understand. I don't mind continuing on my own if that would make it easier."

Daphne looked back at the restaurant.

"I wouldn't be surprised if Wes comes crawling to me, begging me to forgive the back rent."

I wasn't sure how to respond to that comment, so I kept my mouth shut.

"Do you want to interview anyone else today?" she asked.

"I think two is enough for one day. I probably should get home and write down notes from what we learned."

I drove Daphne back to her house and headed to Harry's Bar for lunch and a beer. I needed the drink.

10

THE SURF SHOP

DAPHNE CALLED ME EARLY THE NEXT MORNING AND SAID SHE DIDN'T have the energy to go with me to interview Makani. I told her I understood and that I would call or email later in the week with an update on the investigation. The truth was that I thought her absence would allow people to open up more. No one wanted to say anything bad about the deceased, especially in front of his sister. She also told me she and Kalena were leaving for California for a few days to attend the funeral.

Daphne gave me the address for a surf shop that Makani owned with his brother in Kihei. I put the top down on the convertible and set off for what I guessed would be an hour drive. The traffic in Kihei was usually bad since there was one main road that led in and out of that part of the island. It was a beautiful beach, and the weather was always sunny, so if I did get stuck in traffic, at least it would be in pleasant weather. I was actually a little apprehensive about interviewing Makani. He'd been thoroughly humiliated by Panos at the rehearsal party. I didn't want to 'pile on' so to speak. However, Daphne identified him as a suspect, and I thought he was too. I couldn't shake the feeling that Panos would have simply slapped Makani if he confronted him on that boat. Makani didn't seem to have the courage to hurt anyone, let alone a guy as large as Panos.

I drove past the surf shop twice before I finally guessed it was hidden in the back of a strip mall. The shop was tucked into a far corner, and the sign above the front door faced away from the street. I thought you'd either have to accidentally stumble upon the shop or already know it was there. I couldn't imagine they did much business there.

I walked into the store, and a little bell jangled to alert them of my arrival. A young guy, maybe college-aged, sat behind the counter in the back of the store. He read what looked like an extreme sports magazine. He didn't seem to care that he had a potential customer because he never took his eyes off the magazine. I looked around the store. No customers were there. I walked up to the counter. The guy still didn't look at me. I pressed my body against the edge of the counter and started to count silently in my head until he acknowledged my presence. I thought it had become a sort of contest of wills between the two of us. I got up to thirty-seven before he spoke. He still didn't look at me, though.

"Can I help you?" he asked with zero enthusiasm.

"I'm looking for Makani," I said.

"He's out back on his break."

I looked to the back corner of the store. There was an open door that I guessed led to a storage room. I assumed there was a door in the back of that room that would take me behind the strip mall.

"Do you mind if I cut through there?" I asked and nodded to the back room.

"Nope," he said.

I didn't know if he meant 'nope' he didn't mind or 'nope' he didn't want me to walk through the storage room. I thought about advising Makani to terminate this young man's employment contract but then worried he might actually be a relative of his. I couldn't figure out how else he could keep the job. I walked through the back room and saw an open door that led to the outside. I smelled cigarette smoke as I got closer.

I walked outside and saw Makani sitting on a white plastic bucket that was turned upside down. He was leaning against the wall of the building. He looked up at me as I approached him. I thought about making a comment regarding how cigarettes kill. Instead, I decided not to be a smartass and just smiled at him. Makani must have read my mind. He ground the cigarette out on the pavement.

"I actually quit several years ago but just started back," he said.

I introduced myself and told him Hani had given me his name, which wasn't true, but I wasn't sure how else to start the conversation that wouldn't immediately cause his defenses to go up.

"How's she doing?" he asked.

"Not well. She's staying with her sister, so that should help some."

"Alana was always there for her," Makani said.

"How'd you two meet?" I asked.

"High school. We had several classes together. We ended up going to the same college."

"And you dated all through school?" I asked.

"Yeah, but then I dropped out to open the shop with my brother. Work got kind of busy, and I spent less and less time with her. We just drifted apart."

I wondered if that was the excuse he came up with or if it was just a better way of saving face in front of me. The version I got was that Hani simply got bored with him. I couldn't blame her at the moment. This guy seemed like a deflated dud. He didn't even stand to talk to me. He just kept leaning against the wall.

"Why did you come to the party?" I asked.

"To stop her from marrying that guy. He was wrong for her."

"So you wanted her back?"

"No, I just didn't want her to make a mistake with him. Everyone knew what Panos was like. He cheated on her constantly."

"So you thought you were going to talk her out of marrying him at her own rehearsal party?"

"When else was I going to do it? I didn't even know about the wedding until that morning. I tried calling her several times. I even went over to her house. I couldn't find her until that night."

"You really care for her," I said. "It must have been hard to have seen her with Panos."

"The guy was an asshole."

"I wished he didn't treat you like that. I'm sure you wanted to get back at him."

Makani finally stood up.

"What do you want from me, man?" Makani asked.

"I told you. Hani asked me to come see you. She wanted me to see if you were okay."

I could see Makani trying to decide whether or not he believed me.

"She said she looked for you after the party but couldn't find you," I said.

"Tell Hani I'm fine. I hope she feels better."

Makani abruptly ended the conversation and walked into the shop.

I hated to admit it, but my interview with Makani had been a bit of a bust. I just wanted to take off and be done with it. I didn't want to have to walk back through the shop to get to my car. I also didn't want to have to take the long way down the backside of the strip mall, walk down the street, and then walk all the way down the front side of the mall to get to the back corner where I parked. So I headed into the storage room and made my way into the shop. The guy behind the counter was still absorbed with his magazine, but now I saw a new guy talking to Makani. They were about the same height and weight and had similar facial features, but while Makani projected timidity, this new guy had the air of a cage fighter getting pumped up for a pay-per-view event.

"Is this the guy?" the new guy said.

"That's him," Makani said.

The new guy walked toward me. I stopped in front of the counter. He got a few feet from me. It wasn't hard to pick up his menacing tone.

"What do you want with Makani?" he asked.

"What business is that of yours?" I asked.

"He's my brother. He said you were asking questions about that fool, Panos. You with the cops?"

"Not exactly," I said.

"Then don't let me see you around no more."

"I'm sorry. I didn't catch your name."

"That's because I didn't give it to you. Now tell me you understand what I'm saying."

"Are you always this protective of your adult brother?" I asked.

Cage fighter brother said nothing, and Makani just stood in the background. I wasn't sure if Makani was intimidated by me or his brother or maybe a stiff ocean breeze could make him shake in his boots. I was beginning to wonder what in the world Hani ever found attractive about this guy. Maybe he changed after she let him go. Maybe that rejection was what crushed his spirit.

"How did it make you feel when Panos made a fool of your brother at the party?" I asked.

"He said what that punk did. I told Panos he'd be sorry if he ever laid hands on my brother."

"He didn't lay hands on him. He just laughed at him. A lot of people laughed at him."

"Panos got what he had coming to him, didn't he?" the brother said.

"You're saying you had something to do with that? It sure sounds like that to me," I said.

"Adcock already came around here. He knows we had nothing to do with it."

"Maybe. Maybe not. Adcock isn't the sharpest tool in the shed. And by the way, don't ever threaten me again," I said.

I was expecting a quick reply, but I didn't get one. The brother just glared at me as I walked to the shop entrance. I halfway expected to be attacked from behind on the way out, but nothing happened. The bell jangled again when I opened the door.

No one said 'goodbye' or 'have a nice day' on my way out. They really needed to improve their customer service if they were going to stay in business.

I drove home and went straight to the backyard. Foxx and Michelle were in the pool. For a second, I thought I might have walked in on them going at it again, but I noticed they were too far apart.

"Hey there," I said.

They both turned to me. Michelle waved.

"How are things going with the investigation?" Foxx asked.

I told him about my conversation with Makani and his brother.

"I met the brother once," Foxx said. "His name's Kai, I think. Real hothead."

"Yeah, he threatened me once or twice during the conversation."

"Guys like that are all talk," Foxx said. "The dudes who are quiet, those are the ones to look out for. Those guys end up on a clock tower with a sniper rifle."

"Well, that would point to Makani as the number one suspect. I could barely get a word out of him."

I related to Foxx and Michelle that I didn't see what could have possibly made Hani interested in Makani. They didn't have a good theory either.

"So what's next?" Michelle asked.

"Not sure," I admitted. "I've made my way through every name on Daphne's list. I need a lucky break."

I decided to change the conversation.

"Have you seen Alana today?" I asked Michelle.

She shook her head.

"She wasn't there when I came over. I think she leaves for work pretty early. She told Hani that she's been clashing with the detective on the case. She asked to see the autopsy report, and he refused."

"Can he do that?" I asked.

"She said he can't, but I got the impression he's just being a jerk to her. She said she'd go around him to get the report."

I heard barking and turned around to see Maui the dog standing at the sliding glass door. He wagged his tail when he saw me look at him.

"You need to take that beast of yours for a walk. He's been stuck inside all day," Foxx said.

"Why didn't you let him out?" I asked.

Foxx held up his hands.

"Not my responsibility, buddy."

"I told him, Poe. I think Maui's adorable," Michelle said.

"He'd be tolerable if he'd just stop trying to bite me. One minute he's sleeping on my legs; the next he's trying to have me for lunch."

Michelle laughed.

"He's just suspicious of your character," she said.

"How can anyone not love me?" Foxx asked.

"You guys enjoy yourself," I said.

I turned and walked toward Maui the dog. I would take him on a quick walk, and then I would go for a run. I needed the physical exertion after my conversation with Makani and Kai. Talking to them, especially Kai, was like drinking a gallon of poison. I felt like I needed to sweat the experience out.

11

THE THREAT

WHILE I RAN, I THOUGHT ABOUT EVERYTHING I'D LEARNED SINCE THE start of my investigation.

Peter Bell resented Panos because Panos bought his boat at a bargain price, and then wouldn't sell it back to him as originally agreed upon. I found it unlikely Peter would kill Panos over a boat, but Peter had discovered the body, and he did seem to possess super-human eyesight by seeing the blood stains on a dark dock at night. Did he only see them because he knew they were there? Then again, would you kill a person over a sailboat? People certainly killed for less. I just didn't know if Peter Bell was one of those people.

Wes was a far more likely suspect. He hated Panos for not treating him like an equal business partner, and he felt ignored once Panos moved to Los Angeles. Wes had everything invested in that restau-rant. If it went down, Wes was going with it, along with his wife. It had also seemed unlikely that anything would change as long as Panos continued to own half of the restaurant and blocked every-thing Wes tried to do. But Wes did make a great point when he said owning 100 percent of a failing business was still not worth much. He didn't really gain anything by getting rid of Panos.

I was tempted to scratch the timid Makani off my list, but my list was so small already, I couldn't afford to lose a potential suspect. Makani was deeply embarrassed by Panos at the party, and he was jealous over Panos' relationship with his ex-girlfriend, Hani. So that potentially led to revenge, a proven reason for murder.

His brother, Kai, though, was my number one suspect so far. I had to admit my personal feelings could, and probably did, influence my opinion on the matter. Kai threatened me, and he was an asshole. You'd be upset too.

I finished my run and walked into the house. Foxx was lying on the sofa, watching television.

"Where's Maui the dog?" I asked.

"Outside with Alana," he said, not even turning to me.

"Alana's here?" I asked.

"Didn't I just say that?"

He flipped the television to one of those Discovery Channel shows that deal with wives killing husbands or husbands killing wives. Something like that.

"She's been here for almost an hour," he continued.

I walked outside and found Alana tossing Maui a tennis ball in the backyard. The green ball was almost too big for him, and he struggled to pick it up with his mouth. When he saw me, Maui abandoned the ball and ran to me. I bent down and scratched him on his back.

"Sorry to keep you waiting," I told Alana.

I wondered what was so important that she'd wait here for so long.

"It's no problem. I was glad to get out of the office."

"How's Hani?" I asked.

"Somewhat better. She finally climbed out of bed this morning."

"So she's still staying with you?"

"For the time being. I suspect she'll be going to her own home soon. Her tenant moved out of her house here on the island a month ago, so she'll probably be staying on Maui for a while. She said she has no real desire to go back to L.A."

"I'm sure you've been a big help to her," I said.

"I wish I could do more, but I've been trying to be at work as much as possible to stay in the loop. Michelle has mostly been the one staying with her."

"How is the investigation going? Adcock actually interviewed me, if you can believe it," I said.

"I had a discussion with Detective Adcock regarding you right before I came over," she said.

"You have to admit that him thinking of me as a potential suspect is a giant waste of time."

"That's not what he came to me about," she said. "He got a call from Kai, who told him you came by his shop today. He said you asked him all sorts of questions about Panos. Did you do that?"

"Yes," I said, not willing at that second to elaborate.

"What are you up to, Poe?"

I said nothing while I tried to figure out how to avoid explaining my actions to Alana. I refused to lie to her, but I knew she would explode if she knew the true reason I interviewed Kai. I figured when I accepted the job that she'd find out sooner rather than later. I just didn't expect it to be this soon.

"What are you up to?" she repeated.

My brain completely failed me, as it often does, and I had no great excuse other than the truth.

"Panos' mother asked me to look into it," I admitted.

"When did you meet Panos' mother?"

"She flew to the island to bring back Panos' body. She asked me to go see her, so I did."

"Why would she do that?"

"Something about not having a lot of faith in Adcock."

"Please don't tell me you're conducting your own investigation."

I said nothing.

"You are, aren't you?" Alana asked.

"All right. She hired me to find the killer. Well, technically, she didn't hire me since I'm working for free."

"This is a horrible idea."

"Trying to find the killer is bad?"

"No, clashing with Adcock is bad. He's threatening to arrest you for interfering in a murder investigation," she said.

"Can he do that?"

"Yes he can, and he will."

"You didn't do that to me," I said.

"They're two entirely different situations."

"So you think Adcock can figure this out on his own?" I asked.

"Adcock is a vindictive SOB. He wouldn't hesitate to throw you in jail even if the charges didn't stick. He'd keep you in there as long as he possibly could."

"I'll take my chances."

"Don't expect me to bail you out. I've warned you."

"Fine," I said.

"Fine," she repeated.

We both stood in silence for a few moments. Alana picked up the tennis ball and threw it for Maui the dog. He watched the ball roll toward the pool and decided he didn't want to chase it. Instead, he yawned and lay down on the ground.

"I guess I should be getting back to Hani," she said.

"Please give her my best," I said.

"I will."

Alana walked toward the back gate.

"Where are things with us?" I asked.

She stopped and turned around to face me.

"I don't know. Where are things?" she asked back.

"I was hoping you could tell me," I said. "That's why I asked the question."

"I apologized the other day. You didn't really say whether you could forgive me or not."

"Forgiving is one thing. Forgetting is something different. I was in Wes' office yesterday. I couldn't stop thinking about what I saw in there."

"That's the thing, isn't it? I can't spend the rest of our relationship having you throw that at me. It was a stupid mistake, and it meant nothing."

"I'm not throwing it at you, Alana. I'm telling you how I felt at that moment."

Alana said nothing.

"You still loved him, didn't you?" I asked.

"No."

She answered so quickly that I didn't know if she was lying or just knew the answer.

"Then why did you kiss him?"

"I don't know. It would never have gone any further than that. He kissed me. I should have immediately pushed him away, but I didn't."

"People say hate isn't the opposite of love. It's indifference. I knew something was up when I saw how emotional you were with his return to Maui. You still had feelings for him. I knew it. I just didn't want to admit it to myself."

"He humiliated me, Poe. Have you ever had anyone leave you for your sibling? Do you know how quickly word got around? I was the laughing stock of the island."

"No one was laughing at you," I said.

"How do you know? You weren't even here then."

"Because people respect you, and Panos' actions aren't your fault. If they were laughing at anyone, it was him or Hani, but it wasn't you."

"The thing is, I was madder at myself than I was at him. I knew from the start something like that was going to happen."

"Then why be with him if you didn't trust him?"

"Because it was exciting, at least at first. He lived an exciting life, and I lived a very safe life. I was always the good girl, always the one who did the right thing, did what everybody thought I should do. I was Ms. Predictable. Panos came along and showed interest in me. I was flattered. I knew it would never last, but even then, I didn't expect him to run off with Hani. I was furious with myself for not seeing that betrayal coming."

"It wasn't your fault. Nobody would expect that."

"I should have been smarter. It was typical Hani. If I had something, she had to make it hers," she said.

"How soon did you meet me after that?" I asked.

"Maybe six months. Maybe a little longer."

It suddenly made sense. During our first dinner date, I sensed Alana holding back, like there was a hidden pain deep inside her. Don't get me wrong. No one lays everything out on the table during the first date. I didn't expect Alana to do that. I didn't even know everything about her now, and I really didn't want to. People are deep mysteries. Part of the adventure is solving that mystery slowly over a long period of time, but there was a sorrow that night just below her surface. A hesitation. A fear. Now I knew what it was. Panos had come between us even then. I wondered if we'd ever be able to get past him even though he was now gone.

"We moved too fast, Poe."

"How did we move too fast?" I asked.

"We slept together on the first date," she reminded me, as if I actually needed to be reminded.

"You didn't want that? I thought you enjoyed it," I said, suddenly feeling very defensive, like she was accusing me of doing something she didn't want to do. I knew I had been determined that night, but I thought I was also respectful. I hated now thinking I had talked her into doing something she wasn't ready for. Suddenly I felt like I was part of a sexual harassment training video.

"We should have taken our time," she said.

"That wasn't some one-nighter. It turned into a relationship."

"Maybe I just wasn't ready."

"Ready for the sex or ready for the relationship?" I asked.

"I don't know. Both, maybe."

I didn't know exactly what she was trying to get at. My gut told me this was officially the end, and she was trying to figure out a way to break it to me gently. This sort of felt like a "this is not you, it's me" kind of talk.

"Sometimes I just don't trust happiness," she said.

"I get it. I really do. But that doesn't mean you should never allow yourself to be happy. You have to let your guard down sometime. You can't go through life worrying about something going wrong at any moment."

"I'm sorry. I just don't know what to do."

Alana hesitated a moment.

"Please do me a favor and stay out of this investigation," she continued. "I do care about you. I don't want you to get in trouble."

Alana turned and left. I went back into the house. Maui the dog followed me. Foxx was still on the sofa watching married couples killing each other on television. I hoped this wasn't the universe's way of telling me to get the point.

"You guys work everything out?" Foxx asked. He still didn't take his eyes off the television.

"Not quite," I said.

He didn't respond.

"How can you watch this crap?" I asked.

Foxx put the remote down and turned to me.

"What's the holdup with you two? I was convinced you'd have put this behind you by now."

I brought Foxx up to speed on everything that had just happened outside.

"I don't understand why she needs more time. Time for what?" I asked.

"I think that's the second question you should be asking yourself," Foxx said.

"What's the first?"

"Whether or not you forgive her for kissing Panos."

I said nothing.

"Do you forgive her?" he asked.

"I don't know. It just happened a week ago. How do you forgive someone just like that?" I asked.

"You don't, buddy, but you have to decide whether or not you're going to try. This isn't about her fear of being happy or not happy, and it's damn sure not about Panos. It's about you. She's waiting for you to make a decision. Are you going to cut her loose, or are you going to forgive her?"

"It's not that simple. I told you what she said. She said she's not even sure she's ready to be in a relationship."

Foxx laughed.

"Ready? I've got news for her. She's already in a relationship. No, man, she's waiting to hear from you. She's just trying to protect herself in case you reject her. She's just tricking herself now into thinking she might not even want a relationship. It's self-protection mode. We all do it. She may not even realize she's doing it, but she is."

"You sound like a psychiatrist," I said.

"No, just a dude who's been around a lot of women. I don't pretend to understand them. Not even close. I just understand people not wanting to get hurt. People will do anything not to get hurt."

I thanked Foxx for the pep talk and headed into the bathroom to take a shower. I soaked my head for what must have been twenty minutes. I wouldn't be surprised if I completely drained the hot water heater. I got out of the shower, got dressed, and took Maui the dog for a walk so he could do his business. I walked back into the house and intended to ask Foxx if he wanted to get a drink at Harry's, but I found him asleep on the sofa. The murder shows must have worn him out. I was debating whether to get the drink by myself, when my cell phone vibrated. I walked back into my bedroom so my conversation wouldn't disturb Foxx.

"Hello," I said.

"Poe, this is Shae from the restaurant."

"Hello, Shae. What can I do for you?"

"You asked me to call you if I thought of anything new about the party."

She paused. I guessed she was waiting for me to ask her what, so I asked.

"What did you remember?"

"It's not something I remembered. It's just something I didn't tell you."

"What is it, Shae?"

"Not over the phone. Is it possible for you to come to my home?"

"You can't talk about this over the phone?" I asked.

I wondered what the hell she was going to say. Did she expect the NSA was listening? Actually, they probably were.

"I would rather tell you in person. Please, can you come over now?"

"No problem. Just text me your address. I'll be over soon."

I ended the call and wondered if she was actually going to tell me something useful.

I felt my cell phone vibrate again and saw Shae's address appear on my display. I turned to leave and saw Maui sitting in the doorway of my bedroom. Once we made eye contact, he rolled over onto his back, expecting me to rub his belly.

"Maybe later, Maui. I need to go right now."

I walked past Maui. I had no idea everything was about to change.

12

THE WHITE SEDAN

I DROVE TO SHAE'S HOME. SHE LIVED IN A TINY APARTMENT LESS THAN thirty minutes from the restaurant in Lahaina. It looked like it might have been an old motel complex converted into apartments. Her place was on the second floor. I climbed the outside stairs and knocked on her door. I was immediately greeted by the sound of her dog barking.

Shae opened the door, and a Chihuahua ran out. The dog immediately tried to bite me, but it couldn't get its mouth around my leg.

"Sorry about that," Shae said, but she didn't pick up the dog or try to stop it from biting me. I walked into the apartment. The dog continued to try to eat me.

"What did you want to see me about?" I asked.

"It's about the night of the party," Shae said.

"I'm sorry, but do you mind doing something about this?" I asked. I shook my leg gently to try to get the dog loose.

"Butterscotch, sit!" Shae told the dog.

It ignored her.

"I'm so sorry," she said.

Shae picked up Butterscotch and walked the little beast to the back of the apartment. She placed him in another room, I assumed the bathroom, and shut the door. I could hear Butterscotch continue to bark, a noise probably better described as a yelp. At least it was a muffled yelp now.

"Can I get you anything?" Shae asked.

"A glass of water would be nice," I said.

I felt dehydrated from the run, and I had forgotten to get something to drink afterward due to the conversation with Alana. Shae returned a minute later with a tall glass of water. I tried not to immediately gulp it down. We walked over to a small, worn-out sofa and sat down. The springs on the sofa squeaked. There was nowhere else to sit in the studio apartment, except the bed, but I imagined that it squeaked too.

"I wanted to talk to you about the party," Shae repeated.

"What about it?"

"I didn't exactly tell you everything when we spoke in the restaurant. When I left the party, I did see Panos and Hani arguing in the parking lot, but I left out the part about Hani yelling at me."

"Why did she yell at you?"

"She was screaming at Panos for kissing Alana, and then she confronted me and said she knew I was sleeping with Panos."

Bombshell, I thought. But was it really? I was beginning to think I was the only one on the island Panos hadn't slept with.

"Were you sleeping with Panos?" I asked.

Shae nodded. There was silence for a few moments. I noticed Butterscotch had stopped barking.

"We started an affair shortly after I went to work at the View. That's why Jim left the restaurant. He found out about Panos and me."

"Jim was the chef?" I asked.

I tried to remember if that was the name of the chef Wes mentioned.

"Yes, he and Panos argued about a lot of business stuff, but the affair was the real reason Jim left. Jim confronted him one day in the kitchen, and Panos didn't deny it. He just laughed at him. He told him I wouldn't have strayed if Jim had kept me satisfied in the bedroom.

Jim tried to attack him in the kitchen, but Wes and some others broke it up."

Add Jim the chef to the list of suspects, I thought.

"How did Hani find out about your affair?"

"I don't know. Maybe Jim told her. Maybe Panos did. He didn't seem to care who knew about his women."

"Did he actually say that to you? That he didn't care who knew about his affairs?"

"Not really. He didn't have to. He was so open about everything. I should have known Jim would find out. The affair was never serious. We would be together a few times a month. I knew it wasn't going anywhere."

"So why risk ruining things with Jim?" I asked.

"Because the relationship with Jim wasn't going anywhere either. He cared way more about that restaurant than he did me."

"Did Hani confront you before that night in the parking lot?"

"No. I expected her to, but she never did."

"Panos and Hani were living in L.A. for months. Your affair was over. Why do you think Hani would still be mad?"

"She saw Panos flirting with me during the party. He said he wanted to be with me one more time before the wedding. I told him no. Part of me thought he was joking to begin with."

"He wasn't joking." I guessed.

"I got home after the party, brushed my teeth and collapsed into bed. That's when I heard a knock at the door. It was Panos."

"Did you let him in?" I asked.

But I already knew the answer. Shae nodded.

"We talked for a few minutes. He told me about the kiss with Alana. He started laughing about it. He said he was glad you and Hani opened the door because he was sure Alana might pull out her gun and shoot him for kissing her. Then he kissed me. I told him we shouldn't."

Shae stopped talking. I thought she might start to cry.

"I never meant to hurt Hani. He talked me into it. I made him promise he wouldn't come back here."

"So you and Panos had sex that night?"

"I never would have been with him after he got married. I don't sleep with married men."

I wasn't sure what the difference was between sleeping with Panos the day before he got married versus the day after he got married. Did a piece of paper mean that much difference? Maybe. I guess that's your call to make.

"What time did Panos leave here?" I asked.

"I'm not sure. I think around four. I walked him to the door, and he kissed me goodbye."

"Did you tell the police this information?" I asked.

"No, I was afraid Hani would find out. I didn't want her to know what I did."

"It's important to help establish where Panos was that night, and when."

"Do you think I could ask the police not to tell Hani?"

"I don't know. I've only met this Detective Adcock once. I don't know how willing he is to be discreet," I said.

"There's something else," she said. "I watched Panos drive away, and a few seconds later, another car followed him out."

"Are you sure they were following him?"

"It was so late. It kind of surprised me that another car would be leaving around the same time as Panos."

"Was it one of your neighbors?" I asked.

"No, I'd never seen the car before. We all kind of know each other's cars by now."

"What kind of car was it?" I asked.

"It was a sedan. Four doors. White. I could definitely tell it was white."

"I don't suppose you saw the driver?"

"No, it was dark inside the car. I can't even tell you if it was a man or a woman."

"Do you remember which way Panos turned when he went out of the parking lot?"

"He turned left. I remember thinking it odd because he usually turned right to go home."

Not really that odd, I thought. The marina was to the left. He probably drove straight there, but I still had no idea why he went there versus his home.

"So you think I should call the police?" she asked.

"I do. This could be important for them."

"All right. I'll call them in the morning."

Her delayed call was fine by me. It might be good to have some insider knowledge that Detective Adcock didn't have, at least for the time being. I rose from the squeaky sofa and thanked Shae for the information and the glass of water. The sound of the squeak must have alerted Butterscotch there was movement in the apartment, and the dog started to yelp again.

"Please let me know if you think of anything else," I said.

I walked to the door.

"How are things at the restaurant? Is Wes handling everything okay?" I asked.

"No. I've never seen him this upset. He almost seems paranoid."

"Do you think Wes can turn the business around?"

"I don't know. We've lost so much traffic since Jim left."

Shae opened the door for me.

"Please don't tell Hani any of this. I don't want her to hate me," she said.

I nodded, but did that constitute me agreeing to her request? Probably. But I certainly didn't intend to keep this to myself. I said goodbye to Shae and walked down the steps to my convertible. I climbed inside and drove out of the apartment complex so Shae couldn't see me use my cell phone. I pulled into a convenience store parking lot down the street and called Alana. Her phone rang several times before she answered.

"Hello," she said.

"Hey, it's me. I was wondering if you could answer a question for me."

"Is it safe to say you're still investigating Panos' murder?" she asked.

"Maybe," I admitted.

I heard her sigh on the other end.

"What's your question?" she asked.

"Do you know if Peter or Wes own a white sedan?"

"I know Wes has a black SUV. I think it's an Explorer. I have no idea what kind of car Peter drives. Why do you want to know?"

"I'm looking for a white sedan that may belong to someone Panos knew."

"Hani drives a Honda Civic. It's white."

I suddenly felt sick to my stomach.

"Is her car on Maui or did she ship it to Los Angeles?"

"Poe, what's going on? Why are you asking about a white car?"

"Please just tell me. Where is that car now?"

"Probably at Hani's house. She went home this morning. I assume she's still there."

"The night you went to the rehearsal and the party afterward, did you take your car or Hani's? I know all three of you couldn't fit into Panos' vehicle."

"We took hers."

"I remember Foxx telling me he drove you home, and I know Panos left on his own, so that means Hani was probably in her car by herself."

"Damn it, Poe. Tell me what's going on," she demanded.

"Send me Hani's address, please. I have some questions for her."

I hung up before she could keep arguing with me. I drove to Hani's house and found Alana standing beside her car, which was parked in the driveway. I knew I didn't have to invite her to meet me at Hani's. She would do it regardless. She has that irrepressible sense of curiosity that all detectives have.

"I think I have a right to know what's happening," she said.

"I just have a few questions for Hani."

"I don't want you upsetting her."

"That's the last thing I want," I said. "But I got a new lead, and I think you should hear it too."

We rang the doorbell, and a few moments later, Hani opened the door. Unfortunately, she looked as bad as Alana had described her. Her hair and clothes were a mess, and she had dark circles under her eyes. She sort of looked like I did the day after I saw Alana kissing Panos.

"Poe has a few questions for you. Is that all right?" Alana asked.

"Okay, I guess."

Hani led us into the house. It was about the same size as Alana's, but not as nice. There were clothes scattered on the floor, and the kitchen sink was filled with dirty dishes. She definitely lacked her sister's neat gene. We walked into the kitchen and sat around a table covered with gossip magazines, dirty plates, and an empty bag of chips.

"What did you want to know?" Hani asked.

"The last time I saw you at the restaurant, we were standing outside Wes' office. What did you do after that?"

"Panos left the restaurant. I followed him into the parking lot, and we had an argument."

"What happened after that?"

"I told him I didn't want to marry him anymore," she said.

"You called off the wedding?" Alana asked, clearly surprised.

I was a little taken aback that Hani hadn't told Alana that little piece of information. Unfortunately, it made the other lies I was about to accuse her of more believable.

"Not exactly," Hani said. "After I told Panos that, he just laughed and said we were still getting married. He said you two just shared a simple kiss, and it meant nothing. He told me I would forget about it in the morning."

"So you didn't call off the wedding?" I asked.

"I guess not. I expected him to be there at the ceremony. He never said anything that would make me think he wasn't going to show up."

Hani turned to Alana.

"You called me that morning and told me you weren't going to make it, but you were the only person I spoke to between the rehearsal party and arriving at the wedding."

"What did you do after the argument in the parking lot?" I asked.

"I went home."

"You didn't go back into the restaurant and speak with Alana?" I asked.

"No, I didn't want to talk to her after what she'd done."

"So you drove directly from the parking lot of the restaurant to your home?" I asked.

"That's right."

"You didn't follow Panos to Shae's apartment?"

"No," Hani said.

"What does any of this have to do with Shae?" Alana asked.

"Panos went from the restaurant to Shae's apartment. He stayed there for about an hour or so, and then left. My guess is he went to the marina from there."

"What was he doing at Shae's apartment?" Alana asked.

"They were having an affair, or maybe I should say Panos was starting the affair over again. It ended once Panos and Hani moved to California."

"Why do you think Hani went over there?" Alana asked.

Hani remained quiet during these last several moments. Not a good sign for her.

"Shae saw a white sedan follow Panos out of the parking lot of her apartment complex."

I turned to Hani.

"Shae told me you confronted her in the restaurant parking lot. You saw Panos flirting with her earlier that evening. After your argument with Panos, I'm guessing you thought he might run straight to Shae, which is exactly what he did."

"Did you go over there?" Alana asked.

Hani said nothing.

"You told me you came straight here," Alana said.

"After Panos left Shae's apartment, where did he go?" I asked Hani.

Hani said nothing.

"Where did he go?" Alana repeated the question.

"I followed him to the marina. He got out of his car, and I saw him walk toward his boat," Hani finally admitted.

"Why didn't you tell me any of this? Do you know how bad this looks?" Alana asked.

"That's exactly why I didn't tell you. I didn't want the cops thinking I did it."

"Did you follow him down to the boat?" I asked.

"No. I never got out of my car. I sat in the marina parking lot for a while. I didn't know what to do, so I drove back here."

"Why did you even follow him to the marina?" Alana asked.

"I did come home directly after the restaurant. I was so angry with him. I didn't know what to do about the wedding. Then I thought he might go to see Shae, so I got back in my car and drove over to her apartment. I saw his car there. I debated whether to bang on her door and catch him in the act, but I couldn't do it. I didn't want to see it. A few minutes later, I saw him come out of the apartment and go back to his car. I decided to follow him to his house, but he went to the marina instead."

"Why do you think he went there?" I asked.

"I don't know. Sometimes he would sleep on the boat, but usually when he'd been partying there and had too much to drink. I have no idea why he went there that night."

"What time did he get to the marina?" Alana asked.

"I'm not sure. It was sometime after four but probably before five."

"This is bad. This puts you at the marina close to the time Panos was killed," Alana said.

"I didn't do it," Hani said pleadingly.

"It doesn't matter," Alana said.

"What do you mean it doesn't matter? How can it not matter?"

"Adcock is going to zero in on you. You just became his number one suspect if you weren't already."

"He doesn't have to know any of this," Hani said.

"He will, Hani. Shae is going to tell him," I said. "She feels guilty as hell for not coming forward."

Hani turned on me.

"She should feel guilty for screwing my fiancé. You convinced her to go to the police, didn't you? Why would you do that to me?" Hani asked.

"Don't blame him. If Shae doesn't tell the police, I will," Alana said.

"You're both turning on me," Hani said.

"Adcock's gonna find out. It's better if you tell him," Alana said.

"But I already told him I came straight back here. Now he'll know I lied to him."

"I'll be here with you. We'll figure it out," Alana said.

I left Alana and Hani and went outside. I suddenly felt like a jerk for putting her in this predicament. It was obvious Hani lied to Alana and Detective Adcock about her whereabouts after the party, but I didn't think she actually killed Panos. Panos wasn't drunk at the party, and we know he had other things than drinking on his mind when he went to see Shae at her apartment. That meant he was probably still sober when he got to the boat. Panos was killed with a knife. It would take a strong person to overpower him. Hani was way too small.

Alana joined me outside after a few minutes.

"I gave her Glen Adcock's cell phone number. She said she's going to call him tomorrow morning," Alana said.

"Are you going to call him before that? Try to explain why she didn't say anything before?"

"I can't. I'm already crossing the line by not calling him immediately. I could get fired for not coming forward."

"You didn't know," I said.

"But I should have. She's my sister. I probably know her better than anyone. I should have known she was lying about coming back here. How many days have you been on this investigation? Two or three? And you already figured that out."

"For what it's worth, I'm sure she didn't kill Panos," I said.

"Why?"

I explained my theory on the killer being a large person in order to overpower Panos. As I spoke, Alana broke eye contact with me. It was subtle, but I definitely noticed it.

"What aren't you telling me?" I asked.

"I saw the coroner's report this morning. Panos had significant swelling and an abrasion on the back of his head," she said.

"You mean someone hit him from behind?"

"Either that or he fell backward in the attack and hit his head on the way down," she said.

"So Hani could have struck him from behind to render him helpless and then cut his throat while he was down?"

Alana didn't respond.

"Do you think she could do that?" I asked.

"Hani's not a killer. She doesn't have it in her, but she hasn't always been the most honest person. I'm not surprised to find out she followed him to Shae's apartment and then to the marina."

"Did you even know about Shae's affair with Panos?" I asked.

"No, but it's typical Panos."

I told Alana about Jim the chef attacking Panos in the restaurant once he discovered Shae's involvement with him.

"Jim wasn't anywhere near the party," Alana said.

"I know, but he or Wes or Kai could have easily gone to the boat after Hani left."

"It's unlikely," Alana said. "How would they even know he was there unless they followed him from place to place that night? Hani would have seen them too, especially since she was already following Panos."

Alana looked back at the house.

"I better get back inside. She's probably having a major freak-out session right now."

"I'm sorry," I said.

"For what?"

"For complicating things for Hani."

"It's not your fault. She did that to herself. Thanks for coming here first and not going straight to Adcock."

"Are you kidding me? I wouldn't go to that guy if my life depended on it."

"Still, I appreciate it," she said.

Alana turned and walked back to the house. She opened the door without knocking and disappeared inside.

I didn't immediately get into my car because Peter Bell suddenly popped into my head and distracted me. Alana was right. It didn't make sense that Wes or Kai would follow Panos around, only to jump him at the marina. It also didn't make sense that they would know the boat was Panos' destination at the end of a very long evening.

Peter Bell obviously worked at the marina, though. He might have been there when Panos arrived. Alana told me Panos was killed sometime after five in the morning. I thought it likely the murder took place at dark. The killer wouldn't want to risk being seen leaving Panos' boat, and the daylight would certainly make that more likely.

Five in the morning was early, but not so early that it couldn't be someone's start time for work. My father often went to work even earlier than that when I was a child. He was always an early riser, even on his days off. Hell, he kept getting up early even after he retired.

Maybe Peter Bell was the same way. It wasn't unreasonable to assume he could have been in his office when Panos arrived that morning. The sound of a car pulling into the gravel parking lot would have surely gotten Peter's attention. Maybe he waited for Panos to climb aboard and then gave him time to go to sleep. It would be easy to kill a sleeping man. Or maybe he immediately confronted Panos at the dock, and they got into a fight. Peter was certainly big enough to fight Panos. Then there was the security system. Peter knew the cameras were broken. I needed to figure out a way to discover when Peter reported for work that morning.

I climbed into my car but looked back to the house before I started the engine. I thought about telling Alana immediately about my new theory on Peter Bell but decided against it. The selfish side of me also wanted to go back inside and talk to Alana about our relationship. Foxx's pep talk had sunk in. Maybe Alana was waiting for me to make the decision. Then again, maybe she wasn't. Maybe she had decided to move on. Instead, I did nothing but stay in my car. Alana wasn't the only one afraid to get hurt. This certainly wasn't the time or place for that discussion. At least that was the excuse I gave myself when I started the car and drove home.

13

THE FLASHLIGHT

I GOT UP EARLY THE NEXT MORNING AND DROVE TO THE MARINA TO explore my Peter Bell theory. I got there just before eight o'clock. The marina office wasn't open yet, so I walked around the building and looked into the windows. I hoped to see Peter in his office, which would confirm he got to work early, but I didn't see anyone inside.

I thought he might be walking the dock, checking on the condition of the boats under his watch, so I walked down to the dock. I saw a couple of guys cleaning their boat, but neither man was Peter Bell. I decided to ask them a few questions.

"Hey guys," I said. "I don't suppose you knew Panos Laskaris."

"Hell of a thing that happened to him," one guy said.

"Were you here the morning they found him?" I asked.

"No, but we heard about it later that day. It's all anyone's been talking about," the other guy said.

"Know if they caught the guy yet?" the first guy asked.

"No, the marina's security camera system was broken that week. Did you know that?"

"No, hadn't heard that," guy two said.

"So they don't send an email out or something like that to tell you if the system is down?"

Both guys shook their heads.

"I never knew it to go down before. To tell you the truth, I never paid it much attention," guy one said.

"You guys know Peter Bell?" I asked.

"Sure, we know Pete," guy two said.

"Does he work early mornings?"

"Not that I know of. We're usually out of here before he arrives," guy one said.

And my theory took another blow.

"Thanks for your time, guys," I said.

They nodded, and I walked back to the marina office.

It was now just after eight o'clock, and the office should have been open, but it wasn't. I did another walk around the building. Maybe Peter was in the bathroom when I did my circle before. It was desperate thinking, but I had nothing better to do at that moment. Peter wasn't magically there all of a sudden. The offices were still empty.

I walked back to the front of the building and sat down on the front steps. Less than five minutes later, the receptionist I met on my first trip to the marina drove up. She climbed out of her car and walked toward me. She looked annoyed that I was there. Maybe she expected me to give her a hard time about opening up late, but I didn't.

"Can I help you?" she asked as she reached into her purse and fumbled for a set of keys.

She found the right key and unlocked the doors.

"I was hoping to see Peter Bell again," I said.

"He doesn't come in until nine," she said.

She opened the door, and I followed her into the office.

"Is that right? I thought he told me the other day he was the person who opened the office."

"He told you that?" she asked.

Now she definitely sounded annoyed. She walked behind the front desk and dropped her purse onto her chair.

"I think so," I said.

"Well, he doesn't. I open up every morning. Peter never gets in before nine. It's later if he doesn't have an appointment. Sometimes I don't even see him until ten or eleven."

So much for that idea, I thought. My theory officially died.

"Would you like me to leave him a message for you?" she asked.

I thought about switching gears, but I wasn't sure where to go next with the questioning. My cell phone rang. It was Alana.

"Thank you," I told the receptionist.

She didn't reply, and I walked to the front door as I answered my cell phone.

"Hello," I said.

"It's me. I'm on my way to Hani's house. Shae called Adcock last night and told him about seeing the white car following Panos. He's already gotten a judge to sign off on a warrant. I can't believe he's moved this fast."

"A warrant for what?" I asked.

"To search Hani's house. He knows Hani drives a white car. He saw it in my driveway enough times when she was staying with me. Adcock's at her house now. I've got to go. Hani's calling again."

Alana ended the call.

I stood there by the front door of the marina office. I felt guilty again for causing Hani this trouble. I should have told Shae to keep everything to herself, but I began to realize the search warrant wasn't a big deal. Hani didn't kill Panos. There would be nothing to find in her house. What is that sound I hear? Is that you laughing at me? Yeah, I was being naïve.

I walked outside and saw the two guys I had spoken to earlier heading out on their boat. I assumed they were fishermen. I looked up at the blue sky. It was going to be another beautiful day. I wished I was going out there with them instead of on my way to see Detective Adcock. I told myself to keep my mouth shut and not confront Adcock, but that's not ever an easy thing for me to do.

I walked back to my car and started the engine. I did my best to obey the speed limit on the way over, but I found myself driving faster and faster as I got closer to Hani's neighborhood. Unfortunately, I hit every red light on the way there. I know it happens to all of us when we're in a hurry, but that doesn't make it any less frustrating. I turned off the main road and into Hani's neighborhood. I had tried to call Alana back a couple of times on the way over, but she didn't answer the calls.

There were two police cars parked in front of Hani's house, along with two unmarked cars belonging to Alana and Adcock. Alana stood beside a police officer outside the house. Hani was on the other side of the officer. She looked terrified.

I drove past several neighbors who had come out of their houses to gawk. I thought about yelling at them and telling them to get back in their houses, but I knew it would be a waste of my energy. I parked a few houses down from Hani's and walked toward Alana and Hani as quickly as I could, too quickly for the police officer's comfort, apparently. He put his hand on the butt of his gun. Talk about overreacting. This guy was going to shoot me for walking fast?

"Stop right there, sir," he barked.

I stopped immediately and held my hands just above my waist. Alana put her hand gently on the officer's opposite arm.

"He's with me," she said.

The officer released his grip on the weapon.

I looked around the yard. I didn't see any of the other police officers or Detective Adcock.

"Is Adcock inside?" I asked.

Alana nodded.

"They got here about thirty minutes ago," she said.

Suddenly the garage door opened. We all turned and saw Adcock and two police officers standing inside. Adcock stepped to the front of the garage.

"Officer, would you please bring Ms. Hu up here," Adcock said.

"This way, please," the officer said.

Hani followed the police officer up to the garage. Alana followed a few feet behind them, and I was a few feet behind her. We all walked into the garage. Detective Adcock had a big shit-eating grin on his face. I knew this couldn't be good.

"Is this your flashlight, Ms. Hu?" Detective Adcock asked.

He indicated a black flashlight on a small work bench that was pressed against the garage wall. It looked like one of those heavy metal flashlights. Hani looked at it. She was confused.

"No, I've never seen it before," she said.

"So how did it end up in your garage?" Adcock asked.

"I don't know. It wasn't here before."

Alana walked closer to the flashlight. Adcock held out his hand to stop her.

"Don't," Alana said.

There was no hiding the venom in her voice.

"No problem, Detective. You realize what's on that flashlight, don't you?" Adcock asked Alana.

Alana said nothing. The lighting in the garage wasn't good, and I wasn't close enough to the flashlight to see what Alana was looking at. I already guessed what it was, though. I'm sure you did too.

"What is it?" Hani asked.

"It's blood," Alana said.

"And hair. Black hair. How much do you want to bet that hair is going to match your fiancé's when I get it tested?" Adcock asked.

"That's impossible," Hani said.

"Impossible? It's right here, Ms. Hu."

Adcock turned to one of the police officers in the garage with us.

"Officer," he said.

The police officer unclipped his handcuffs from his belt and walked over to Hani.

"What's going on?" Hani asked.

"You have the right to remain silent," the police officer said as he pulled Hani's arms behind her back and slapped the handcuffs on her wrists. "Anything you say and do can and will be held against you in a court of law."

"Alana," Hani started.

Her voice was filled with panic.

"You have the right to speak to an attorney," the officer continued.

"It's okay, Hani. I'll get this straightened out," Alana said.

Adcock laughed.

"You really think so?" he asked Alana.

She ignored him.

"If you can't afford an attorney, one will be appointed for you. Do you understand these rights as they have been appointed to you?" the officer asked.

"I know a good lawyer. I'll call her for you," Alana said.

The police officer walked Hani down to his car and deposited her into the backseat. Alana and I stayed in the garage with Adcock. I saw Hani looking back at us through the window of the car. She started to cry.

"You're lucky you're not in there with her," Adcock said. "I told you to stay out of this."

"Really, Glen," I said. "You're going to pick this moment to try to flex your muscles?"

"That's Detective Adcock to you."

I wanted to tell him to kiss my ass, but what good would that have done? I'd have ended up arrested too, and then I'd be no help to Hani or Alana. I looked at Alana. I couldn't believe how well she was handling this. Her expression was calm, but I could see the look of determination and resolve in her eyes. I had seen it a hundred times before. It always appeared when she wanted me to do something that I didn't want to do. Now it was turned on Detective Obnoxious. Alana was going to prove him wrong. I had no doubt about that.

Adcock turned to one of the other officers still in the garage with us.

"Seal this place off," he barked. Then he turned to me. "You need to leave. I don't want you tampering with any of the evidence."

I knew I didn't have the right to stay there.

"I'll call you later," I told Alana.

She nodded, and I walked down the driveway. I got as close as I could to the police car and mouthed the words 'it's okay' to Hani. She saw me, but I didn't know if she understood what I had just said. If she did understand, I hoped she believed me. I just wasn't sure I believed myself.

I didn't know where to go after leaving Hani's house. I didn't want to head home. I feared I'd do nothing there but pace back and forth. I couldn't follow Alana to the police headquarters. There was no way I could justify my presence. I wasn't even sure what they would allow Alana to do. She was one of their lead detectives, but she had an undeniable conflict of interest. I didn't know if that meant she would be forbidden to speak with Hani, let alone view the evidence against her.

I found myself driving back to Lahaina and toward Harry's Bar. The bar was closed when I got there. It was still too early, so I walked down Front Street until I hit a section that overlooked the harbor. It was one of my favorite places to sit and look out at the water.

The more I thought about what had happened that morning, the more my head began to spin. I felt beyond guilty for bringing this on Hani. If I hadn't spoken to Shae, the truth about Hani following Panos to the marina wouldn't have come out. That's what gave Adcock the evidence he needed for the search warrant. I didn't think Hani was capable of murder. Alana agreed with me, but she was her sister. What did I expect her to say?

I thought back to my one and only previous investigation. The resolution to that case had thoroughly surprised me, and it taught me the lesson that the killer is not always the guy with the black hat who has the word "killer" tattooed on his forearm. So maybe I was wrong about Hani. Maybe she was guilty. It made the most sense. She walked in on Panos kissing her sister and then found him betraying her a second time with Shae. It was hard to believe she followed him all the way to the marina, only to turn around and drive home. Did I really believe Hani was capable of putting those two things behind her and showing up for the wedding ceremony? I wouldn't have been able to do it. I would have told him to go to hell and caught the first plane back to California.

I also had to admit that I didn't really know Hani very well. I couldn't make the mistake of applying my values and feelings to her. I needed to find a way to put myself in her shoes and figure out her motivations and desires. She seemed like a case of contradictions though. On the one hand, she was the young woman who had the long-term relationship with Makani, a mild-mannered guy who seemed to have no ambition. A life with him seemed like it would be calm and steady but also incredibly boring and unadventurous. I wasn't sure how that girl ended up with a self-absorbed jerk like Panos. The guy had money, though, and life with him seemed to be a permanent vacation. Was that Hani's main reason for being with him? Maybe she thought the life of luxury was worth looking the other way regarding his indiscretions. She certainly wouldn't be the first person willing to do that.

I didn't know what my next move should be. Did I concentrate on proving Hani's innocence? What about the other suspects? I had interviewed everyone on Daphne's list. Did I try to interview them again? Like I said before, my head was spinning.

I called Foxx and brought him up to speed on Hani's arrest. I asked him to meet me at Harry's. I looked at my watch and saw the bar was about to open. I didn't want to be standing outside the door when they unlocked it, so I got up and walked back toward Front Street. I just strolled up and down the street, gazing at the window displays like all the tourists. There were at least twenty or thirty of them walking around. They all looked happy. I looked at my watch again. I had killed about thirty minutes, so I headed to the bar. I was indeed the first customer of the day. I sat down at the bar and ordered a beer. One beer led to two which led to three. I looked around the bar. I was still the only customer. I sent Foxx a text message but got no reply. The bartender asked me if I wanted another beer, but I declined.

A second later, I heard the bell jangle on the door. I turned around because I assumed it was Foxx. I was wrong.

"They told me you like to hang out here," Kai said.

Kai stood just inside the door. A guy several inches taller than him was at his side. The guy looked like he could have been a pro wrestler. I turned away from them and just stared at the dozens of bottles of liquor behind the bar. It didn't take a genius to figure out what was about to happen. I heard their footsteps as they walked across the wooden floor. Kai smacked his hand on the bar.

"I'm so glad we can have this conversation," Kai said.

I turned to him.

"I'm really not in the mood to talk," I said.

"That's funny. You expect my brother to talk about Panos, but now that I want to talk to you, you're not in the mood."

He has a point, I thought.

"Who told you to talk to my brother?" he asked.

"Who says anybody asked me to? Maybe I just did it on my own."

"My brother had nothing to do with Panos. You need to stay the hell away from him."

"You made that perfectly clear yesterday."

"Maybe," he said. "But I think you could use more convincing."

"And who's going to do that. You and this gorilla?" I asked.

The gorilla shoved me hard against one of my shoulders, and my back slammed into the bar behind me.

"You're not making a very good case for your innocence," I said.

The friend shoved me again. This time even harder. I heard the bell on the door jangle again, but I couldn't see who it was, because Kai and his enormous friend blocked my view.

"This is going to be fun," Kai said.

"What is? I love to have fun," Foxx said.

I couldn't see Foxx, but I easily recognized his voice. Kai and his friend turned around and saw Foxx walking toward us.

"How do you know my friend?" Foxx asked them.

They said nothing. Foxx stopped when he was a few feet from them. He was the same height as Kai's grunt, but he outweighed him by at least thirty or forty pounds. Foxx turned to Kai.

"You didn't answer my question. How do you know my friend?"

Kai still said nothing.

"I'll talk slowly so you can understand me," Foxx said. "If my friend ever tells me you're bothering him again, I'll find you both and break your damn necks."

Foxx shoved Kai's friend in the shoulder in the same spot he had shoved me seconds before. The gorilla almost lost his balance and fell into me.

"Get the hell out of here," Foxx said.

They both waited a few seconds before doing anything. I guess maybe they were showing some defiance in an effort to save face. Finally they turned and walked out of the bar.

"I appreciate you not destroying the bar. Can I get you anything?" the bartender asked Foxx.

Foxx looked at the empty beer bottle in front of me.

"We'll have two more of those," he said, and he sat down beside me.

"That was interesting," I said.

"They're all talk," Foxx said.

"No, I'm pretty sure they intended to beat the hell out of me."

The bartender put two beers in front of us.

"Put them on his tab. He owes me one," Foxx said.

The bartender nodded and walked away.

"Sorry I'm late. Michelle heard about Hani getting arrested and fell to pieces," Foxx said.

"Where is she now?" I asked.

"Back at the house. I told her to play with the dog. It makes her feel better. So what are you going to do?"

I took a sip of my beer.

"I don't know," I admitted.

Foxx shook his head.

"I know just what Hani's going through. Everybody thinks you're guilty. You feel completely trapped."

"Not everybody," I reminded him.

"True."

Foxx held up his beer, and I tapped mine against his.

"What does Alana say?" Foxx asked.

"I haven't spoken to her since I left Hani's house."

"You've got to be there for her. She won't show it, but I'm sure she's losing it right about now."

"If she asks for my help, I'll give it to her."

"The hell with that. Don't wait to be asked. Just do it."

"She's warned me off the case twice," I said.

"Because that's her official line. I'm telling you, she wants your help." Foxx put his empty bottle on the bar. I looked at mine. It was still half full. "I'll take another one," he told the bartender.

My cell phone vibrated on the bar as the bartender placed a second beer in front of Foxx. It was Alana.

"Hello," I said.

"Can you be at the station in a few hours? We'll get a chance to speak with Hani."

"No problem. I'll be there."

"Thanks," Alana said.

She ended the call. Foxx took a long pull from his beer.

"Told yah," he said, without turning to me or even asking who was on the phone.

Foxx and I hung out at the bar for another hour or so, and then he decided he better get home to Michelle. I had at least another hour to kill before leaving for the police station, so I paid the bar tab and walked around Front Street again. The tourist count had doubled. I eventually made my way over to the View restaurant. There were only a few cars in the parking lot, but it was on the tail end of the lunch rush. Nevertheless, it didn't seem promising for Wes and his business.

I decided to leave early for my meeting with Alana and Hani. The traffic in Maui could be unpredictable, that, and the fact I had literally walked up and down Front Street several times and had nowhere else to go. The traffic was heavy, but I still arrived at the station early. I found a parking space and headed toward the front doors just in time to run into Detective Adcock as he was walking out. He smiled when he saw me.

"Look who it is," he said.

"I'm surprised to find you outside," I said.

We both stopped on the sidewalk.

"I was certain you'd be in Hani's cell beating her with a rubber hose and demanding she confess," I said.

"You're a world-class smartass. You know that, don't you?" he asked.

"I have a question for you, Detective," I said. "What's more embarrassing, telling your chief you arrested the wrong person or admitting to the media you did?"

Adcock smiled.

"It must be fun living in fantasy land," he said. "Hani is guilty. The sooner you admit that to yourself, the sooner you can move on."

"Have a nice day, Detective."

I smiled and headed toward the front door. I didn't turn around to see Adcock's reaction, but I did hear him make some sort of grunting sound. I went inside and immediately saw Alana in the lobby. Foxx was wrong. She wasn't hiding the pain. I knew her facial expressions well enough to know she was hurting badly.

"We'll go to room three," she said.

Alana led me into the back of the station. We walked past a few small rooms and then went inside the last room on the right. There was a table tucked against one of the walls. A pair of handcuffs was attached to the surface.

"My boss isn't happy about you being here, but I think he's cutting me some slack considering the circumstances," she said.

"Have you talked to Hani yet," I asked.

Alana shook her head.

"Not since at her house. I shouldn't even being talking to her now. Like I said, though, they're giving me a break."

"No thanks to Adcock I'm sure."

"I'll deal with him later," she said.

A police officer arrived with Hani. She started crying when she saw Alana and ran over to her. I was a little surprised the officer didn't do anything to stop her, but I could tell by the look of concern on his face that he understood the connection between the two women.

"Anything else, Detective?" the officer asked.

"No, thank you."

Alana led Hani over to one of the chairs. Alana sat in the opposite one, and I stayed standing.

"Your attorney should be here soon, but I wanted a chance to talk to you first," Alana said.

"Can she get me out of here?"

"They have to set bail first. The DA will probably try to persuade the judge you're a flight risk. The judge may deny you bail."

"Do you think that will happen?" Hani asked.

"I don't know, but the attorney I called is very good. She'll do everything she can to get you out of here."

"Have they had a chance to analyze the flashlight yet?" I asked Alana.

"There are no fingerprints on it. We're still waiting for the blood and hair analysis."

"I swear I've never seen that flashlight before in my life," Hani said.

"The killer takes their time to clean the flashlight of fingerprints but doesn't think to wipe off the blood and hair?" I asked.

"I know. It makes no sense," Alana said.

"Your lawyer will have a field day with it, Hani. It's clearly a setup," I said.

I turned to Alana.

"What other evidence do they have?"

"All circumstantial."

The police officer returned.

"Detective Hu, her lawyer is here."

"Bring her back in please."

The officer nodded and walked away. Alana turned to Hani.

"I need to have a quick conversation with Poe. I'll be right back."

Alana stood and led me back to the lobby. It was crowded, and probably full of people wanting to eavesdrop on our conversation, so we walked outside.

"I need you to do something for me," Alana said. "They won't let me touch this case with a ten-foot pole, and the chief has already denied me leave to handle this off-the-clock."

"What do you need?" I asked.

"I want you to keep up with your investigation. Adcock already thinks he's got the right person. He's not going to do any more digging."

"I already intended to keep at it."

"Thanks," she said.

"Do you think this can make it to trial?" I asked.

"If we don't find out who really did this, then yeah, I think it's going to trial."

"You said yourself they just have circumstantial evidence and a bullshit flashlight."

"That may be all they need. A man was murdered. People want someone to pay."

She was right, of course. Unfortunately, I knew I was in serious jeopardy of failing her and Hani. I had already made my way through Daphne's short list of suspects. Sure, any one of them might have wanted to kill Panos, but I lacked any kind of proof and no gut instinct. I decided an additional perspective was needed.

"Who knew Panos the best other than his sister?" I asked.

"I guess Hani." Alana paused for a moment. "And Aaron. He followed Panos to the island. I'm pretty sure they were friends since childhood."

"Does he still live on Maui?"

"I'm sure. He and Daphne dated. They probably still do. His last name is Tench. He lives about ten minutes from Panos' house. I'll look up his address and text it to you."

Aaron Tench. I memorized the name. Alana looked back at the front door to the police station.

"I better get back. I want to hear what the lawyer has to say."

"I'll call you later once I have something to report."

"I'm sorry to drag you into this," she said.

"You didn't. I was already working on it. Remember?"

"Please figure this out, Poe. She won't make it in there."

Alana went back inside.

I walked back to my car and decided to drive home while I waited for Alana to send me Aaron Tench's address.

My cell phone vibrated. It was Daphne.

"Detective Adcock just called and told me the news," she said.

"I'm sure he'll hold a press conference soon. Wouldn't be surprised if he started signing autographs," I said.

"Is it possible for you to come over here?"

"I thought you and Kalena were in California."

"We were, but we got back late last night. I'd really like to see you," she said.

"Actually, I was just about to head somewhere else."

"It's important, Poe."

"All right. I'll see you shortly."

I didn't really want to see Daphne just now, but a trip to see her wouldn't be a major delay in time, especially if Aaron Tench lived only a few minutes away from her.

The traffic had gotten even heavier, so it took me almost an hour to get to Daphne. Who knew I'd drive so much on an island?

Kalena, Daphne's assistant, must have been looking for me because she opened the door before I even got out of my car. She led me into the living room where Daphne was sitting on a comfortable-looking sofa.

"May I get you anything to drink, Mr. Rutherford?" Kalena asked.

"No, thank you," I said.

Kalena turned to Daphne, but before she could ask, Daphne waved her off. I found it a bit rude. Kalena turned and left the room. I sat on a chair just off to the side of the sofa.

"I know it won't bring Panos back, but I'm just glad they caught her. I still can't believe Hani would do this," Daphne said.

"That's because she didn't," I said.

"What do you mean?" she asked.

I told Daphne about the flashlight and my theory about it having been planted in the garage.

"Maybe she was just careless. I'm sure she was panicked after what she did."

"I don't buy that. If she knows enough to wipe her prints clean, she'd certainly take the two seconds it would've required to remove the hair and blood. And there's another thing that bothers me. Why was the flashlight even there to begin with? The knife wasn't there. She thinks to ditch the knife but not the flashlight? This is such an obvious setup that it's not even funny."

Daphne didn't have a response. I really didn't expect her too. I imagined it was somewhat of a relief to hear about Hani's arrest, but I didn't think it was the right thing to let her believe the guilty person had been brought to justice.

"You know, I am kind of thirsty. Do you mind asking Kalena for a lemonade?" I asked.

"Of course. I don't think she has any made, but it won't be a problem."

"Water will be fine then," I said.

Daphne stood.

"Maybe you should try to go see Hani at some point," I said.

"Why would I want to do that?" she asked.

"I'm sure once you talk to her, you'll realize she couldn't have done it," I said.

"Do you know Hani well?" she asked.

"Not really."

"I didn't think so," she said.

Daphne walked across the room and pressed a button on the intercom mounted to the wall. She looked at it like something was wrong, and then she pressed the button again.

"Kalena," Daphne said into the intercom.

A second later, Kalena's voice came over the small speaker.

"Yes, ma'am."

"Can you make our guest a glass of lemonade?"

"Yes, ma'am."

Daphne walked back toward me and sat on the sofa.

"Do you know a guy named Aaron Tench?" I asked.

"Of course."

"Does he still live on Maui?"

"Yes, he lives on the other side of the island."

"I thought he was just ten minutes from here."

"No, he recently moved."

"You and he used to date?"

"Why are you asking me about Tench?"

"I have some questions for him."

"About what?"

"Just background on Panos. Maybe he can give us some new leads."

Daphne was silent and looked away. A second later, Kalena entered with my glass of lemonade on a small tray. She walked over to me and handed me the glass.

"That was fast," I said. "Thanks."

Kalena nodded and exited the room. I turned back to Daphne.

"Is something wrong?" I asked.

"That's what I wanted to talk to you about," she said. "I don't want you to continue the investigation. The detective is convinced Hani is guilty. I think she is too. There's no reason for you to go on interviewing people."

I was stunned.

"I never trusted her anyway," Daphne said.

"Why?"

"I always thought she was after his money."

"Did Panos change his will to make her the beneficiary of his estate?" I asked.

"Not that I know of."

"Then what does she gain by killing him, especially if she only cared about the money? And why would she kill him before the wedding? Now she has no legal claim to anything of his."

"I don't know. But I know she didn't love him," Daphne said.

I didn't see the point in arguing with her anymore, so I said nothing. Daphne leaned forward and picked up an envelope from the table in front of the sofa.

"My mother wanted you to have this," she said.

She stood, walked the few feet to me, and handed me the envelope.

"What is it?" I asked.

"Your payment for the work you did. I know you told her your fee was zero, but she insisted."

"There's no need," I said.

"Please take it. She'll get upset with me if she finds out I couldn't convince you to accept it."

I hesitated a moment and then slid the envelope in my back pocket.

"I appreciate all your help. I am sorry how it turned out," Daphne said.

"What about you? Have you thought more about what you want to do?" I asked.

"I haven't fully decided on anything, but I'm leaning toward going back to California."

"I'm sure your mother would like that," I said and stood. "If you do decide to move, please call me before you leave. I'd like the chance to say goodbye," I said.

I followed Daphne out of the living room and toward the front door where I saw Kalena waiting for us. Kalena opened the door as I approached it.

"Thanks for the lemonade," I said.

Kalena smiled and nodded. I turned to Daphne again.

"If you need me for anything else, please call me," I said.

"Thank you."

I exited the house and headed down the sidewalk to my car. I tossed the envelope onto the passenger seat and drove away. Once I got clear of the house, I pulled over and opened the envelope. It was ten thousand dollars in cash. I couldn't believe she paid me so much for what amounted to a few days of interviews.

I didn't feel good about keeping the money, so I swung by the animal shelter on the way home. The lady at the front desk remembered me from when I picked up Maui just a few weeks ago. I told her I wanted to make a donation to the shelter and handed her the envelope of cash. I did ask for a receipt so I could write it off on my taxes. The government already takes enough of our money.

After I got back into the car, I checked my phone to see if Alana had texted me the address for Aaron Tench. She obviously hadn't heard he'd moved. She hadn't texted me yet, so I decided to head home. Foxx wasn't there, so I took the dog for a walk. Alana still hadn't texted me by the time I got back to the house. I called her and was a little surprised when she answered. I told her about my conversation with Daphne. I left out the part about the cash payment.

"How did the meeting with the attorney go?" I asked.

"Not great. She also suspects the DA will push for Hani to be viewed as a flight risk. Even if the judge grants bail, it will probably be a huge amount, which my family can't afford."

"Have you learned any more about the case against her? What are they saying about the lack of a murder weapon?"

"It's all garbage. You know that. All Adcock has is that flashlight, but nobody will listen to me."

"What about Aaron Tench's address?" I asked.

"I just found it in the system. He's moved to Wailua. I'll send it to you shortly."

"Good. I'll go see him tonight."

"Do you mind if I tag along? I really need to get out of here, and if I go home, I'll just end up bouncing off the walls."

"I thought you had to stay away from this case."

"I do, but the way I see it, I'm just going to visit an old friend. I must have seen Tench twenty times. I just lost touch with him when Panos and I ended things."

"Okay, do you want me to pick you up at the station?"

"No, let's meet in the K-Mart parking lot. I'll leave my car there, and we can ride to Wailua in yours."

"See you there shortly," I said.

I ended the call and looked down at Maui the dog.

"What do you think of that?" I asked.

14

AARON TENCH

I WASN'T REALLY SURPRISED BY ALANA'S SUDDEN CHANGE OF HEART. I never thought she was going to stay out of the investigation to begin with. I saw her car as I pulled into the parking lot. She'd parked in the section of the lot that was closest to Dairy Road. She climbed out of her car as I drove up. The top was down on my convertible, as was usually the case. The sun was almost down, and the temperature was ideal.

"Hey there," she said.

I reached over and opened the door for her. It was one of the advantages of owning such a small car. She got in, and I drove out of the lot and back onto Dairy Road. I knew it was going to be a long drive to Wailua, and I wondered if the time in the car was going to be awkward between us.

"So tell me about this Aaron Tench," I said.

"He's a nice guy. Probably Panos' best friend. They grew up together in California and Tench followed Panos and Daphne out here."

"What does he do for a living? Is he independently wealthy like Panos was?"

"No, he owns a landscape architecture business. I think he specializes in stone patios and walkways. Real beautiful stuff."

"Maybe he moved to Wailua after Panos moved to California," I said.

"I don't know," Alana admitted. "I never saw Tench unless I was with Panos. I don't even have his phone number. It's been over a year since I've seen him."

We drove in silence for the next thirty minutes or so. The road twisted and turned with the coastline, so we could hear the waves in the distance. By then, the sun was down, and it was completely dark other than the convertible's headlights. I looked over at Alana and saw she'd fallen asleep. I never knew how people could fall asleep in cars, especially one as small as mine. She's a lot smaller than me, though, so I guess it wouldn't be as difficult to get comfortable. Plus, I had no doubt she was beyond exhausted. I remembered how upset I'd been when Foxx was arrested. I couldn't imagine what it was like to have a sister taken away to jail. The sheer adrenaline that had rushed through Alana's body all day was enough to make anyone feel spent. I took one of the road's curves too fast, and the movement woke Alana up.

"Where are we?" she asked.

I looked at the tiny GPS on my windshield.

"We'll be there in another ten minutes," I said.

Alana looked at the trees as the car raced by them. She turned back to me.

"Thanks for doing this," she said.

For a moment, I thought she might bring up the relationship problems we'd been having, but she didn't. She just turned away from me and stared straight ahead. The GPS alerted me to the right-hand turn into Aaron Tench's neighborhood. We pulled into his driveway a few minutes after that. The lights were on inside his house, and I could hear the TV through the open windows. A good sign.

I turned off the engine, and we got out of the car. We walked to the front door, and Alana rang the doorbell. I heard the TV mute and then heard footsteps on what I assumed were wooden floors. Before the door opened, I looked around the front yard. It was a mess, tall grass, and overgrown flowerbeds. There were two large planters on either side of the door, but they were both filled with dead plants. I can't say I was surprised. I'm sure the last thing he wanted to do when he got home was work on another yard.

The door opened, and I saw Aaron Tench for the first time. He was about my height and the same age as Panos, which made sense since they were childhood friends. He was deeply tanned and lean, but also muscled, if that makes any sense. I guessed it was from all the labor he did for his landscaping business. Those stones couldn't be light. He smiled when he saw Alana.

"What do I owe the pleasure?" he asked.

"Hello, Tench," Alana said. "It's been a long time."

Tench turned to me.

"This is Poe," Alana said.

I had wondered how she was going to introduce me. Boyfriend? Ex-boyfriend? Friend? But she kept it entirely neutral. I wasn't sure if I was relieved or upset.

"Come on in," Tench said.

He stepped back and held the door open with an outstretched arm. Alana and I went inside. It was a lot neater in there than outside. The furniture was modern with bold colors. There were several large photographs of Maui's gorgeous coastline on the walls. Overall, it seemed like a very tasteful and comfortable space.

"Have a seat," he said.

Tench indicated a red sofa. Alana and I sat on it, and Tench sat in a matching chair just off to the side. There was a small table in front of the sofa, and I noticed several large landscaping books on it.

"So what brings the beautiful Alana Hu to my home?" he asked.

I must admit that I found the guy charming.

"I guess you heard about Panos," Alana said.

Tench nodded, and his mood instantly went dark.

"I'm sorry I didn't call after they found Panos's body. I got caught up in the investigation," Alana continued.

"I heard about Hani on the news today. Is it true?" Tench asked.

"No, it's not true. She didn't do it," Alana said.

Tench said nothing, and his expression was neutral. I couldn't tell if he believed Alana or not.

"Just because Hani's been arrested, doesn't mean the investigation's over. That's why we're here," Alana said.

"I don't understand."

"There are some in the department who think she's guilty, but some of us don't believe that."

"You mean you," he said.

"You know Hani, too. You know she would never hurt Panos," Alana said.

"We're wondering if Panos got in touch with you when he came back to Maui. Did he say anything that might have led you to believe he thought he was in danger?" I asked.

Tench thought for a moment.

"No. I mean he seemed stressed about other stuff, but he never said anything about someone wanting to hurt him."

"What was he stressed about?" I asked.

Tench immediately looked at Alana and then looked away.

"Was it about Hani?" Alana asked.

Tench nodded.

"He said they were constantly fighting."

"About what?" I asked.

"About everything."

"There must have been something specific," Alana suggested.

"Hani didn't tell you any of this?" Tench asked.

"No, but you know Hani would never admit something was wrong."

Tench hesitated some more.

"This would really help us with the investigation," Alana said.

"Panos said after they lost the baby, everything changed."

"Baby? What baby?" Alana asked.

"You didn't know?" Tench asked.

Alana said nothing.

"Hani got pregnant while they were in L.A. That's why they decided to get married, but she had a miscarriage."

Alana looked to the ground. There was silence for several uncomfortable moments. Finally, Alana spoke.

"Panos must have wanted to call off the wedding."

Tench nodded.

"According to Panos, he made the suggestion, and Hani completely lost it. She'd been pushing for Panos to marry her for a while. He accused her of trapping him by getting pregnant. She demanded that he still marry her, or she was going to leave him."

Alana and I both said nothing.

"Panos did love her. He told me that several times," Tench said.

"So why did he cheat on her?" I asked.

"Come on, man. You know some guys are just like that. It has nothing to do with the girl. The guys just always stray."

I wondered if Alana was going to jump off the sofa and punch him in the nose on behalf of all the women Panos wronged over the years, but she did nothing.

"So the fights were all about the wedding?" I asked.

"Yeah, Panos changed his mind and was committed to marrying her. He didn't want to lose her, but then they started arguing about other stuff too. Where to live. Money."

"What about money?" Alana asked.

"Panos gave her a prenup, but she refused to sign it."

"When did she sign it then?" I asked.

"I don't know that she did."

I remembered Panos declaring his love for Hani at the rehearsal party. I also remembered him saying how he was looking forward to marrying her. Had Panos gotten her to sign it before then, or was that potentially a source of conflict after the party?

"Do you think she could have signed it, and Panos didn't mention it to you?" I asked.

"Maybe," Tench admitted. "We talked maybe once or twice a week. He was so busy when he got back that I didn't even get a chance to see him."

"Why didn't you come to the party?" Alana asked. "I don't remember seeing you there."

"I had a job in Hana. By the time I got home, I was beat."

I remembered going to Hana on my first trip to Maui. It takes forever and a day to get there. I believed his excuse, but it did seem odd that he and Panos hadn't found some time to see each other, especially if they were such good friends.

"I should have seen him," Tench said, as if he was reading my mind. "I can't believe I didn't see him before he was gone."

"It's not your fault," Alana said.

"If you don't think Hani did this, then who did?" Tench asked.

"You said Panos never mentioned being fearful of anyone, but do you know of anyone who was angry with him?" I asked.

Tench laughed.

"The line of people who were pissed at him would stretch from here to California. Look, I loved Panos like a brother, but even I knew he could be a pretty self-centered guy. It didn't exactly endear him to a lot of people."

"No name jumps out at you?" Alana asked.

Tench shook his head.

"Not really. No one who would be angry enough to kill him," he said.

"Okay, we appreciate your time," Alana said.

She stood, and I followed her cue.

"It was a pleasure meeting you," I said. "I'm deeply sorry about the loss of your good friend."

Tench shook my hand and nodded. Alana then walked up to him and hugged him goodbye.

"If you think of anything that might help us, please call me," she said.

"I will," he said.

Tench opened the door for us, and Alana and I walked out into the night. We climbed into my car and backed out of the driveway. Tench stayed in the open doorway until we drove down the street and lost view of him. I wanted to ask Alana about Tench's news about the baby, but I didn't want to be the first one to bring it up. I turned left out of the neighborhood and put us back on the main road toward Paia and Kahului. Alana still said nothing, and it took every ounce of my strength to keep quiet. Finally she turned to me.

"I'm starving. Want to grab dinner at Eddie's?" she asked.

I thought it an interesting choice. Eddie's was the site of our first date. As I am prone to do, I immediately started to overanalyze her suggestion. Was this supposed to mean something? Of course, Eddie's was the best restaurant between our current position and Alana's car, so maybe her choice didn't mean anything beyond a guarantee of good food.

"Sure," I said. "Eddie's sounds good."

We drove for another twenty minutes before we arrived at the restaurant. It was late, and the parking lot was mostly empty. We snagged the booth in the back where we normally sat. We both ordered pancakes, which was our food of choice at this restaurant. I know what you're asking yourself. Pancakes? At night? But hey, don't judge us until you try them for yourself. I guarantee that you'd order the exact same thing.

"Do you believe him?" Alana asked.

"About the baby?"

Alana nodded.

"Yeah, I'm not sure why he or Panos would lie about that."

"I believe him too," she said.

"It's terrible news, but it doesn't mean anything regarding this case."

"It goes toward establishing Hani's state of mind. She was a wreck. She'd just lost a baby and then Panos backs out of the wedding. So she threatens to leave him. Next thing you know, they're arguing over Panos' money and the prenup."

"So you think she did it?" I asked.

"I don't know what to think," she admitted.

"How much was Panos worth anyway?" I asked.

"I don't know, but it was a lot. His parents moved to Northern California from Santorini. They were from a long line of winemakers.

Panos said there was some sort of rift between his father and his uncles, which is why they moved to America. His father started a vineyard in California, and it just took off from there."

"Did Panos help run the business?" I asked.

"No, I don't think Panos ever worked a day in his life. His parents set him up with a trust fund that paid out millions every year."

"Who gets that money now?"

"I don't know. Maybe Daphne. I think she and Panos were the only children. I guess everything might go to her."

Our pancakes came, and they were as good as I remembered them.

"Do you need me to drive you home? I don't mind taking you back to your car in the morning."

"No, thanks. I'll be okay. I was going to stop by and check on Hani anyway. What is your plan for tomorrow?"

"Not sure. I may try to interview the people on Daphne's list again."

"They'll see you coming. It'll be hard to get anything out of them."

"Have faith in me. I have a way of weaseling information out of people."

Alana smiled for the first time in a long time.

15

TEMPTATIONS AND TRIALS

I SLEPT LATE THE NEXT MORNING BECAUSE I WAS EXHAUSTED FROM THE long day before. I went for a run after dragging myself out of bed, and then I walked the dog for my cool-down. I found Foxx sitting by the pool when I got back to the house. I brought him up to date on everything that had happened, including my meeting with Aaron Tench and my late dinner with Alana.

"That's terrible news about the miscarriage," Foxx said. "I'm surprised she didn't tell Alana about it."

"Me too, but Alana said it was typical behavior for Hani. Have you ever met Aaron Tench?" I asked.

"No, I've never even heard of him."

"He seemed like a nice guy," I said.

"Seems kind of weird though that we wouldn't have seen him before since he was supposedly Panos' best friend," Foxx said.

"I thought the same thing."

"Maybe they had a falling out or something."

"Maybe, but this Tench guy didn't mention it."

"What are you going to do now?" Foxx asked.

"I thought about going to see Wes again."

"The guy that owns the restaurant?"

"Yeah, he's still a solid lead."

"Good luck," Foxx said.

I walked into the house and took a long shower.

It didn't take long to drive to the View. I was hoping I would have some groundbreaking revelation on the way over, something that would steer my conversation with Wes, but nothing came to me. I pulled into the restaurant parking lot with absolutely no idea what I was going to do or say once I got inside.

There was no one at the hostess stand, so I walked past it and entered the dining room. A few diners were scattered here and there. A waiter walked by me and said nothing. So much for Wes turning the place around.

I headed over to the bar and slid onto one of the high-backed chairs. A bartender approached me. Her name tag read *Dolly*. She was the first Dolly I had ever met in person.

"Can I get you anything?" Dolly asked.

"Yes, I was wondering if Wes was in."

"He took the day off."

"What about Shae?"

Dolly's expression immediately changed. She looked uncomfortable, maybe even a little intimidated.

"She no longer works here," Dolly said.

"Really? When did that happen?" I asked.

"This morning. She left right before the lunch shift started."

I didn't know Shae all that well, but I had a hard time believing she would just skip out on her shift. I remembered something Shae told me during our last conversation.

"Jim's working here again. Is that why?" I asked.

"He came back this morning. Wes didn't tell any of us. Jim fired Shae. It was the first thing he did," Dolly said.

So Wes didn't even have the guts to be here when Shae got fired, I thought.

"That's bad news, but Shae's a smart girl. I know she'll land on her feet," I said.

"I hope so," Dolly said.

I decided to change the subject because I eventually needed a reason to get Jim out of the kitchen.

"I assume you guys have a burger and fries on the lunch menu," I said.

"Of course."

"I'll take that, please. Cooked medium rare. And a Diet Coke."

Dolly nodded and walked to the computer to punch in my order. She then poured me a Diet Coke and placed it in front of me.

"Thanks," I said.

My lunch came out a short while later. The burger could be described as 'okay' at best. It was a little overcooked and needed more seasoning. The fries were a bit better.

"Is Jim still here by any chance? I'd really like to meet him."

"I'll see if he's still in the back," Dolly said.

Dolly left the bar and disappeared into the kitchen. A guy in a white jacket and black pants came out a few minutes later. He was a decent-looking guy, but his neck was covered in tattoos from the top of his jacket to the bottom of his jawline. It was hard to tell what the tattoo was exactly. It looked like some kind of tribal pattern. I assumed his arms and chest were covered as well. He walked behind the bar and approached me.

"I'm Jim," he said.

He extended his hand, and I shook it.

"I'm Poe."

"Nice to meet you. Did you enjoy the burger?" he asked.

"Delicious," I said.

"Is this your first time at the View?" Jim asked.

"No, I had dinner here the other night, and then I was back for Panos' rehearsal dinner."

His mood immediately darkened.

"So you were friends with Panos?" he asked.

"Not exactly. More of a friend of a friend. I hardly knew him to tell the truth. How did you know Panos?"

"He used to be one of the owners of the restaurant here."

"You know, I think I remember Wes maybe mentioning you. Are you the chef who had a run-in with Panos?"

"You could say that."

"Yeah, he could be a tough guy to be around. He tried to get with my girlfriend, and he did it at his own wedding rehearsal dinner. Can you believe that?" I asked.

"Doesn't surprise me," he said.

"I hate to be so morbid, but his being out of the picture kind of helps you, doesn't it?"

"Wes has offered to sell me half the restaurant," he said.

"You going for it?" I asked.

"Thinking about it."

"It's a big step, especially with the restaurant struggling," I said.

"We'll turn it around," Jim said. "I better get back to the kitchen. It was nice meeting you."

Jim shook my hand again and left.

Dolly came back out.

"Can I get you a refill?" she asked.

I looked down at my empty Diet Coke.

"No, trying to cut back on the caffeine."

I looked toward the kitchen.

"Jim seems like a nice guy," I said.

"Think so?" Dolly asked.

"He's not?"

"Let's just say I don't expect to be here in another week. I think most of us will be gone."

"He's a control freak or something?" I asked.

"Or something. You ready for your check?"

"Sure."

Dolly went back to the computer and printed out my receipt. I pulled cash out of my wallet and laid it on the bar.

"Keep the change," I said.

"Thanks."

"One more thing," I said.

I removed a twenty from my wallet and placed it on the bar where she could see it.

"Just between you and me. How much did Jim dislike Panos?"

"He hated him."

"Was that just because of Shae?"

"Jim's a real hothead. Worst I've ever seen. When he found out about Panos and Shae, he attacked Panos in the kitchen with a knife. He had to be held back by two other kitchen staff. That's the reason he was fired."

"Did the police show up?"

"No, Wes managed to convince Panos to drop it. It wasn't a big deal to Panos anyway. He just laughed it off like he did everything. I actually think he enjoyed knowing he'd gotten Jim so riled up."

I stood.

"Thanks for the information."

She shoved the twenty in her pocket as I walked toward the door. I exited the restaurant and debated whether or not to call Shae and wish her good luck on searching for a new job. I decided against it. I really didn't want to get dragged into more drama that had nothing to do with the case. Selfish of me? Maybe.

I climbed into my car but didn't immediately start the engine. It had been an interesting lunch. I learned Wes didn't have the guts to fire a hostess. I wasn't sure if that translated to him not having the guts to attack Panos in the boat, though. It probably did. I also learned that Jim had a violent temper and apparently wasn't above using his kitchen knives to go after another guy. That certainly earned him a place of honor on the suspect list, but there was a problem with labeling Jim as the killer. The timing was all wrong. If Jim did kill Panos, why did he wait until that night? It seems more likely that he would have killed him the same night he got fired from the restaurant, maybe even a few nights after that. Of course, I might not have been giving Jim enough credit. Maybe he was much smarter than that. Maybe he had the patience to wait. As far as I knew, the police never even considered him a suspect, and he now had the chance to become a restaurant owner with Panos out of the equation.

It seemed like an ideal result for Jim, so I couldn't dismiss him as a suspect.

I started my car, but before I could put it in reverse, my cell phone vibrated. I recognized the number - Daphne's. Let me guess. She needed to see me at once, and it had to be in person.

"Hello, this is Poe."

"Poe, it's Daphne. I was wondering if you had time today to swing by the house."

Told yah.

"Sure, Daphne. I'm not too far from you now."

"Perfect. I'll see you soon."

I ended the call and drove out of the parking lot of the View. It didn't take a genius to know what she wanted to talk about, but I was curious to know why she didn't want me continuing to interview people about Panos' murder. It couldn't be because she thought Hani did it. Anyone with half a brain would have doubts about the evidence, and Daphne impressed me as being a smart lady.

The traffic was still light, and I made good time getting to her house. I rang the bell, and Daphne opened the door. She was wearing a low-cut white dress that looked fantastic against her tanned skin. She had a few inches of cleavage showing. It was difficult not to stare, and you know me well enough to know that I looked. Fortunately, she either didn't notice or decided to give me a break. She led me to the living room, and we both sat down on the plush sofa.

"Where's Kalena?" I asked. "I was surprised when she didn't open the door."

"She's moved back to Hana to spend more time with her family. She was living here with us because there was no way she could do the drive every day."

"So she just quit with no notice?" I asked.

Daphne nodded.

"Just yesterday. I understand, though. It's for the best, really. Panos needed her most. It didn't make sense for her to stay now that it's just me. Where are my manners? Can I get you anything? I need to start getting used to asking that question."

We call that rich people's problems, I thought.

"I'm fine. What did you want to see me about?"

"I got a call from Aaron Tench last night. He said you and Alana came by to see him."

"That's right."

"I don't know why you would do that," she said.

"I would think the answer is pretty obvious. I thought he might have known something about Panos that I, or even you, didn't know."

"But we agreed you were going to end the investigation. I even gave you a great deal of money for your services."

"You did, and I thank you."

I thought about telling her the Maui Animal Shelter also thanked her, but I saw no reason to make things even more tense.

"Now you're going to remind me you're continuing my investigation for no money, so it shouldn't be any of my concern," she said.

"Technically I finished your investigation when you asked me to, but someone else hired me."

"Let me guess. Alana."

"I'm not allowed to say. Client confidentiality and all that."

"I really don't understand why you're doing this."

"You know why. Hani didn't do it."

"Detective Adcock thinks she did," Daphne said.

"Why do you have so much faith in him? Your mother told me you thought he was a buffoon."

"I regret that early judgment of him. I was so upset I'm sure I would have felt that way about any detective."

"I understand, but how are you going to feel if this thing goes to trial and Hani's found innocent? Then we'll have lost a great deal of time."

"You can't make the assumption she won't get convicted. There's a good amount of evidence against her."

"It's all one level above worthless," I said.

"I need to be honest with you, and let you know that I may need to report your unauthorized investigation to Detective Adcock. I can't have you messing up his case."

"Are you threatening me?" I asked.

"Don't look at it that way."

"How else am I supposed to look at it?"

"I don't want us to be enemies, Poe."

"I don't want that either. I really don't see how I'm harming anything. If Hani did do it, then she'll probably be found guilty at the trial. But if she didn't, and I can help find the real killer, then that can only help you and everyone else who cared for Panos."

Daphne smiled.

"You're right, of course," she said.

That seemed a little too easy, I thought.

Daphne leaned over and picked up a glass of water off the table in front of the sofa. I feel safe in saying that we've established the fact I'm not an expert when it comes to women, but even I'm smart enough to realize what she was doing. She'd flashed me some serious cleavage on that lean forward. It was a cheap and obvious tactic, and I was a little pissed that she thought it would work. I will admit, though, that the view was spectacular, and a certain part of me instantly imagined myself taking her right there in the living room. Nevertheless, I am a strong man, at least most of the time, and I managed to maintain my dignity and reserve.

"Do we have a truce?" she asked.

She held out her slender hand.

"We do," I said.

I shook her hand, and the warmth of her flesh against mine began to chip away at that dignity and reserve I just bragged about.

Daphne looked at the clock on the wall.

"Can I convince you to stay for dinner? I could make us some drinks. We never got a chance to really get to know each other outside this dreadful case."

I wanted to stand and run out of the house, but my legs were so weak, I feared I might fall forward and crash face-first into the table.

"I'm sorry, but I really need to get going," I said.

"You sure there's nothing I can do to convince you?"

"Some other time," I said.

I managed to pry myself off the sofa and made my way to the door. Daphne opened it for me. I turned to her to say goodbye and found her standing just a couple of feet from me. It was a clear invasion of personal space.

"I'm glad we worked this out," she said.

"I am too."

I backed away from her and walked outside. I did my best to walk casually to my car. Once I reached it, I turned and waved goodbye to her. It was a close call.

I drove to Wailuku, which is where the district court is located. Hani's criminal arraignment was scheduled for that afternoon. I knew Alana would be there, and I didn't want her to have to sit through it alone.

I arrived at the courthouse early. Alana was already there. She was in the front row behind the defendant's table. I slipped in the space beside her. She nodded to me. We sat through a few other arraignments that had been scheduled before Hani's. It was amazing how fast they blew through those things.

Then Hani was led out from the back and escorted to the table. She looked at Alana and me but didn't say anything.

A tall woman with dark red hair joined Hani at the table. She looked about forty-five years old. She had an air of confidence about her that was immediately apparent even to the most casual viewer.

"That's Mara Winters, Hani's attorney," Alana whispered to me.

The attorney said a few things to Hani, and then she turned around and acknowledged Alana.

"Alana," she said.

Alana shook hands with Mara.

"Thanks for doing this for us," Alana said.

Mara nodded and turned back around before Alana could introduce me.

Then the show began.

The judge asked the prosecutor to outline the charges against Hani. He described the murder of Panos and the evidence against Hani. It didn't take long considering there wasn't much of a case, or maybe this just wasn't the time to go too in depth. The judge asked Hani how she pled to the charges, and Mara Winters answered for her. *Not guilty.*

The prosecution asked the judge to deny bail. He pointed to the heinous nature of the crime and described Hani as a potential flight risk since she no longer lived on Maui. Mara Winters informed the judge that Hani still owned a house here and intended to relocate back to the island. She also described Hani's strong ties to the community, including her sister, a local, respected police detective. The judge, however, agreed with the prosecutor and denied bail. The judge set a preliminary date for the trial. The gavel came down, and Hani was escorted out of the courtroom. The whole thing had been almost as speedy as the few cases that were before hers. There was an impressive efficiency to the event, but I couldn't help but feel the wheels of justice were running over Hani in their haste.

We followed Mara Winters into the lobby of the courthouse. Alana introduced me to her.

"Are you surprised they denied bail?" I asked.

"Unfortunately no. This judge is a tough one," Mara said.

"So what now?" I asked.

"We start building her defense."

"What do you think her chances are?" Alana asked.

"Good. We both feel the evidence is weak. I know this prosecutor. He's not the best there is. I've beaten him the few times I've gone against him. I assume that's why you asked me to represent Hani."

"I did my research," Alana said.

"I don't doubt it. I need to get back to the office. I'll be in touch soon."

Mara turned to me.

"It was nice meeting you," she said.

"Pleasure to meet you as well. Wish it was under different circumstances," I said.

Mara nodded and headed out of the courthouse.

Alana turned to me.

"Thanks for being here," she said.

"It was no problem."

Then Alana broke down. It was completely unexpected, and it came without warning. She's a tough woman, stronger than anyone I've ever met, but I knew it was only a matter of time before the emotions overwhelmed her.

I pulled her against my chest and wrapped my arms around her. She sobbed. I didn't know if people gawked at us or not. I really didn't care. I wanted so badly to tell her something that would make her feel better, but I had nothing.

16

AN INTERESTING TURN OF EVENTS

THE NEXT MORNING I DECIDED I NEEDED ANOTHER HEART-TO-HEART with Hani. I preferred Alana not be there because I thought her presence had an influence on Hani, but I didn't want to go behind Alana's back either. I sent her a text message and let her know what time I was going to see Hani. She wrote me back and said she'd meet me there. So much for a private meeting.

On the drive over, I thought about my encounter the day before with the lovely Daphne. I couldn't figure out why she tried to seduce me. It wasn't too overt. She didn't actually kiss me or anything, but it was an obvious flirtation to anyone with half a brain.

Part of me wanted to believe she simply found me irresistible, but the less egotistical side of me knew she wanted me to end the investigation. But why? Every indication told me she loved her brother and wanted his killer to spend the rest of his or her life behind bars. I couldn't fathom that she actually thought Hani was that person.

I wondered, though, if I was fooling myself. Did I want Hani to be innocent because she was Alana's sister? I didn't know if this investigation, and my potential success at it, was just my way of convincing Alana I was the guy she should be with. I thought back to the rehearsal party and the kiss I saw Alana share with Panos. My mind was flooded with questions. Could I get past that kiss? Could I learn to trust Alana again? Can we ever trust anyone 100 percent? What happens if you trust someone 95 percent? Is that really trust?

Unfortunately, none of these questions were answered by the time I got to the jail. Interestingly enough, Alana wasn't there. I waited several minutes and then sent her another text message. I got no reply. I waited for a few more minutes and then went inside.

Hani seemed different this time. It was way more than the baggy orange suit. I noticed during my visits with the jailed Foxx that there seemed to be different emotional stages of being imprisoned, much like there are stages of grief.

The first stage is the freak-out, where you can't believe you're actually being arrested. It usually kicks in the moment they slap the handcuffs on you, as if everything up to that point was merely a threat you believed the police officer had no intention of carrying out.

The second stage happens after you've been booked at the police station. You've just had your fingerprints and your mug shot taken, and now you're pleading with everyone you know to somehow magically get you out.

The third stage is desperation. You're in jail, and you're surrounded by drug dealers, thieves, rapists, and derelicts of society. You know you don't belong, at least you think you don't belong, and you hope there's still a chance for someone to get you out soon. You beg people for updates and convince them that there's got to be some option for freedom that everyone's simply overlooked. Maybe you think there's a magical piece of evidence that will be revealed. Maybe you pray the cop will find the real culprit.

The fourth stage is a combination of resignation, depression, and a general feeling of hopelessness and despair. It's finally sunk in that you're not getting out any time soon, and you feel like the weight of the whole world is crushing you. That's the stage Hani currently seemed to be in. She looked even smaller now. She was defeated, like someone who put every nickel she owned on black and the wheel came up red. She was quiet, and she had trouble looking at me.

I sat down in a chair opposite her in the visitation room. We sat in silence for a few moments. I fought the urge to ask her how she was doing. The answer was obvious, but we always seem to feel the need to ask the question.

The visitation room was crowded and noisy. I had taken a quick look at everyone when I entered. There was lots of emotional devastation. Most of the imprisoned women looked hard. I didn't know how Hani was going to make it. Hani eventually thanked me for coming and asked where Alana was. I told her I didn't know but assumed some unexpected police business probably kept her away.

"I met with Aaron Tench," I said.

Hani nodded.

"How well do you know him?" I asked.

"Not well. I only met him a few times."

"Really? I thought he and Panos had been best friends."

"I wasn't really around Panos that much here on Maui. We really didn't start dating until I moved to L.A."

"So Panos just decided to visit you in L.A. and things took off from there?"

"Something like that," she said.

"Come on, Hani. Alana's not here. Tell me how it really happened."

Hani hesitated.

"I'm not going to judge you," I continued. "I really wouldn't care under normal circumstances, but I need to understand the dynamics of everything."

"You won't tell her?" Hani asked.

"No. I'm not here as Alana's spy."

"I was with Panos a few times when he was dating Alana," she said. "I met him when Alana invited me to a party he was throwing. We hit it off, and he asked for my number."

"And then you eventually left Maui, and he followed you?" I asked.

"Basically."

Hani's a clever lady, I thought. By getting Panos to follow her, she eliminated the competition, and she made herself more desirable by playing hard to get.

"I'm sure you knew about Shae and the other women. Why did you stay with him?" I asked.

"Because I loved him," she said.

"Daphne thinks you were only interested in Panos for his trust fund."

"She can think whatever the hell she wants. It's not true," Hani said.

I didn't believe that for a second. I'm sure Hani didn't believe it either, or maybe she was just self-deluded enough to think that.

"Did Panos ask you to sign a prenup?" I asked.

"Yes."

"Did you sign it?"

"Not at first. I was really offended."

Most people would be, I thought. Marriage was a legal contract, though, so shouldn't the financial aspects be worked out too? Wouldn't it be more prudent to do that before the wedding? But I understood the emotional aspect of it to. It doesn't seem like a good omen to already be planning your potential divorce before you even walk down the aisle.

"What made you eventually sign it?" I asked.

"He refused to get married without it."

"Did you have a lawyer look over it?"

"Yes, one I found in Los Angeles."

"There's something else I need to ask, and it's a pretty sensitive subject, so please forgive me. Aaron Tench said you were pregnant but lost the baby."

Hani paused a moment, and then nodded.

"Now you're going to ask me if that's why Panos agreed to marry me," she said.

I said nothing.

"He wasn't happy when I told him, but he came around. He even became pretty excited after a while. Then I lost the baby."

"Did you guys talk about cancelling the wedding after that?"

"Once. Panos was drunk. He became depressed after I'd lost the baby. He told me there was no reason to get married anymore. The next morning, I told him I was leaving him. We were separated for a couple of weeks, and then he asked me to marry him again. He said he didn't want to lose me."

So far everything she'd told me backed up Tench's story.

"How well do you know Daphne?" I asked.

"I barely spent any time with her."

"Did she ever visit you two?" I asked.

"Never. I saw her a couple of times when we got back, but she wasn't interested in helping with the wedding, which was fine by me."

"Back to Aaron Tench for a minute. How is it possible he and Panos were best friends when you hardly know him?"

"I kind of got the impression he and Panos had a falling out."

"Do you know what it was over?" I asked.

"Not really. Panos made a comment once that he thought Aaron was jealous of him."

"Aaron told me he spoke to Panos a few times a week, even after he moved away."

"I don't remember him calling at all, but I wasn't around Panos twenty-four hours a day."

"What about Jim, the chef who worked at Panos' restaurant. Did Panos mention him when you two came back to Maui?"

"No, Panos said he needed to talk to Wes at some point, but he didn't say anything about Jim."

"Did you know Jim attacked Panos in the kitchen because of an argument over Shae?"

Hani looked away, and I took that as a confirmation.

"You said Panos mentioned he needed to talk to Wes. Did he say anything specific about the meeting?"

"Not really. I figured it was about the business."

"Why do you think Panos ignored Wes? Did he not care about the business?"

"When you get millions every year for doing nothing, why would you care about a tiny restaurant in Maui? I don't know why Panos invested in that thing to begin with. He got bored so easily. I knew his interest in the restaurant would never last. Wes was a fool to think it would."

"Did you hear about Wes ever threatening to harm Panos?"

"No, Panos never said anything about it. We hardly ever talked about Wes at all."

"So Panos never mentioned anything about anyone threatening him?"

Hani turned back to me.

"Don't you think I would have told you or Alana if he did?" she asked.

It was a stupid question, but I was grasping at straws. I still had a long list of suspects but no solid evidence against anyone, except Hani.

"I'm sorry," she said.

"There's no reason to be," I said.

"Makani came to see me yesterday," she said.

Now that was a surprise, I thought.

"What did he say?"

"He asked me how I was doing. Said he was sorry."

"Sorry for what?" I asked.

"That I was in here."

"Why did you leave him?"

"I really loved him, but when I looked at our future, I could tell you exactly how our life would play out. There would be no surprises. It would be a life without stress but also one with no adventure. I knew Panos was cheating on me, but he offered me something I could never get on my own."

I was now more convinced than ever Hani was innocent. Panos was her meal ticket. I just couldn't picture her hurting that golden goose.

"How are things with you and my sister," Hani asked.

"I don't know. Okay, I guess."

"Are you guys back together?"

I shook my head.

"Why not?" she asked.

"She says she needs time to think. Once you got arrested, we've pretty much spent all our time trying to get you out of here."

Hani rolled her eyes.

"It's typical Alana. She's terrified of being happy," she said.

"What do you mean?" I asked.

"I can't tell you how many times I've seen Alana sabotage herself because she's convinced the universe is about to ruin things for her. She'd rather end things on her own terms."

It was an interesting comment. I thought I knew so much about Alana, but here was a person who knew her a million times better. Maybe Hani was right. Maybe things were going so well for Alana and me that she convinced herself it couldn't be for real. Maybe that's the main reason Alana said she thought we were moving too fast. Even if this new information was true, I wasn't sure how I could make use of it. I didn't know what to do other than give Alana her space.

Hani and I spoke for a few more minutes before visitation hours came to an end. I promised to come see her later in the week and give her an update on my progress. I hoped I'd have something positive to report by then.

I was about half-way back to my house when my phone rang. It was Alana.

"Hey, I waited for-"

Alana cut me off. "Where are you now?" she asked.

"Heading home," I said.

"I'm going to send you Peter Bell's home address. You need to get over here, now," she said.

She abruptly ended the call.

17

TAG WATCHES AND OTHER THINGS

PETER'S HOUSE WASN'T FAR FROM THE MARINA WHERE HE WORKED. When I turned the last corner in his neighborhood, I saw several police cars and an ambulance parked in front of his place. Fortunately, the media hadn't caught wind yet. I parked at a respectable distance and sent Alana a text message indicating I was there. I then walked slowly toward the house so I wouldn't startle any police officers and give them a reason to shoot me. I half assumed Adcock had ordered a hit on me. I wondered if Adcock was there with Alana and how I would respond if he made another cutting remark. I didn't think I'd be able to control myself around him after my morning visit with Hani.

By the time I was in front of the next door neighbor's yard, I saw two EMTs remove a body from Peter's house. It was on a gurney and was covered with a blue sheet. I assumed it was Peter Bell but couldn't tell for sure since the blue sheet also hid the face. The EMTs carted the body down the driveway and lifted the gurney into the back of the ambulance.

I looked around the area. Several of Peter's neighbors stood in their driveways. They all looked horrified. I didn't blame them. It was an act of violence that would shake this neighborhood for months, maybe even years.

Alana came out a couple of minutes later. I waved to her, and she motioned to a police officer to come get me. I was pretty sure it was the same police officer who had read Hani her Miranda rights just a few days ago. The officer said nothing when he approached me, and he had a scowl on his face. I didn't know if it was directed at me, but he escorted me to the front door anyway.

I looked back at the ambulance just as one of the EMT's shut the back doors to the ambulance.

"That was Peter?" I asked.

Alana nodded.

"Come on in," she said.

Alana led me into the house. We walked past a few other police officers and two forensics techs who were snapping photographs.

"Don't touch anything," Alana said, as if I needed to be reminded.

We walked into the living room, and I saw a large pool of blood on the tan carpet. There was a broken glass coffee table a few feet from the blood.

"He cut himself on the glass?" I asked.

"Probably broke during the fight, but he was killed by a gunshot to the chest."

I looked around the room. There was a small bookshelf against one wall. Most of the books had been pulled off the shelf and were lying on the floor. The kitchen was connected to the living room, and I could easily see into it. All of the drawers were open.

"So he interrupted a robbery?" I asked.

"Seems like it," Alana said. "But follow me."

Alana led me down the back hallway. I looked in each room as we passed. One bedroom was converted into a home gym. Nothing looked out of the ordinary or out of place. The second bedroom was an office. The drawers on the desk were pulled out, and papers littered the floor. The last bedroom was the master. The mattress was pushed off the bed frame. The single drawer of the nightstand was open. Personal items were on the floor. I looked over to a cabinet where Peter stored his clothes. Those drawers were also open, and the contents tossed around.

"The thief was thorough," I said, and I continued to look around the master bedroom.

"Think so?" she asked.

Then I saw it, a silver watch on the top of the cabinet. I walked over to it.

"Don't touch it," Alana said.

"I know," I said.

I got as close to the watch as I could without disturbing it. Fortunately, the face of the watch was up.

"It's a TAG Heuer," I said.

"Know anything about them?" Alana asked.

I held up my wrist.

"I've worn one for years. Paid a few thousand dollars for mine. I don't know what they cost now. Probably more."

Alana nodded.

"I know what you're thinking," I said. "Two possibilities. The thief either doesn't know the value of the watch, which would probably be incredibly easy to pawn, or this wasn't a robbery at all. It was just staged to look like one."

"Exactly, or the killer was searching for something specific and the watch wasn't it," Alana said.

"Peter was already here when the thief entered," I said.

"Why?"

"These watches have self-winding mechanisms. The movement of your arm activates it, so they stay running as long as you wear them each day."

I looked at the watch again.

"The time is accurate. The fact it's in here means Peter had been wearing it regularly. So he must have already been in the house instead of coming home after being gone all day."

I turned to Alana.

"The question is, 'why kill Peter Bell?'" I asked.

"Any theories jump out?" she asked.

"Nothing immediate, but this has to be connected to Panos in some way. It can't be a coincidence."

"My thoughts exactly," she said.

Alana escorted me out of the house, and we stood on the front lawn.

"Sorry I missed your visit to Hani," she said. "I've been here the last couple of hours."

"Understandable," I said. "Who found him?"

"The maid service."

"Any idea on time of death?" I asked.

"Nothing solid yet, but I'm guessing he was killed at least twelve hours ago."

"So sometime during the night. Was he dressed in clothes you would sleep in?"

"He was. You're getting good at this," she said.

"Foxx watches a lot of crime television. It's hard not to pick up stuff. What do you do now?"

"I need to contact the family."

"They don't know yet?" I asked.

"Peter wasn't living with anyone. We need to track down his relatives. I don't even know if they live on the island."

"Is there anything I can do to help?" I asked.

"Just keep pushing on the investigation. If you think of anything I need to know about Peter Bell, let me know. How did the meeting with Hani go?"

I told her about the conversation, including Hani's confirmation of the pregnancy.

Alana shook her head.

"She never tells me anything. You'd think I'd be the first one she'd call with news of a pregnancy."

"I thought you two weren't on speaking terms at that point," I said.

"She still should have called."

"Agreed."

We spoke for a few more minutes about Hani and her obvious

pattern of either not telling important information or downright lying about it. Nothing new or earth-shattering was said. Alana just needed to vent about her sister.

I wished her luck with the Peter Bell investigation and walked back to my car. I felt kind of guilty for not telling Alana exactly what I was thinking. I did have an idea, and I was about to explore it.

I drove to the marina and parked close to the main office building. I found the receptionist I had spoken to on previous visits sitting behind her desk in the lobby. I didn't want to mention Peter Bell's murder, and judging by her calm demeanor, she hadn't heard the terrible news yet.

"Hi, you may remember me from earlier visits with Peter," I said.

The receptionist said nothing. She didn't even smile. This lady clearly hated her job.

"I'm helping the police with the murder investigation concerning Panos Laskaris. Did you know him?"

"Yes."

"I was wondering if you could help me with something. Peter told me your security system was down during the time frame when Panos was killed. Do you know anything about that?"

"No."

"Does Peter normally deal with the security system, or is that something you work with too?" I asked.

"I don't think that's something I should talk to you about. Perhaps you can talk to Peter about that. He should be in any time now."

"It's okay. Like I said, I'm working with the police."

"Maybe I should call them and verify that," she said.

"Of course. I could give you the number for Detective Alana Hu, if you like."

I hoped she would accept my bluff, but I couldn't tell. She just stared at me.

"Can you just tell me the name of your security company?" I asked.

The receptionist didn't answer me, but she picked up the phone. I assumed she intended to call 911 since I hadn't given her Alana's number. I decided this lady needed an emotional punch to the head to get her to cooperate.

"I just came from Peter's house," I said.

She hesitated before dialing.

"He's been killed," I continued.

The receptionist dropped the phone and covered her mouth with her hands.

"I'm sorry to tell you that, but we could really use your help to figure out who did this."

I hoped the word "we" further implied I was working with the police. She still said nothing, and I didn't know if I had miscalculated and ruined any chance I had to get information out of her by overwhelming her with the bad news.

"I don't think that the security system was ever down. I just need you to verify that," I said.

"Peter normally handled it. He never told me if it was down," she said.

"Had it ever gone down before?" I asked.

"Not that I know of."

"Do you know the name of the security company?"

"It's in Peter's office. I can get it for you."

"Please."

She stood and walked toward Peter's office. I was glad my strategy worked, but I felt guilty for using Peter's death to get her to cooperate.

"Do you mind if I come with you?" I asked.

I hoped I wasn't pushing my luck. She didn't reply, so I followed her into Peter's office. She quickly found a business card tacked to a small bulletin board near his desk. She handed me the card. It had the name and phone number of the security company.

"Can I use his phone?" I asked.

She nodded. I wanted to use the office phone because I thought the number would show up on the security company's caller ID as a customer of theirs. The phone started to ring, and I turned to the receptionist.

"Could I please bother you for a glass of water?" I asked.

She turned without saying a word and left the office. I couldn't believe I had gotten this far. I just needed to press my luck a little more. A woman on the other end of the call answered.

"Hello, this is Day Security. How may I help you?"

"Yes, this is Detective Glen Adcock with the Maui police department. I'm calling in reference to the Lahaina marina, a client of yours," I said.

"Yes, Detective, can I have your badge number please for the record?"

Ordinarily I would have panicked at this point and hung up the phone. But I had seen Alana's badge enough times to know how many digits it had. I gave the person a random series of numbers. I hoped they didn't have some computer system that could instantly verify Adcock's name to his number. It was highly doubtful, though.

"Thank you, Detective. How may I be of service?"

"Can you verify for me if the security system here was ever reported as malfunctioning?"

"Stand by. Let me check their records."

I heard her typing on the other end.

"No reports here. As far as we know, the system has been working fine."

"What type of system do they have here exactly?"

"There is a motion detector installed in the main office building. We also set up a surveillance system around the marina."

"Is there a computer drive or DVDs that record the video images from the cameras?"

"Of course. All the video feeds are automatically backed up to the hard drive."

"Do those video feeds also go to your company?"

"No, just the hard drive."

"So if someone erased it from the drive here, it would be gone for good."

"Unfortunately, yes."

"Thank you for your help."

"My pleasure, Detective."

I hung up just as the receptionist returned with a small bottle of water.

"Thanks," I said.

I unscrewed the cap and downed it in a couple of gulps. I looked at the computer on Peter's desk.

"Is this the computer that stored the video images from the security system?" I asked.

"I think so," she said.

"Do you mind pulling up the video files?"

The receptionist walked over to the desk and sat in Peter's chair.

"I'll see if I can find them."

The monitor came alive when she moved the computer mouse. We both looked at the desktop icons.

"There," I said.

I pointed to the folder that I thought was for the security system. She double-clicked it. There were several other folders inside the main system folder. Each sub-folder was labeled with a date.

"Can you open one of those?" I asked.

She double-clicked on the folder with yesterday's date. This new folder had several QuickTime video files.

"Now click on one of those files," I said.

She clicked on a video file labeled *Dock 1*. The video took a second to load, and then we saw an image of one part of the dock. The video clip was during the day, and a person was walking down the dock toward the camera. It looked like the camera was only recording a few frames per second because the person's movement was leaping forward on the dock as opposed to a smooth walk. I assumed this was done to keep the video files as small as possible.

"Let's go back to the main folder," I said.

She closed the video file and the sub-folder labeled with yesterday's date.

I searched for the folder labeled with the date Panos was killed. It wasn't there. The date before and the date after his murder was.

"Thank you," I said. "You've been a tremendous help."

The receptionist turned to me.

"What do I do now?" she asked.

"A detective named Alana Hu is going to call you. You'll eventually want to show her everything you showed me. In the meantime, I would call the owner of the marina and tell them about Peter. Do you know the owner's name and contact information?"

"Yes."

"Good. We'll find out who did this. I promise."

"Do you think I'm in any danger?" she asked.

"No, you'll be fine."

I left her sitting in Peter's office chair. I didn't think she believed me about not being in any danger. There was a miniscule chance the killer might think Peter had shared a copy of the video file with her, but I didn't think that was the case. I went outside and called Alana. I told her about my visit to the marina and how I discovered Peter Bell lied to me, and everyone else, about the security system.

"I don't suppose you found a laptop or a thumb drive at his house?" I asked.

"I don't remember the officers finding one, but I'll follow up on that."

"Looks like Peter knew from the start who killed Panos," I said.

"How long do you think it took him to blackmail them?" Alana asked.

"I doubt he did it right away. He probably waited a bit to see if the police were going to catch the person. When he saw in the news that Hani was arrested, he knew the police had the wrong person."

"So he contacts the real killer and demands payment in exchange for the video," Alana said.

"We know he had a gambling problem. Maybe he got in way over his head again and thought this was the only way to score some quick cash."

"Dangerous game to play," Alana said.

"Does this get Hani out of prison? Seems to me it's pretty clear proof she didn't do it."

"I'll share it with Adcock and Hani's attorney, but I don't think the prosecutor will rush to do anything about Hani. By the way, don't think I don't know you kept this marina thing from me. You probably drove straight there after leaving Bell's house."

"It was a wild hunch. I didn't want to waste your time," I said.

"Sure it was. So what's your next wild hunch? Who was Peter Bell blackmailing?"

"That's the million-dollar question," I said.

We ended the call, and I looked back at the marina office. I assumed the receptionist was having a breakdown right about now. I didn't blame her. I was on the verge myself. I had confirmed the killer was still out there. I just didn't know who they were.

18

BUT OFFICER, IT WAS SELF-DEFENSE

ALANA STAYED BUSY WITH THE PETER BELL MURDER INVESTIGATION FOR the next few days. I wish I could say I was as productive as she was. She spoke with the security company and confirmed there was no report from Peter Bell or any other staff member at the marina that the security system was down. The security company even visited the marina and did a thorough check of the system. It was fine. They checked the files on Peter's computer and confirmed the only files that were missing were from the day Panos was murdered. Alana had a computer expert from her department look over the marina office computer as well. They hoped they could recover the deleted video files, but Peter had done an excellent job of removing them from the system. Alana had a team go over Peter's house again. They searched for a laptop or some other storage device. Nothing was found, which was highly unusual in my book. Do you know anyone these days without a laptop, iPad, or smartphone lying around the house?

Our theory about Peter being in financial trouble again was correct. Alana learned Peter was in significant credit card debt. He owed over $50,000 to various credit card companies. He had missed his last three mortgage payments and his last three car payments.

The police found a letter from the mortgage company saying his house was about to enter foreclosure.

Foxx got in on the investigation too. After I told him about Peter's debt, Foxx spoke with a friend of a friend, who claimed Peter was part of an underground card game. Peter's game was poker, and he apparently wasn't very good at it because he owed another $40,000 to a few different players. On a side note, I asked Foxx if he was part of this game. He said he wasn't, but I was pretty sure he was. I understood why he didn't tell me. He probably wanted me to have plausible deniability should Alana ever ask me.

All of this new information indicated a desperate Peter Bell who would probably do anything to pay off those debts, including blackmailing the killer of Panos. Alana pointed this out to her chief and the prosecutor as proof that the real killer was still out there. Unfortunately, she got nowhere. They both argued that Peter's killer could have easily been one of the poker guys he owed money to. I disagreed, but I understood their stance. Hani stayed in jail.

I know exactly what you're asking yourself right now. What of Detective Adcock? After all, he was the one who thoroughly blew it when he failed to check Peter's office computer to confirm Peter was telling the truth. Well, nothing happened to him. According to Alana, Adcock got a mild talking to. So much for accountability from our government representatives.

A lot of information came out, but I wasn't excited about any of it. I had already guessed most of it, so all this really did was confirm what I already knew. I didn't see Alana at all during those few days, but she called me several times each day to give me an update. You might suspect our relationship was on the mend. I wished I could say that was the case, but it wasn't. She never brought up our relationship, and I didn't either. I really didn't know what to say.

I was frustrated on so many levels. I needed a new lead desperately if I was to solve this case. Sometimes if I write stuff down, I have a better time of sorting through my thoughts, so I grabbed a piece of paper and wrote down everything I knew about Panos' death.

Wes: He was the co-owner of the restaurant. He was angry with

Panos for abandoning their business and leaving him on the verge of bankruptcy. Did I think him capable of killing Panos? Absolutely. Did I think he could drive over to Peter's house and gun him down? Probably not.

Jim: He hated Panos because Panos was sleeping with his girlfriend, Shae, and Panos forced him out of the restaurant. Dolly the bartender told me Jim had attacked Panos with a knife in the restaurant kitchen. Interesting connection considering the fact Panos was murdered with a knife, but a knife isn't exactly an uncommon murder weapon. There was also nothing to make me think Jim even knew Panos was back on the island. He might have heard it, but I wasn't sure if Jim's anger was still strong enough to make him drive to the marina late at night and slit Panos' throat.

Makani and Kai. I lumped these two together since they were brothers. I still didn't think Makani was capable of confronting Panos, let alone killing him, but I could easily see Kai doing it, especially after Makani told him how Panos humiliated him at the party.

Aaron Tench: He definitely wasn't the killer, but had the two best friends fallen out? Hani said Panos told her Aaron was jealous of him, but jealous about what? On the other hand, they couldn't have had too much of a falling out if he knew Hani had gotten pregnant and then lost the baby. So why did he avoid Panos once he'd come back to the island if he was still on speaking terms? Or was he really just busy at work like he said he was?

Detective Glen Adcock: Why was he such an asshole? Was he simply compensating for a small penis?

Now that you know exactly what was going on in my head, you'll understand why I decided to go to Harry's for an early evening drink. I asked Foxx if he wanted to join me, but he said he was on his way out the door to meet Michelle for dinner.

I hopped in the convertible and headed for the bar. I love driving around the island at night with the top down on the car. There's something about the night air that clears my head. When I got to the bar, I saw the parking lot was full. I parked in a dirt lot that was right next to the paved one and was used for spillover. I walked inside. It was jammed, but I was lucky to find an open spot at the bar. All the televisions were tuned to a football game, and people were cheering and booing, depending on what team was doing well at that moment. I ordered a beer and went over the list of suspects you just read. I felt like I was banging my head against the wall. I knew the answer was somewhere in there, but nothing came out.

I ordered a second beer when I heard a voice that made me cringe.

"We meet again."

I recognized the voice instantly. I looked over my shoulder to see Kai and his burly friend approaching.

"Where's your bodyguard?" Kai asked.

I gave him no response except to turn back around and pretend to go back to watching the game on the television. I had no doubt what was about to happen.

One of them put his hand on my left shoulder. I could feel the placement of his thumb on my back, so I knew he grabbed me with his right hand. That meant he was off to my left side versus standing directly behind me. I spun my elbow back as hard and as fast as I could. I heard the cartilage of his nose break under the impact of my arm. I didn't waste any time. I spun my body fully around and slammed my fist into the nose again. The burly friend howled in pain. At least I had the good fortune to take the big one out first.

I turned to go after Kai next, but he hit me above the eye before I could square up against him. I felt my skin tear, and the blood immediately began to flow into my eye. He hit me again in the same spot and then dove on me. The air burst out of my lungs as I collapsed on the ground with all of Kai's weight on top of me.

Kai smashed his fist into my rib cage again and again. I felt my vision go blurry from the pain he was inflicting on me and the blood flowing down my face. I don't remember consciously deciding to do this, but I jammed my thumb into his eye. He screamed and rolled off me. I tried to stand up to grab a beer bottle or something else to hit him with.

"Freeze!"

I turned to see a guy pointing his gun at my head, at least I thought it was a gun. It was difficult to tell with all the blood in my eyes. It turned out there was an off-duty cop in the bar. Apparently, he had stopped by to watch the game with one of his neighbors.

He handcuffed all three of us and dumped us on the curb in front of the bar. He then walked to his car and called in the report. About twenty minutes later, an unmarked police car pulled up. Alana climbed out of the car. She walked over to the cop, and they spoke for a few minutes. I saw him nod a couple of times, and then she shook his hand. They both walked over to me, and the cop removed my handcuffs, only to have Alana slap her handcuffs on me. She pulled me to my feet and then dragged me to her car. She didn't say anything as we walked across the parking lot. She opened the back door, pushed my head down with the palm of her hand, and then shoved me hard into the backseat.

She slammed the door and climbed into the front seat. As she pulled away, I looked over my shoulder as best as I could and saw the cop talking to Kai and his friend. They both looked seriously pissed off. I hate to admit this, lest you think ill of me, but I had a certain amount of pride at having inflicted so much damage on them even if I did take a beating myself.

"Where are we going?" I asked.

"To jail. Where did you think we were going?"

"In that case, aren't you going to read me my rights or give me my phone call?"

"No, and you can take up any complaints up with the chief of police."

"I thought you were off-duty," I said.

"I am, but I still have a radio in the car and heard Kai's name mentioned along with the phrase 'fight at Harry's Bar.' Something told me you were involved. Lucky for you, that officer owes me a favor. He's going to convince them not to press charges. He already talked to the bar owner. You three maniacs didn't do any damage to the bar. The owner did request that you return later and pay your tab."

"Sorry to make you cash in your favor."

"You should be."

"It was self-defense," I said.

"Well, the officer backs you up on that front. He saw the whole thing. Did you really take those guys out on your own?" she asked.

"You sound surprised."

"Let's face it. You're not exactly a fighter."

"I'm offended. I can take care of myself."

"Apparently."

I thought Alana was going to take me to Foxx's house, but instead she drove me to hers. She pulled into the driveway and turned off the engine. She opened the car door.

"Turn around," she said.

I turned away from her, and she undid the handcuffs. I slowly started to feel the blood flow back into my wrists and arms as I clenched my fists open and closed.

"Let's get that cut cleaned up," she said.

I followed Alana into her house.

"Come into the kitchen. I don't want you bleeding all over my carpet."

Alana walked over to the sink and placed a kitchen towel under the faucet. She turned on the cold water and soaked the towel thoroughly, and then she cleaned the blood off my forehead and face.

"It's a nasty cut," she said.

"I think he must have been wearing a ring or something."

"I should take you to the emergency room. I think you're going to need stitches."

"I'll be fine."

"You don't want it to scar."

"I could use a good scar on my face. Maybe people won't mess with me then."

"You're crazy. You know that, don't you?"

I smiled and then winced. The movement of my face from the smile went right up to the cut on my head.

"If you won't go to the emergency room, at least let me bandage it up."

Alana left and came back a minute later with a first aid kit. She opened the small box and removed a tube of ointment and a box of bandages. She spread the ointment on the cut, and then placed the bandage on my head just above my eye.

"All patched up," she said while balling up the paper wrapper of the bandage.

"Thank you," I said.

She walked over to the kitchen island and leaned her back against the counter top.

"So, what's next for tomorrow? Do you want to re-interview anyone?" she asked.

I looked out the window of her kitchen into her backyard. I'd always liked the landscaping she'd done. There was a nice round patio that was surrounded by several planters, all filled with colorful red and yellow flowers. The grass was neatly manicured, as usual. Tall trees blocked her neighbor's view into her yard.

I thought back to the first time I'd exchanged more than one or two words with her. It was at Foxx's house, and she'd shown up to arrest Foxx. I'd defended him, spouting out ridiculous words and phrases like I was some know-it-all television lawyer. She called me out on my bullshit, but I deserved it. I didn't know what I was talking about. I'd just wanted to help a friend in the middle of a serious crisis.

We exchanged flirtations with each other over the next few weeks, even though we were on opposing sides, and then there was our first date. I couldn't believe how beautiful she looked. My nervousness was hard to control that evening, but an excitement and thrill also ran through my body.

Now, I was here again in her home, a bandage plastered across my head. She and I stood at a crossroads, all because of a kiss, and fear. When you broke everything down, it was always about fear. We protect all or part of ourselves because we're always so damn afraid of getting hurt. I realized then and there that if it doesn't kill you, then what's the point of being afraid? And if it does kill you, well, we all have to go sometime, anyway.

"You know that you could have just as easily taken me home instead of here," I said.

"What are you talking about?" she asked.

"Harry's is almost exactly at the half-way point between your home and mine. You could have just gone there."

"I guess I knew I had the first aid kit here."

"Really?" I asked.

"What are you getting at?"

I really don't know what came over me at that moment. Maybe I was filled with extreme confidence after the fight. Maybe the adrenaline was still pumping through my body. I really didn't know then, and I certainly don't know now as I write this for you.

I walked across the kitchen. Alana was still leaning against the counter. I stopped just a couple of feet from her. I clearly and intentionally invaded her personal space as I had done the night of our first date. She didn't back away from me then. She didn't back away now. Of course, she couldn't back away with the island behind her, but you get the point.

"I think you brought me back here because you knew we'd be alone. Foxx is probably at his home this time of night. We both like him, but he would have just gotten in the way."

Alana said nothing.

"If I may play the role of detective, this investigation was really the first clue. You don't need me looking into this case. You have a thousand times the experience I do when it comes to detective work."

"You'd already started. It didn't make sense for me to repeat your work."

"Maybe. Maybe not."

"And I'm too close to Hani. I need someone else to keep me objective."

"I don't believe that 'too close' nonsense, and neither do you," I said.

"So what is it?"

"You wanted to be near me again."

"Oh, look who's suddenly full of themselves after their first bar fight," she said.

"Who said it was my first bar fight?"

But just between you and me, it was.

I closed the remaining distance between us and pressed my body against hers. She didn't try to push me away. I placed my hand on the side of her face. She still didn't pull away.

"I've missed you," I said.

She said nothing.

I leaned forward and kissed her, and then I leaned back and looked at her. She never took her eyes away from mine. I kissed her again. She reached up and placed her hand behind my neck, pulling me back to her. We kissed for a few moments, slowly getting more aggressive with each passing second.

I lifted her shirt and ran my fingertips across her smooth stomach. I slowly made my way upward and eventually cupped her breasts. With the other hand, I reached down to her pants and undid the button. She helped me tug them down, while she stepped out of them.

Then she reached for my shorts, but I was already pulling them away. I kissed her again and lifted her onto the edge of the counter. Alana spread her legs open and wrapped them around me.

You can figure out what happened after that. I would like to go into more detail, but I'm trying to be more of a gentleman these days.

Afterwards, we held onto each other. Both of us tried desperately to catch our breaths. I hadn't planned on this happening tonight. I didn't know if it would ever happen again. But I had gotten her back, and I would never let her go.

19

I'M SORRY

I SPENT THE NIGHT AT ALANA'S. IT WAS THE FIRST TIME I HAD DONE SO in weeks. I wondered how things would be in the morning. We had made a giant step toward getting back together, and as far as I knew, we were back together, but I wasn't sure if she felt the same way. I usually woke up before she did, and this morning wasn't the exception. I stayed in bed though. When she eventually woke, she reached for me. Our love making wasn't as intense as it had been the night before in the kitchen, but it was perhaps even more pleasurable. We took our time exploring each other's bodies, and by the end, I knew for certain we were back.

After showering and getting dressed, we sat on her back patio and had coffee.

"You're thinking about the investigation, aren't you?" she asked.

"Is it that obvious?"

"You have that faraway look in your eyes," she said.

"Just realizing that there's something I should have been asking myself but haven't."

"What is it?"

"The first two questions were obvious. Who would want to kill

Panos and who could have followed him to the marina without Hani noticing?"

"I actually don't think it would have been too difficult to follow without her realizing it. If she was following Panos, she would have been giving his car all her attention. She probably didn't even think someone might be behind her."

"Exactly," I said.

"So what's the question you should have been asking yourself?"

"How did the person get in Hani's house to frame her with the flashlight? You said there was no sign of forced entry, right?"

"Yeah."

"How do people normally break into a house?"

"Usually they break a window. Sometimes doors have glass panels in them. It's pretty easy to knock one of those out and then just reach inside to unlock the door."

"But that didn't happen at her house," I said.

"No."

"What about picking a lock?" I asked.

"It's not that hard if you know what you're doing. Hell, you can learn to pick a lock on YouTube."

"Were there any signs the lock had been tampered with?"

"Not the lock, but the doorknob," she said.

"What do you mean?"

"I'm pretty sure the person went in through the backdoor in the garage. The outside of the doorknob was free of fingerprints. The inside was not."

"Whose prints were on the inside?"

"We found two sets of prints. One belongs to Hani, the other is someone else. They aren't in the system," she said.

"Didn't you tell me Hani had a tenant for a while?" I asked.

"I've reached out to her and asked if she could go to her local police station and get printed so we can compare."

"Has she done that?"

"Not yet."

"You said the outside of the doorknob didn't have prints?"

"It was wiped clean," she said.

"So the person picks the lock somehow, opens the door, plants the flashlight, and then wipes the doorknob after they shut the door."

"Probably."

"I assume Adcock knows all of this," I said.

"Of course. It doesn't seem to bother him."

We finished our coffee, and then decided to visit Hani. I followed Alana to the jail since she needed to go to work afterward.

Hani looked a little better than the last time I'd seen her, but just barely.

"You're my second guests of the morning," Hani said.

"Really? Who else came by?" Alana asked.

"Makani. He wanted to check on me."

"The guy's really stuck on you," I said.

"It was nice of him to come by," Alana said.

Hani turned to me.

"He said you and Kai got into a fight."

"Him and some other guy. Much bigger dude."

"Don't know his friend. When Makani and I were together, I tried to stay away from Kai as much as possible," Hani said.

"Understandable," I said.

"It wasn't easy, though. Sometimes I thought Makani and Kai were glued at the hip."

"Strange they could be so different," I said.

Hani nodded, and then she looked at us both, like she was suddenly examining us.

"Something's different. Did you two work things out?" she asked.

"It was the bar fight," I said. "She couldn't withstand my manly charm."

Hani looked at Alana.

"It wasn't the bar fight," Alana said.

"I'm glad for you both. At least someone around here should be happy."

I thought back to my morning conversation with Alana. I turned to Hani.

"After your tenant moved out, did you change the locks?" I asked.

"No, I didn't have a chance because I was busy planning the wedding."

"I assume she returned your keys to you," I said.

"She gave me back the two keys she had. I had a third."

"Was the garage door key the same as the front door?" I asked.

"Yes, all the locks can be opened by the same key."

"Did anyone else have a key other than you and your tenant?" Alana asked.

"I gave Panos one of the keys when we got back."

So much for that theory, I thought.

We spoke with Hani for as long as we could. We talked about random things, like how I was having trouble keeping Maui the dog from occasionally attacking Foxx. We didn't speak much about her case. There wasn't much new to say. We were at a dead end. We didn't tell Hani that, but I think she already knew. The visiting hours ended, and we told her we'd be back as soon as we could.

I followed Alana out to her car in the parking lot.

"Anything new on the Peter Bell case?" I asked.

"Not much. We tracked down the card players Peter Bell owed money to. They have solid alibis."

"So you still think it's connected to Panos' death?"

"Undoubtedly."

Alana looked at her watch.

"I better get over to the station. I'm way late."

"I'll see you later," I said.

I kissed Alana goodbye. She climbed into her car and drove away. I found my car, which was on the opposite side of the parking lot. I wasn't surprised by the news the card players checked out. I never thought it was them to begin with. Peter Bell had blackmailed the killer. There was no other explanation.

I left the jail and drove to Harry's Bar. I figured I owed them an apology for last night's fight. I also owed them for my unpaid bar tab. Harry's had become a favorite locals' hangout of mine, and I was a little worried the owner might ban me from the bar. The last thing I wanted was to get stuck going to a tourist trap. I had spoken to the owner a few times, and he seemed like a nice guy. Maybe I could convince him I wasn't the one responsible for the fight, even though I threw the first punch, or elbow in this case.

Harry's was owned by a guy named Bart. At first, I thought he'd bought an established place that already had a reputation as Harry's, and he didn't want to mess up the vibe. But Bart told me he built the bar himself. Apparently, he thought people were more inclined to frequent a Harry's than a Bart's. He was probably right.

I got there before the place officially opened, but fortunately the door was unlocked. I entered and found Bart wiping down the tables. He looked up at me when he heard the door open.

"Looks like they got yah," Bart said.

He pointed to my head. I touched my head and felt the bandage just above my eye. I had forgotten about it.

"Not too bad," I said.

I reached into my back pocket and removed my wallet.

"I came by to apologize for yesterday and also pay my bill."

Bart held up an open hand.

"No worries. I've come to expect a bar fight once in a while. Comes with the territory."

"Still, it's not something I want to be known for. Let me at least pay for the beers."

"Already taken care of," he said.

"Really?"

I put my wallet back in my pocket.

"Some guy came by this morning. Apologized for the fight and paid your bill," Bart said.

"Was it one of the guys I fought with?" I asked.

"No, I didn't recognize him."

"What did he look like?"

"Hawaiian guy. Medium build. Quiet fella."

"I don't suppose his name was Makani," I asked.

Bart thought about it for a moment.

"Might have been. I think that's what he said his name was."

"That's Kai's brother."

I could tell from Bart's confused look he had no idea who Kai was either.

I pointed to the bandage on my head.

"He's the smaller one who gave me this yesterday."

"Got yah. Yeah, this Makani fella kept telling me how sorry he was. You'd think my bar had gotten blown up or something."

I walked over to Bart and extended my hand.

"Either way, I appreciate your understanding. It won't happen again," I said.

Bart shook my hand.

"I'll catch you later," I said.

"Sure thing. Thanks for stopping by."

I left the bar and walked back to my car. I wondered how much apologizing Makani did for his hotheaded brother. I got into my car and drove home.

I decided to test Alana's theory that anyone could pick a lock. I logged onto YouTube, and sure enough, there were several videos that showed you how to pick a deadbolt. They made it sound like any first grader could do it, but it was actually trickier than it looked. It took me about twenty minutes to get the lock on Foxx's house to open. I figured I could probably get that time down to a couple of minutes if I practiced more. Still, my brief experiment on lock picking taught me it might not be the easiest thing for an amateur to do, especially if that amateur was in the process of trying to frame Hani. He or she had to be nervous. They would have been in possession of the flashlight with Panos' hair and blood on it.

I didn't know what else to do at this point, so I drove to Hani's house. When I got there, I noticed she had a privacy fence around her backyard. It was something I hadn't really paid attention to on my previous visit. That time, I had concentrated solely on the actions of the police. Both her neighbors had one-story houses, so it would have been relatively easy to play with the lock without anyone noticing. I walked into the backyard and examined the lock. I didn't notice anything weird. It had been a wasted trip, but sometimes you feel compelled to do something.

I got home and decided to take the dog for a walk when my phone rang.

"Hello."

"This is Mara Winters, Hani's attorney. I just got out of a meeting with her. She asked me to call you and pass on some information. She said she remembered Makani had a house key once. He would cat-sit for her when she was out of town, but she got the key back."

"Okay, thanks for the information."

"Does this make sense to you?" she asked.

"Perfect sense. Thanks."

I ended the call. He might have given the key back, but that doesn't mean he didn't copy the key beforehand. There was something else. *I'm sorry.* Makani said that to Hani and the bar owner.

Was that the answer?

I drove straight to Kihei. The traffic was heavy, as usual, but it gave me time to work out my theory. It made sense, and I was completely convinced I was right by the time I arrived.

I parked in the lot of the strip mall where Makani's surf shop was located. This time I parked in a slot near the road versus the back of the mall in case I found him behind the store like before. I had no idea what Kai's car looked like, so there was no point in scanning the parking lot. I really hoped he wasn't there, for multiple reasons, but it wasn't going to stop me from exploring my new theory. Before I entered the store, I took out my phone and turned the video recorder on. I didn't think there was much chance I would get a confession this morning, but it was better to be safe than sorry, as the old saying goes. I slipped the phone back in my pocket. Hopefully it could pick up the audio between us.

I opened the door and saw Makani sitting behind the sales counter. Kai was nowhere to be seen, neither was his Hulk Hogan-sized friend or the young guy with the magazine I saw on my last visit. It was just Makani and me. I expected more of a reaction from him when he saw me, but he seemed pretty calm.

I walked across the store and stopped in front of the counter. We were only a few feet away from each other. He didn't stand. He didn't say anything. He just stared at me.

"Thanks for paying my bill at Harry's," I said.

Makani still said nothing.

"Thanks also for visiting Hani this morning. I know she gets really lonely in there. You feel bad about that, don't you?"

"Who wouldn't?" he asked.

"She told me you kept telling her you were sorry," I said.

I waited for a reaction from Makani, but I got none.

"When she told me you said you were sorry on your first visit, I didn't think much of it. That's kind of the thing to say, isn't it?"

I waited a moment for Makani to answer me. He didn't.

"I'm a little mad at myself. I should have caught it then, but it wasn't until after the bar owner told me you had said you were sorry that I figured it out."

I watched Makani for a reaction, but he gave me nothing. I wondered if he had a really good poker face, or if my new theory was total garbage.

"When you told Hani you were sorry, you weren't saying it in a generic sense, like telling a widow you're sorry for her husband dying. Your sorry was more specific. You actually feel responsible for her being in jail. I never seriously considered that you killed Panos. I knew you hated the guy, but I thought you were too mild-mannered to slit his throat. It would take some serious fury to do that. Your brother is another story. You told him what happened at the rehearsal party. He lost his cool and went to the marina. Did you follow Panos there? Is that how you guys knew he was there?"

Makani said nothing.

"Here's why else I know Kai did it. The flashlight. I know you love Hani. You're probably mad at her too for leaving you, but I don't think you'd actually frame her. Kai, on the other hand, wouldn't have an issue with doing that. He's the one who put the flashlight in her garage. He got the key from you, but Kai didn't have to frame her. As far as he knew, he'd gotten away with it. Or maybe it was Peter Bell.

Maybe once Peter contacted you guys after the murder, Kai felt he needed some extra insurance so someone else would take the fall. It's kind of killing two birds with one stone. He gets back at Panos for humiliating you, and he frames the girl who broke your heart. He's an asshole, but he really cares about his brother. I'll give him that."

"None of that's true," Makani said.

He said it so calmly, like he was simply talking about the weather.

"You don't sound passionate about that. If my family had just been accused of committing a crime we didn't commit, I'd be pretty upset."

"You've got no evidence of any of this," he said.

"Maybe not today, but I'll get it, especially now that I know who to concentrate on. I've been spreading myself too thin since Panos had so many enemies. Now I'm just going to look at you and Kai. You'll have made a mistake, if not during Panos' murder, then during Peter Bell's."

I left the surf shop. I thought about immediately calling Alana and telling her I figured it out, but I wanted more time to think things through. I wanted to wrap everything up in a nice little package for her.

The traffic was just as heavy leaving Kihei as it was getting there. I finally got home and took Maui the dog for another walk. I thought about the case as I walked, and I realized I'd made a colossal mistake by letting them know I had figured it out. My ego had gotten the better of me. I saw Makani as a weakling. I thought there was a good chance I could have shaken and intimidated him. I expected him to confess, but he'd remained pretty reserved and in control throughout the meeting at the surf shop.

I wasn't sure I'd ever be able to nail these guys for the crimes. The police hadn't found the murder weapon. The camera footage from the marina security system was gone for good, or at least stolen by Kai and/or Makani. I had no doubt they'd destroyed the computer drive by now. It was probably in a million pieces at the bottom of some random dumpster.

There was also the problem of whether or not I'd even be alive to keep investigating the case. Why? Well, there was the little thing of Kai and his burly friend standing in my driveway when I got back to my house. It was pretty obvious why they were there. They'd wasted no time in heading my way once Makani called them.

"I told you to stay the hell away," Kai said.

He charged me. His bodyguard friend was only a few steps behind. I waited until the last moment, and then I slammed my fist into Kai's throat. He gasped for air and immediately lost interest in me.

His friend was another story. The burly friend hit me in the exact same spot that Kai had hit me. I felt the cut split open again. This guy had a lot more force behind his punch as well. The dizziness and wooziness were immediate.

I balled up my fist to strike back, but he punched me a second time. This one was aimed at my nose. I assumed he was getting back at me for the damage I caused to his. I turned my head right as his fist connected. His punch glanced off the side of my nose and landed solidly under my eye. He was much faster than I thought possible for a guy his size. He hit me a third time in my stomach, and I doubled over. I heard him laugh as he swept his leg behind my legs, and I fell hard on the ground. I was on my back, and I saw his ugly face as he leaned over me.

"No cop to rescue you this time."

He lifted his leg and stomped down on my stomach. Every ounce of air left my body. He stomped on my stomach a second time. I tried desperately to catch my breath but couldn't. I heard Maui the dog bark in the background, and then I heard my arm snap as the big guy stomped on it. I don't remember exactly what happened next, but I think he kicked me in the side of the head.

I saw Foxx's face when I woke up.

"Was it those two guys from the bar?" he asked.

I tried to answer him but couldn't. My brain was too clouded.

"Hold on, buddy," he said.

I don't know what happened next because I passed out again. The next time I woke, both Foxx and Alana were looking at me.

"Where am I?" I asked.

"Emergency room," Foxx said.

"You're gonna be okay," Alana said.

"I'll go tell the doc you're awake," Foxx said.

Foxx stood and left my bedside. Alana moved her chair closer to me.

"Who did this to you?" Alana asked.

"You have to ask?"

"Kai," Alana said.

I didn't answer her because the emergency room doctor pulled the curtain back. Foxx was right behind him.

"Good afternoon, Mr. Rutherford."

"I wouldn't exactly call it good," I said.

"You're alive. That qualifies as good in my book," he said.

"I see your point."

I tried to sit up by pressing my arms against the bed. A sharp pain raced through my left arm, so I didn't get very far.

"I wouldn't advise that. The radius and ulna, which are the two bones in your lower arm, were snapped in half. You're going to need surgery."

"Great," I said. "Any other damage. My head feels like it was run over by a truck?"

"I suspect you have a concussion as well. They really did a number on you. We'll keep you in here a few more hours for observation. I can give you the name of an orthopedist if you don't have one already."

"Thanks," I said.

The doctor left my area to attend other patients. Foxx turned to Alana.

"Can you do me a favor and take him home? I've got a couple of things I need to take care of?"

"Sure thing," Alana said.

"Take care, buddy. I'll see you later tonight," he said.

Foxx left, and I had the pleasure of hanging out in the emergency room another four or five hours. A nurse appeared at some point and put my arm in a splint and wrapped it tightly with an Ace bandage. It hurt like hell going on, but the pressure of the bandage eventually made the pain subside somewhat.

They eventually let me leave, and Alana drove me home. It wasn't until we pulled in the driveway that I thought about Maui the dog.

"Holy shit, where's my dog? He was with me when those guys jumped me."

"Foxx found him when he got home. He was sitting by your side," Alana said.

"Really? He didn't run off?"

"He was right there."

I walked into the house, and Maui the dog ran to greet me.

"Hey, buddy. Thanks for sticking with me."

Alana stayed with me until Foxx came home, which was a few hours later. They had a brief conversation in the other room, but I couldn't hear what they said. Alana came back into my room and asked me if I needed anything before she left. I told her I was fine.

Foxx poked his head into my room after she left.

"Feeling any better?" he asked.

"Yeah. A little. Thanks for taking me to the ER."

"No problem. Holler if you need anything."

Foxx left the room. I looked down at Maui the dog, who was sleeping on the floor beside my bed. There's something to be said for loyalty.

20

THE VIDEO

The next day I went to the orthopedist. He, too, recommended surgery since the break was so bad. My left arm ended up with a few pins and plates, and I wondered if I would permanently set off the metal detector every time I went to the airport.

The few days after the surgery were a haze of painkillers and frequent naps. My head started hurting worse than before. At first, I was worried it was complications from my possible concussion. The throbbing in my head was so bad I actually vomited a few times. I stopped taking the pain medication, thinking that might be the real culprit in causing the headaches. Within a few hours, the agony subsided in my head. Of course, the pain immediately returned in my arm. I say all this to explain why I was so distracted and didn't think to look for my cell phone in those initial days after the fight with Kai.

Foxx had gone to the grocery store the third morning after my surgery, and I wanted to call him to bring me back a few things. That's when I realized I hadn't used my phone in a while, and I really didn't know where it was. I slowly remembered having it on my walk with Maui the dog, so I assumed it might be somewhere in the front yard. It could have easily fallen off me when Kai's friend was beating the living hell out of me. I went outside and searched for the phone, but I couldn't find it. Alana drove up while I was on my knees combing through the grass.

"What are you doing out here?" she asked.

"Searching for my phone."

"Why would it be in the grass?"

"I think Kai's friend knocked it off me when he knocked me out."

"Let me call it."

Alana pulled out her phone and called my number. She quickly hung up.

"Went straight to voice mail," she said. "Let's get you back in the house. We'll find the phone later."

"I'm fine," I protested.

"You need to be resting and not crawling around in the yard."

Alana and I went back inside. Maui the dog ran up to her. He did his usual thing of collapsing on his back in dramatic fashion so she could bend down and scratch his belly.

"Hello, Maui," she said.

Alana stood after tickling Maui's stomach.

"Did the headaches go away yet?" she asked.

"Much better since I quit taking those painkillers."

"So what are you doing for the pain?"

"Pretending it doesn't exist," I said.

"Is it working?"

"Not well. You know, I never followed up with you about Kai and his friend. When did they get arrested?"

"They didn't," she said.

"How's that possible?"

"I went looking for them and found them in the hospital."

"The hospital?"

"Apparently they checked in just after you checked out. They claimed a certain retired football player paid them a visit."

"Foxx?" I asked.

"He broke both their arms, meaning both arms on each guy. So that's four broken arms to your one."

"Really?"

"You're surprised? I'm pretty sure that's why Foxx asked me to drive you home from the hospital. He went looking for them."

"I guess he found them. I can't believe he didn't tell me."

"They wanted to file an assault charge against Foxx when I reminded them you could easily file one against them."

"So you cut a deal."

"I didn't think you'd want Foxx going back to jail, even if it meant keeping Kai and his friend out."

"I see your point."

"I don't think they're going to bother you anymore," she said. "Here's another interesting development. Makani's mother called in a missing person's report on Makani. His family hasn't seen him for a few days."

"Think he fled the island?" I asked.

"Maybe. I've got a guy checking the flight schedules as we speak. Certainly lends credence to your theory," Alana said.

I already felt bad for confronting Makani before I had gathered the evidence. Now I felt even worse, but why would he leave when I was convinced Kai was the killer? Was Makani there too when the murder occurred? Probably. I couldn't think of another theory that fit.

"I better get back to the office. I just wanted to see how you were doing," she said.

"You coming back after work?" I asked.

"Absolutely."

I walked Alana to the front door.

"Do me a favor and stay off the grass. You need to rest," she said.

I smiled and promised I would stay in bed. A few minutes after Alana left, though, I took Maui the dog outside so he could do his thing. He roamed around the yard for a while and then disappeared into the bushes.

"What are you doing in there, Maui? You find a bird or something?"

Maui the dog came out of the bushes with a black object in his mouth. I bent over to examine it. It was the plastic case for my phone.

How did it get all the way in there? I thought. I got down on my knees and felt under the bush for my phone. I found it against the trunk of the bush. I pressed the button on the bottom of the phone, but the phone was completely dead. I guessed that was why it went straight to voice mail when Alana called.

I took Maui the dog back inside and plugged my cell phone into the charger. It powered up after charging for another ten minutes or so. A few minutes after that, a text message appeared on the display.

"Meet me at the marina. M."

I assumed *M* stood for Makani. I wondered when he sent the text, though, because it registered as having just been sent. I thought that was because the phone had just been turned on. I got a sick feeling in the pit of my stomach. Alana said Makani had gone missing. What if he'd been at the marina all this time? I called Alana but only got her voicemail. Foxx still wasn't back from the store. I called Makani's number back. It went to voicemail after several rings.

I knew I should wait for one of them, but my impatience got the better of me. I grabbed my car keys from the kitchen counter and headed out to the car. The BMW Z3 is an automatic, so it wasn't that hard to drive with one hand.

I got to the marina in no time. I walked down to the dock where Panos' boat was. I didn't notice the smell until I hopped on the boat. I opened the door to the cabin, and then the smell became over-whelming. The scene was difficult to describe, but I'll give you the somewhat censored version because I doubt you'd want to hear the true horrific details. Makani's body was slumped on the sofa. His blood and brain matter were spread across the cabin wall behind him. I looked down and saw a handgun on the floor, just off to the side of his body. There was a small table bolted to the floor in front of the sofa. A cell phone was on the table, along with a note that said "play."

I pressed the home button on the phone and immediately saw my phone number listed as a missed call. There were several other missed calls listed but only from a couple of different phone numbers. I didn't recognize the numbers, but they probably belonged to Kai and his mother. I tapped the video icon on the display. There was only one video shown on the phone's drive, so I played it. Makani's image appeared. The video was somewhat dark, but it was clear enough to tell it was shot in the boat cabin. Makani spoke directly to the phone's camera. His voice cracked as he spoke, and he did so in a slow cadence as if he were searching for the right words to say.

"I can't allow my brother or Hani to be blamed for something I did. The flashlight belonged to me. I took it out of my glove box when I got to the marina. I found Panos sleeping. I hit him in the back of the head so he wouldn't wake up. I pulled his head back and cut his throat. I threw the knife in the ocean. You'll never find it."

Makani looked down. He mumbled into his chest, and I couldn't tell if he was talking to the camera or to himself.

"He wasn't a good person. He shouldn't have done the things he did to Hani," Makani said.

He looked back at the camera.

"Hani is innocent. Please let her go."

Makani reached toward the phone, and the video ended. I tapped on his text icon and confirmed he had sent me the text message a few days ago. He must have come here shortly after our conversation at the surf shop. I felt sick to my stomach for multiple reasons. The sight was gruesome for sure, but I also felt somewhat responsible for driving Makani to suicide.

I put his phone back on the table and pulled mine out. I called Alana, but it went to voice mail again. I left her a message to get to the marina as quickly as possible. I then hung up and called 911.

I left the cabin and stood on the dock beside the boat and waited. The sky was beautiful, and the waters were calm. Makani was gone. I had such a hard time processing that.

The first police car arrived about twenty minutes later. It was a single police officer. He looked like he was in his early twenties. I wondered if he'd just joined the force. He was about to see something he'd never be able to purge from his mind. I knew I wouldn't be able to, no matter how hard I tried. I told him where the body was. I told him to prepare himself for the smell.

Detective Adcock and Alana showed up a few minutes after the initial officer. They were in two different cars, but they got to the marina around the same time. The police officer came out of the cabin. He walked to the stern and hopped onto the dock. He stood still and sucked in the fresh air. I tried not to look at him. I wanted to give him his space, but it was easy to notice the sweat rolling down his face as he walked by me. The police officer headed up the dock and greeted Adcock and Alana who were walking toward him.

"Body inside, Detective," the police officer told Adcock.

Adcock walked past the officer without stopping and headed over to me.

"What's going on?" he demanded.

"There's a cell phone on the table in the cabin. Play the video. Everything will be clear."

Adcock stepped onto the boat and disappeared into the cabin.

"Makani?" Alana asked.

I nodded.

She followed Adcock into the cabin. They both came out a couple of minutes later. In that short time, another police car and an ambulance had arrived.

Adcock walked up to the original police officer. He pointed at me.

"Arrest him," Adcock said.

"Arrest me?" I asked.

"For murder," Adcock said.

"You're going to pin this on me?"

"You found the body. How did you know it was here?" he asked.

"Check the text messages on his phone. He told me to meet him here."

The officer approached me.

"Put your hands behind your back," he said.

"I don't think you're going to get cuffs around this thing," I said, and I held up my arm with the cast.

"This is bullshit, Glen, and you know it," Alana said.

"Don't interfere. This is my case," he said.

"You saw the video. The guy confessed," Alana said.

"And why wouldn't he with your boyfriend pointing a gun at his head?"

"You have zero proof he was coerced," she said.

The police officer read me my rights as he escorted me up the dock and to his car. He removed a thick canvas belt from the trunk of the car. It had a metal loop on it, and he wrapped it around my waist. He then pulled my good arm behind my back and handcuffed it to the metal loop. He then zip-tied my cast to the belt. My arms weren't going anywhere. He shoved me into the backseat of the car and shut the door. I looked back toward Panos' boat but couldn't see it from the angle the car was parked. I knew the murder charges wouldn't stick, but I couldn't help but be nervous. This was my first time in the back of a police car, if you don't count the time Alana pretended to arrest me outside Harry's.

They took me to the station and booked me on murder charges. They then threw me into a large cell populated by about twelve other guys. I had no idea what they were in there for, and I had no desire to get to know them.

Despite what I may have implied earlier, I don't think Detective Glen Adcock is a dumb guy. In fact, I think he's somewhat clever in certain aspects. I do think he's an incredibly lazy detective, and there's no doubt in my mind he royally screwed up this investigation. Did I think he'd ever acknowledge that or even apologize to me? No chance. He's clearly a vindictive tool. He uses the law to settle grudges and perceived grievances. But is he dumb? No. Case in point, he arrested me on a Friday afternoon. He knew nothing was going to get done over the weekend, so I would sit in that cell for close to seventy-two hours before they finally let me out.

I probably would have been locked up even longer had it not been for Alana. She visited me a few times over the weekend and told me she was doing everything she could to set me free. I believed her, but it didn't make the weekend any better or go any faster for that matter. They finally let me out late Monday morning. Adcock wasn't there. In fact, I didn't see him anywhere in the police station. I guessed he decided to do a coffee run or just take a personal day to work on his insecurities. Maybe he needed time to reflect on how he messed this thing up. Maybe he was just brainstorming other bogus charges he could hit me with. Either way, I was glad I didn't see him.

"The medical examiner is a friend of mine," Alana said as we walked toward the exit.

"I convinced her to do the examination over the weekend. Makani's time of death is around the time you were in the emergency room. You've got multiple witnesses to confirm that, as well as your medical records. By the way, we owe the M.E. an incredibly expensive steak dinner."

"No problem. I'll be glad to buy her, and a date of her choice, dinner anytime."

We walked outside. The sky was overcast, and it looked like it might rain any second. I didn't care about the crappy weather. I was just thrilled to be out of there. We walked toward Alana's car, which was parked in the back of the lot.

"What about Hani? That video has to exonerate her," I said.

"Mara Winters has seen the video and has filed a petition for her release. I don't see the judge not granting it, but the hearing isn't until this afternoon."

"If the judge agrees, how fast will she be out?"

"Later today if all goes according to plan. She knows what you did for her. She told me to tell you how grateful she is."

"It's no problem," I said.

"No problem? You got your arm broken, and you were thrown in jail."

"You know what I mean. I wanted to help."

We reached her car. Alana put her arms on the roof and looked across the car to me.

"I know what you did too. Thank you," she said.

"I did it for you," I said.

"I know."

We climbed into Alana's car, and she drove out of the parking lot. We drove in silence for several minutes.

"I guess Kai and his mother know what happened," I said.

"I told them. It was bad, especially with the mother."

I nodded. I couldn't imagine how difficult that must have been for them to hear. As much as I disliked Kai, I didn't want something as awful as Makani's suicide to happen to his family. Their pain had to be beyond belief.

"Did you get a chance to look over Makani's phone? Was there any other information on there that's useful?"

"We went through everything. Nothing stood out but the text to you and the video recording of his confession," she said.

"What about the gun Makani used to kill himself? Does it match the weapon used to murder Peter Bell?" I asked.

"I'm still waiting on the ballistics report. My guess is yes."

We drove for several minutes, and we approached the turn-off for the marina.

"Foxx and I picked up your car. It's back at the house."

"Thanks."

I looked out the window as Alana drove past the marina. I certainly couldn't see Panos' boat from the road, but I knew it was down there. I thought the thing should be torn apart and recycled piece by piece.

"Foxx is pretty pissed at you. He can't believe you didn't wait for him."

"Yeah, I'm pretty pissed at myself too," I said.

"That makes three of us mad at you."

I turned to her.

"Sorry," I said.

"You should be. Oh, I forgot. There's actually four of us mad at you. The dog's angry too. There was no one there willing to walk him."

"Foxx didn't take him out?" I asked.

"I'm sure he did, but the dog is still bent out of shape."

"I'll give him a bone to chew on. That should repair our relationship."

21

DOUBTS

AFTER VIEWING THE VIDEO CONFESSION, THE PROSECUTOR recommended all charges against Hani be dropped. The judge agreed, and Alana threw Hani one of the biggest parties I had ever seen. At least for the time being, the animosity I had first seen between the two sisters had completely disappeared. Hopefully that would remain the same for a long time to come. I only knew a few people at the party, including Hani, Alana, Foxx, and Michelle, but I had one of the best times of my life that evening. We stayed up well past dawn. I don't even remember going to bed. I think I fell asleep in Alana's backyard at some point. The next few days were a bit foggy. The older you get, the harder it seems to be to get over those all-night parties.

Hani decided not to move back to Los Angeles. I don't know if she was ever serious about the modeling career. She was certainly beautiful enough, but I still thought her main goal of moving to California was to get Panos away from Alana and other women like Shae. I had no doubt, though, that Panos probably had a list of beautiful women in L.A. too. The city certainly had no shortage of them. Panos must have loved Hani, at least in his own way. He committed to marrying her after all. The guy was still a mystery to me, and with his passing, I knew there was no way I'd ever figure him out completely or even partially. He obviously had a charm that made him irresistible to people, but he was also self-centered and egotistical. Regardless of his tendency to ignore the feelings of others, he didn't deserve his fate.

This story, though, was also about the death of Makani. He was the classic example of the quiet guy who was pushed too far. I thought back to the verbal confrontation he had with Panos the night of the wedding rehearsal party. Panos had thoroughly humiliated him. I wondered if Makani had made the decision to stay home that night, how things would have turned out? Would Panos and Hani actually have gotten married? Would they be happy today? I guessed they were silly questions to ask considering how they were totally irrelevant now. I just couldn't shake the feeling all of this was one giant example of how a human life can be snuffed out for such an insignificant reason. I did my best to put the entire ordeal behind me. After all, life goes on.

My relationship with Alana seemed back on track. I don't want to say it was like the kiss between her and Panos never happened because it did, and it wasn't something I could forget. But I did my best to forgive. I assumed it was only a matter of time before I screwed up something in the future. So who am I to cast stones? There's enough of that going around these days.

As good as things had become for me again, I couldn't shake lingering doubts about my investigation into Panos' murder. I knew there was something that just didn't feel right. It's kind of like when you're leaving your house and you just know you're forgetting something, but the harder you try to figure out what it is, the less likely you are to remember what you're missing. The doubt kept growing, and it was annoying, like a splinter in my palm. Yes, Makani confessed to the crime. I knew my initial suspicions were that Kai killed Panos. I didn't think Makani had it in him, but I did believe the confession. Also, I didn't think Makani would commit suicide just to take the fall for Kai.

Here's what really bothered me, though. Alana eventually got the ballistics test from the gun Makani used to kill himself. That gun was not used to shoot Peter Bell. Granted, Makani could have used a different gun, but was it likely he had two guns? Maybe, but I didn't think so. Furthermore, Makani hadn't expressed remorse for killing Peter Bell during his video confession. He didn't even bring it up. I'm sure you noticed that before I did. Makani was a sensitive guy. I didn't think he would just ignore Peter's death.

The flashlight also stuck out. I didn't believe Makani would frame Hani by stashing the bloody flashlight in her garage, so I really thought a second person was still out there. It was probably Kai. He may not have killed Panos, but I had him pegged for the killing of Peter Bell. I just didn't know how to get evidence on him, especially now that Makani was gone and couldn't be interrogated. I hated the thought there might be a second killer walking around free. I just didn't know what to do.

There was something else that kept popping up in my mind that I mentioned before. Daphne's behavior toward me. I didn't understand why she was against me continuing the investigation after Hani was arrested. Daphne seemed to be a smart lady, so I had a difficult time comprehending how she believed such flimsy evidence as the planted flashlight. I knew she wanted the killer to be found. Could she have really believed Hani did it? Yes, she said she always thought Hani was only interested in Panos' money, but that was another factor that pointed to her innocence. Daphne had to have realized that. Hani wouldn't kill someone when she'd already signed a prenup, and there was no life insurance policy in place that would have given her a dime should Panos die. Plus, Hani never officially became Mrs. Panos Laskaris to begin with. She got nothing by killing Panos the night before the wedding. It wasn't like Hani just discovered Panos was cheating on her either. That was apparently obvious to everyone who knew Panos well. Certainly Daphne fit into that category. You're probably wondering why I obsessed so much over the Daphne thing. I just don't like loose ends, and this was definitely a loose one.

It was during one of the moments I was obsessing over Daphne's strange behavior that Alana called and asked if I was in the mood for dinner at Eddie's. It was a Friday evening, and we were both looking forward to the weekend. She asked me to pick her up from work in a couple of hours. I was pretty bored at home, so I decided to drive to Harry's to grab a beer before meeting Alana. I hadn't been in the bar since apologizing to the owner. I was a little embarrassed to go back, but I figured I liked the place, so why continue to avoid it?

When I entered Harry's, I saw Shae working behind the bar.

"What happened to your arm?" she asked.

I looked at my cast. I still had to wear it for another two weeks.

"Oh, just clumsy, I guess. How long have you been working here?" I asked.

I slid onto a bar stool.

"A few days. What can I get you?" she asked.

"Coors Light, please."

Shae fished out a beer and popped the top. She put the beer down in front of me.

"Thanks. How do you like bartending?" I asked.

"I'm a lot more tired at the end of the night, but the tips make up for it."

"Good. I'm glad things worked out for you. I had a feeling they would," I said.

"It was good I got out when I did. I heard the View is about to close."

"Really?"

"I ran into Dolly in the grocery store. She said Wes has decided to close the place and open a new restaurant back in Paia."

"That's surprising. I thought Jim might turn things around for them," I said.

"Dolly said Wes and Jim are constantly at each other's throats."

"I didn't see that coming," I admitted.

"Wes swapped one prima donna partner for another," she said.

"So what's Jim going to do?"

"Don't know. He sure as hell isn't going to Paia with Wes. I don't think Wes wants to ever see Jim's face again."

"I remember Wes told me he wasn't happy with the business in Paia. It doesn't make sense he would try to go there again."

"He's desperate," Shae said.

There was a giddiness to Shae's voice. I couldn't blame her after the way Wes allowed Jim to fire her with no warning. The fact that Wes didn't even have the courage to do it himself just added to the bitter feelings.

"Speaking of moving on, I heard Daphne moved back to California to be with her mother," I said.

"I can see that. With Panos gone, there's probably not much reason for her to stay."

I took a long sip from my beer.

"That's not her mother by the way," Shae said.

I almost choked on my beer.

"What do you mean?" I asked.

"Daphne's parents died in a car accident in Greece. She went to live with Panos and his family when she was just a teenager."

"So Panos' mother is her aunt or something?" I asked.

"Panos father and Daphne's father were brothers."

"That makes Panos and Daphne cousins," I said.

"Yep."

I thought back to my first visit to Daphne's house. I remembered looking at the family photographs in the sitting room. There were several photos of Panos as a child but none of Daphne. She didn't appear in the photos with Panos until she was a teenager. Now it all made sense. I stood and pulled my wallet out.

"Thanks for the info and the beer."

I slid some cash onto the bar.

"Good luck with the new job," I continued.

"Thanks."

Shae grabbed a wet cloth and cleaned the bar top.

I walked outside and headed to my car. Panos and Daphne were cousins and not brother and sister. That was interesting. I brought that little fun fact up to Alana when I picked her up. She said she didn't know it either, but she didn't understand why I found it so intriguing. She told me it made perfect sense for them to give people the impression they were siblings when they had grown up together, at least for part of their childhoods.

We drove to the restaurant and had a pleasant meal. Our conversation consisted of what we wanted to do that weekend. We debated over seeing a movie but realized there wasn't much out we wanted to see. We were almost finished with dinner when Aaron Tench approached our table. I hadn't seen him in the restaurant earlier.

"I was glad to hear Hani was released," Tench said.

"So were we," Alana said.

"How's she doing?" he asked.

"She's better. She misses Panos, of course, but she's just taking it day by day," Alana said.

"I guess that's all you can do," he said.

"Do you come here a lot?" I asked.

Tench patted his stomach.

"Way more than I should. I usually pass the restaurant on my way back from work. Sometimes it's hard not to stop, especially when I don't feel like making myself dinner at home."

"Speaking of your work, my friend, Foxx, has a nice pool in his backyard, but the landscaping around it isn't that great. I thought I might hire you to spruce it up, sort of a thank you to Foxx for letting me live at his place."

"Sure. Sounds like it could be a nice project. Just let me know when would be a good time to stop by and look at the place."

"We're in Ka'anapali, though. Do you do work that far out?"

"I'm out that way all the time. Most of my clients are over there," he said.

"Didn't you used to live out there?" I asked.

"Yeah, it's a nice area. I just wanted something a bit more isolated."

I found that somewhat strange. I can understand someone wanting to have privacy, but he'd moved a pretty good distance away from his main client base. I imagined landscaping was a tough job that often required long hours. Who the hell would want to do such a long drive afterward?

"I heard Daphne moved back to California," Alana said.

Tench said nothing.

"Have you considered it yourself? I know you guys were child-hood friends," she continued.

"I'm happy here," he said.

"When was the last time you were there?" I asked.

"It's been years," he said.

"You know, you should give Hani a call sometime. She'd probably be glad to hear from you," Alana said.

"I will," he said.

Tench reached into his wallet and removed a business card. He handed it to me.

"Just give me a shout when you're ready to start your project," he said.

He started to leave.

"I have a random question," I said.

Tench stopped.

"Sure, what is it?"

"Is everything okay between you and the Laskaris family? Hani told me you had somewhat of a falling out with Panos. Is that true?"

"No."

I could have accepted the one word answer, but it was the way he said it. He didn't say "no" like he was bewildered as to why I would ask such a thing. And without the confusion in his voice, I would have expected him to elaborate if the answer was, in fact, "no." He should have said something like, "No, I don't know why she would say that." Instead, he said "no" as if I had just asked him if he would like a red hot poker to the eyeball.

"So you were still talking to Panos up until he came back to Maui?" I asked.

"That's right," he said.

I shrugged my shoulders.

"Why'd you want to know?" Tench asked.

"Just wondering. It's no big deal," I said.

I looked at his business card.

"I'll give you a call soon," I said.

Tench nodded and left the restaurant.

"What was that all about?" Alana asked.

I explained to her my questions about why he would move so far from his work, as well as his insistence that he and Panos had been on good terms when Hani clearly remembered them no longer speaking to each other. Panos had told her, too, that he thought Tench was jealous of him. But jealous of what?

"Maybe he just didn't want to speak ill of the dead," she said.

"Maybe," I admitted.

"But Hani had to have been wrong. Tench was the one who told us about Hani's miscarriage and Panos thinking about calling off the wedding," Alana said.

She had me there.

Alana studied me.

"What are you thinking?"

"Nothing in particular. It's just a feeling."

"Describe it to me," she said.

"Hard to describe. There's just something about him that doesn't sit right with me."

"You think he's not telling you something?"

"Maybe. He just seems very guarded, and I don't know why," I said.

"Why wouldn't he be guarded? He doesn't know you."

"I know, but I don't understand why he's been so distant if he was supposedly a great friend of Panos. He didn't go to see him after Panos got back to Maui. He wasn't at the rehearsal party. He just told us he hasn't been back to California in years. Why would he blow off Panos' funeral. Hell, Kalena went to the funeral, and she was just the housekeeper. He didn't come to Hani's welcome home party either. You told me you invited him, right?"

"Yeah, but he said he had to work late."

"So his best friend's fiancée finally gets released from prison after being falsely accused of killing him, and Tench doesn't think to call even once?" I asked.

"I don't think he and Hani knew each other that well," she said.

"That just proves my point. Tench seems to have distanced himself from Panos and Daphne."

"What does any of this have to do with anything?"

"You have to admit it's a bit strange," I said.

"Maybe. Maybe not. People can drift apart. It's not uncommon."

"I guess," I said.

"Plus Tench and Daphne broke up. Maybe he felt awkward around Panos because of that."

We drove back to Alana's house, and I spent the night. She got up at some point to use the restroom, and when she climbed back into bed, she noticed I was still awake. I couldn't stop thinking about the conversations with Shae and Aaron Tench.

"You okay?" she asked.

"Just thinking about something."

I rolled over and looked at her.

"You want to go to Hana with me tomorrow?"

"Hana? What's in Hana?" she asked.

"Someone I need to see."

22

KALENA

THAT MORNING I ASKED ALANA AGAIN IF SHE WANTED TO DRIVE WITH me to Hana. I told her I was going to try to meet with Kalena, Panos' former housekeeper. Alana was hesitant to go. I didn't blame her. Although Hana is a beautiful little town, it's an all-day affair to drive there and back. The road to Hana twists and turns along the coast. It makes for gorgeous scenery with the rugged coastline, waterfalls, and black sand beaches, but it's also extremely slow going. There are many places where the two-lane road is so narrow you can only get one car through at a time. This causes severe backups. I didn't know how many times Alana had been to Hana, but I'm sure it was enough to not want to do the ride again, especially on her weekend off.

"Is this another one of your theories?" she asked.

"You say that like I'm crazy."

"No, your theories tend to be dead-on. That's why I'm thinking I need to go."

The drive took a few hours as expected. We took my car so we could enjoy the view better with the convertible's top down, but we passed through several rainstorms, so we constantly put the top back up. There was a good reason Hana was so green.

We found Kalena's house easy enough. It was a small place, maybe only one bedroom. I didn't know how much Panos and Daphne had paid her, but I didn't think it was much judging by the size of her home, which made the brand new blue Honda Accord in the driveway seem a touch out of place.

Kalena looked understandably surprised when she opened the door and saw Alana and me standing there, but she was gracious and invited us inside. The inside was neat and tidy. Despite the small space, it was free from clutter. We sat down on a comfortable sofa. Kalena sat in a chair across from us. There was no TV in the living room. I did see a couple of mystery books on the table in front of the sofa. There was a large window behind Kalena's chair. It offered a nice view of the thick, green palm trees outside.

"How's your family?" I asked. "Daphne said you moved back here to take care of them."

"They're fine," she said.

"So they don't live with you?" I asked.

"No, my son and his family live in a neighborhood not too far from here."

"He and his wife have kids?" Alana asked.

"Yes, two boys. Eleven and eight."

Kalena smiled, and it was obvious she was proud of them.

"I missed you on my last visit to see Daphne," I said. "I was sorry to see you go."

"I'm sure Ms. Daphne will do fine without me."

"She moved back to California. Did you know that?" I asked.

"No. I haven't spoken to her since I left."

"Does that make you feel relieved?" I asked.

"Why should it?"

"Sometimes when I've left jobs I didn't like, especially ones with bad bosses, I was kind of glad to know if they also left the area. Let's face it. You can sometimes run into them here or there, and it always makes for an awkward scene."

"We got along fine," Kalena said.

"Maybe," I said. "But Daphne mentioned to me that Panos was

really the main one who wanted you there. I thought maybe she didn't."

"She never said she didn't."

"That was a nice Honda in your driveway. Daphne bought you that car, didn't she?"

"No, I saved up for that," she said.

"I'm sure you can afford it. You just impress me as being a very practical person though. This house, for example, is small, but it's probably exactly what you need. Why pay for something more? Not like that car, though. It's not an extravagant vehicle, but it's probably more than you need."

"I've always wanted one," she said.

"And you deserve it. I just think Daphne bought it for you," I said.

"It was a going-away present. She said she wanted to thank me for all the time I worked for her and Panos."

"So she did buy it for you?" Alana asked.

"Yes," Kalena admitted.

"You always impressed me each time I visited. You always seemed to know what people wanted before they even asked you. That time Daphne asked you to bring me a lemonade, you had that glass to me in under a minute," I said.

Kalena smiled. She was clearly proud of her work reputation.

"But Daphne said you didn't have any lemonade already prepared. So you would have had to make some, and then put it in a glass with ice, and then walk through the house to get it to me. How could you have done that so fast?" I asked.

Kalena said nothing.

"I was thinking about that last night. The only way you could have been that fast was if you were listening to my conversation with Daphne. I didn't think you were just outside the room. We probably would have heard you. I couldn't figure it out, but now I think I know the answer."

I watched Kalena for a reaction. She was quiet, and she wouldn't make eye contact with me.

"It was the intercom in the room. You could hear us through the intercom. I saw Daphne fumble with the button when she first tried to call you. I think you had the button already pressed down. It probably sticks. Maybe that's how you found out you could listen to people through the intercom without them knowing. You liked to eavesdrop on the guests, didn't you?"

Kalena said nothing.

"I'm not judging. I think you just did it at first so you could serve Panos' guests better. You impressed him, which meant you got to keep your job, maybe even got better raises, but you did more than listen to the guests, didn't you? You listened in on Panos and Daphne too."

"Is that true?" Alana asked.

Kalena still said nothing.

"Daphne suspected that you knew, didn't she? That's why she bought you that car. She was buying your silence."

"I told you it was a thank-you gift," Kalena said.

"You heard about Peter Bell, didn't you? That's why you're afraid."

Kalena nodded.

"Daphne's in California. She can't hurt you," Alana said.

"You don't know her," Kalena said.

"I think what saved you is that you're too close to her. There's nothing connecting her to Peter Bell, but if you show up dead, that's a different story. That's when the police start snooping around her house," I said.

"You don't know her," Kalena repeated.

"You heard something over that intercom. What did you hear?" I asked.

"I didn't hear anything," she said.

"We need to know, Kalena. If Daphne hurt someone, we need to know," Alana said.

"Daphne and Panos fought about the wedding, didn't they?" I asked.

She said nothing.

"Did they fight about something?" Alana asked.

"She didn't want him to marry Hani," she said.

"Why not?" Alana asked.

"She kept saying Panos promised her."

"What did he promise?" Alana asked.

"I don't know," Kalena said.

"Do you know why Panos went to the marina that night?" I asked.

"Sometimes he would sleep on his boat, especially if they were fighting," Kalena said.

"Who? Hani and Panos?" Alana asked.

"No, Panos and Daphne."

"That night of the party, did Panos and Daphne have a fight?" Alana asked.

Kalena nodded.

"They fought right before he left the house," she said. "It was awful."

"Do you know what they argued about?" I asked.

"The wedding. She couldn't believe Panos was going to marry Hani. She said, 'You promised me.'"

"What about Aaron Tench?" I asked. "Why did he and Daphne break up?"

"I don't know," Kalena said.

"You may not have heard, but you know why," I said.

Alana turned to me.

"What are you talking about?" Alana asked.

"He found out. That's why he left her. That's why he moved across the island and stopped speaking to Panos."

I turned to Kalena.

"He found out, didn't he?" I asked.

Kalena said nothing.

"Please tell us. Tell us what you heard," I said.

Kalena looked away.

"We'll protect you," Alana said.

"You liked Panos, didn't you?" I asked.

Kalena nodded.

"Don't do it for us, Kalena. Do it for Panos. The truth needs to come out," I said.

Kalena turned back to us, and then she told us everything.

23
___

WINE COUNTRY

ONE OF THE FEW BAD THINGS ABOUT LIVING IN MAUI IS THAT FLIGHTS
back to the mainland tend to be red-eyes. I generally can't sleep on
planes, and this flight was no different. Fortunately, I got an aisle seat,
so at least I wasn't crushed between two other people or pinned
against the curved wall of the plane. I landed in San Francisco at the
crack of dawn. The airport was quiet, and all of the shops and restau-
rants were still closed. I rented a car and drove down to wine country.
I'd never been to this part of California, although I have several
friends who've described it to me. I believe the word they most
frequently used was "spectacular." However, now that I was seeing it
for the first time, I didn't think that description did it justice. It easily
rivaled Maui in beauty. I wished I could have enjoyed it more than I
did, but my mind was preoccupied with the conversation I was about
to have. Confrontation might be a more accurate description, though.

I passed several wineries before I arrived at the Laskaris Winery. I
drove down a curved, paved road that took me past acres of vineyards
and the large cabin that served as a place to have a wine tasting. The
Laskaris private home was in the back of the estate. It was three
stories high and easily ten thousand square feet. People obviously
enjoyed their wine, and the Laskaris family benefited handsomely.

I rang the doorbell, and their butler, I guess that's what you'd call him, answered. He was a few inches taller than me, probably around six foot five, but he weighed about forty to fifty pounds less than me. I didn't know how his skeletal frame allowed him to remain upright. At first I wondered if the guy was sick or something, but his voice was strong, and his eyes were bright. He led me to a sitting room in the back of the house that overlooked the vineyard. The room reminded me of a larger version of the one Panos built for his mother on Maui, and I assumed this room was the inspiration for the latter. There was a large bookshelf on one wall. I looked over the framed photographs. They were different shots than the ones in Maui, but they still showed Panos as a child and Panos and Daphne together as teenagers. The room also had a large sofa and two comfortable-looking chairs.

"May I offer you a beverage or snack?" the butler asked.

"No, thank you," I said.

"Very well. Please don't hesitate to ask if you change your mind. I'll inform Ms. Laskaris you're here."

The butler gave me a small bow and exited the room.

I was here to see the younger Ms. Laskaris, and I waited a full twenty minutes before Daphne graced me with her presence. Ironically enough, she was wearing the same low-cut white dress she'd worn on my last visit. Her tan seemed even richer, though, and those tempting inches of her cleavage were still present.

"I was stunned when they told me you'd arrived this morning," she said.

Daphne walked across the room and gave me a hug.

"I decided to do a little tour of wine country. Thought I'd pop in and say hello," I said.

"You should have called first. I could have planned a full day for us," she said.

"Oh, that won't be necessary. My return flight is this afternoon."

"When did you arrive?" she asked.

"Just this morning."

"I don't understand. You're here for less than a day?"

"Do you mind if we sit?" I asked.

"Of course not."

Daphne and I both sat down. She was doing a good job of hiding the anxiety I was certain she was feeling. I wasn't sure how I was doing, though. I felt a slight sickness in the pit of my stomach. I thought about delaying the jump into why I was there. I could bring up the weather in Maui, discuss how I wished she'd told me she was moving, maybe even talk about the View restaurant and her decision to raise the rent on Wes and Jim, but what would be the point really? I was either going to be able to get her to admit to her role, or I wasn't.

"Has it been stressful?" I asked.

"Has what been stressful?"

"Wondering if you'd gotten away with it."

"Gotten away with what?"

Daphne smiled, and I knew the game was on.

"Makani was a weak guy. I hate to say that since he's not here to defend himself anymore. That was how you managed to talk him into it, isn't it? But it's also why you had to go with him. You couldn't count on him to follow through with it on his own."

"I don't know what you're talking about," she said.

"You really should have asked me to continue the investigation. If you had, I probably never would have tied you to it."

"How do you think I'm tied to it?" she asked.

"You've got your hands all over it. I don't think there was one element you personally didn't oversee."

"Did you stop by for a wine tasting before you came here because you must be drunk or something?"

I smiled. Part of me really liked this lady. I appreciated intelligence and a good sense of humor, but who doesn't?

"Peter Bell didn't impress me as a dumb guy. If he was going to shake someone down for the murder of Panos, it had to be someone with money. Makani doesn't scream money to anyone. Then there's Kalena. She knew, or at least, she suspected," I said.

"You've been talking to Kalena? What does she think she knows?"

"About you and Panos, of course. Aaron Tench knew too. After our conversation with Kalena, we stopped by Tench's house. He was a lot harder to get to talk. That's the thing about loyalty. Even though he wanted Panos out of his life, he was still loyal to Panos' memory. He eventually described an evening the three of you had. You went out drinking and stumbled back to your house. At some point in the night, Tench woke up and you weren't in the bed, so he went looking for you. He found you on top of Panos."

Daphne laughed.

"Let me get this straight. You're accusing me of having an affair with Panos?" she asked.

"It was the reason Tench broke up with you. He was so worried he'd run into you or Panos that he even moved to the other side of the island. He refused to talk to either of you, despite Panos calling him over and over again. I was a little confused at first because Tench knew so many details about Panos, such as Hani's pregnancy, and then Tench told me that Panos would email him all the time, trying to get Tench to change his mind about cutting him out of his life. He told Tench all those details about himself and his problems. I suspect it was to garner sympathy from Tench. Kalena also confirmed your affair to us. She heard you the morning of the wedding rehearsal. I believe the quote was, 'You think you're going to keep screwing me after you get married.' You didn't use the word 'screwing' though."

Daphne said nothing.

"You also told him he promised you something. What was it? I'm guessing he promised he wouldn't marry Hani," I said.

"You came all the way here to repeat some lie the maid and my bitter ex-boyfriend told you. Kind of sad, Poe."

"I really don't care that you were sleeping with Panos. It's none of my business, but I do care that you tried to frame Alana's sister. The police report said there was no sign of forced entry at Hani's house, but someone had to have gotten in that house to plant the flashlight. I was pretty mad at myself for not figuring that out sooner. You had a key, or it might be better to say Panos had a key. Since you two lived together, it wasn't hard to get your hands on it. Maybe you even secretly made a copy. You simply drove over to her house when she was staying with Alana, let yourself in, and then left the flashlight in the garage for the police to find. It was overkill, though, wasn't it? The flashlight was so obviously planted, and it made me realize someone other than Makani was also involved. He never would have framed Hani. He loved her too much, but you couldn't resist the urge to take out an enemy. Why didn't you just toss the flashlight in the ocean with the knife? Did you really hate Hani that much?"

"I think the pressure of this case has gotten to you. You're creating these bizarre theories that no one in their right mind would believe."

"Maybe, but here's what the police will believe. Makani didn't just confess the crime on video. He also told his brother Kai. Except his confession to Kai was much more elaborate. He said you helped him."

"Nothing but Kai's word against mine."

"Not really. There's that payment to Kai you made to keep his mouth shut. I assume he wasn't as greedy as Peter Bell. His tastes aren't quite as large. He closed his surf shop after you left. Word was there just was not enough business, which makes sense to me. Had you ever been to his shop? It's tucked in the back of this depressing little strip mall. No one could see it from the road. Here's the interesting thing, though. Kai bought a new car despite having just closed his struggling shop. So Kai gets a car. Kalena gets a car. Where's all this money coming from? I imagine you considered killing Kai too. You knew you couldn't trust him. He's too much of a hothead, but it wouldn't make sense to anyone to pin that death on Makani. He wouldn't kill his own brother. The guy was practically his full-time bodyguard. Peter Bell is another story, though. You weren't about to give him anything, especially since you knew he had a gambling problem. It would only be a matter of time before he came back demanding another payment. He'd be like an albatross hanging around your neck for the rest of your life."

"It's my understanding Peter Bell was killed during a robbery," she said. "It had nothing to do with Panos' death."

"A robbery where a three-thousand-dollar watch is left out in the open? No, the only thing that was stolen from Peter was the laptop where he had the security footage of your car driving Makani to the marina to kill Panos."

Daphne laughed.

"I drove Makani to the marina? And how would I even know Panos was there?"

"Because that's where he always went after you two fought. He knew you were furious with him, so after he left Shae's apartment, he drove straight to the marina."

I saw the look of confusion on Daphne's face.

"That's right. While you were talking Makani into killing Panos, Panos was having sex with Shae at her apartment. Did you even know about Shae?" I asked.

Daphne said nothing.

"It was easy to get Makani riled up. Panos had just humiliated him at the party, and you probably convinced Makani he could be with Hani again after Panos was gone. The guy was desperate to get her back. He'd do anything, especially kill the guy she was about to marry."

"You have no proof of anything," she said.

"No proof? I have video of your car at the marina. I recognized it, and I barely know you. Peter Bell surely knew your car too. It must have been fairly easy for him to put it all together. Did you actually think Peter Bell made only one copy of the security footage? He might have had a serious gambling problem, but he wasn't stupid. He made a second copy that he mailed to his sister. She lives in Seattle by the way. It was fairly easy for me to track her down. She was out of the country for several weeks on a business trip. That's why she was late opening the package he mailed. He specifically mentions you in a note."

I wondered if this would be the time Daphne jumped out of her chair and attacked me, but to her credit, she remained calm.

"I'm not wearing a wire," I said.

I stood and lifted up my shirt.

"I also turned off my phone. You can see for yourself."

I reached into my pocket and removed my phone. I placed it on the table in front of us. Daphne hesitated a moment, and then leaned forward and pressed the button on the bottom of the phone to confirm it was off. I sat back down.

Daphne stood and walked over to the door. At first, I thought she was leaving the room, but she simply closed the door and walked back to her chair.

"So what now?" she asked.

She sat down and crossed her legs like she was some high-powered executive in a business negotiation.

"I go to the police, and you get arrested," I said. "By the way, why not pay Kai to kill Peter Bell? Why do it yourself?"

"It wasn't my intention to bring Kai in at all. But I should have realized that little shit Makani would blab."

"Do you feel no remorse for killing Peter?"

"Why should I? He tried to blackmail me."

Daphne laughed.

"You should have seen the look on his face. I opened the briefcase, and he expected to see stacks of money. Instead, he saw a gun."

"Clever. You have a flair for the dramatic," I said.

"Let's cut to the chase. Name your price."

"My price?" I asked.

"You just said you haven't gone to the police. I assume that's because you're following in the footsteps of Peter Bell. How much do you want?"

"Funny you should mention Peter Bell. I take it that's your not-so-subtle hint of how I'll end up should I cross you."

"I would never threaten you, Poe. I actually like you. I just wish you'd taken me up on my offer of having a little fun on Maui. Why didn't you? Was it your commitment to Alana?"

"Something like that," I said. "Did you actually love Panos?"

"My feelings for him are none of your business," she said.

"Understandable. It's just my curiosity getting the better of me. I really was wondering what he promised you."

I turned to the wall behind me.

"Did you get enough?" I yelled.

Daphne was confused by me yelling toward the intercom in the room, but a second later, the door opened, and Alana walked in with two California police officers. I apologize for not mentioning Alana was on the flight with me, as well as the drive to the winery, but I didn't want to spoil the surprise.

"Arrest her," Alana said.

The two police officers walked over to Daphne. They hauled her to her feet.

"By the way, Daphne, there was no other video. Peter Bell was an only child," I said.

I could see the fury building behind Daphne's eyes.

"I wasn't wired, but I employed a little trick Kalena taught me. She maneuvered the talk button on the intercom so it would stay depressed. Alana and these two police officers were in the other room recording our entire conversation."

"It came through loud and clear," Alana said.

"You son of a bitch," Daphne said.

She struggled to get to me.

"Don't feel that bad. They had enough to arrest you with the payment to Kai. I just wanted to make sure you went down for the murder of Peter Bell too."

Panos' mother entered the room.

"I think your trust fund just got canceled, Daphne," I said.

"It's all lies," Daphne told her aunt.

Mrs. Laskaris said nothing. She just turned away from Daphne and walked out of the room. In full disclosure, I'd already called Mrs. Laskaris before my arrival. I told her everything, including the sexual affair between Panos and Daphne. It gave me no pleasure to reveal these secrets about her beloved son, but I didn't know how else to justify Daphne's jealousy of the other women, especially Hani, and how that jealousy and anger eventually led to her arranging the murder of Panos. Mrs. Laskaris was also integral in catching her niece's potential confession on audio. She arranged for the butler to bring me to the sitting room, and she rigged the intercom to permanently broadcast to the other room where Alana and the police were hiding. Mrs. Laskaris also suggested we hide a second recording device under the table in the sitting room in case the audio didn't come in clear over the intercom. I appreciated her willingness to help, as well as her ability to not immediately confront Daphne before I had an opportunity to try to drag a confession out of her.

Alana and I watched the two police officers escort Daphne away in handcuffs.

"Nice work," Alana said.

"Thanks. I didn't think I was going to get it out of her."

"She was dying to tell you. She's too arrogant not to."

"Want to change our flight? Stay a few days in wine country?" I asked.

"Love to. Let's do it. What was that about you and her having a little fun by the way?"

"That? That was nothing."

Alana looked at me like she didn't believe me, and then decided to drop it.

Before we left the winery, we walked about a hundred yards behind the house where Panos and his father were buried side by side. There were several large trees around the small family cemetery. Mrs. Laskaris was there.

"I asked you to find my son's killer. You did that. Thank you," she said.

"For what it's worth, she didn't kill him," I said.

"No, but she lured the one who did there. It's the same thing in my book. I always knew she loved him."

"I'm sorry you had to hear all of that."

"Daphne came to live with us when she was just fourteen years old. Panos was fifteen. It was the first time they had met because their fathers had been feuding for so long. A couple of years after she moved here, I caught her and Panos together. I was furious, of course, and I forbade them to be together that way. But I thought it was mostly teenagers experimenting. I had no idea it was still going on. Panos had many flaws, but I loved him."

"We know," Alana said.

"What will happen now?" Mrs. Laskaris asked.

"Daphne will be extradited back to Maui where she'll stand trial for killing Peter Bell and being an accessory to the murder of Panos."

Mrs. Laskaris nodded.

We stayed by the gravesite for several more minutes, and then we said goodbye to her.

24

JOB OFFERS AND SAILING LESSONS

Alana and I spent our limited time in wine country touring two or three wineries per day. We did wine tastings and had picnics outside. We changed our flight a second time and hung out in San Francisco for a few days after that. We did the usual tourist thing, including walking around Fisherman's Wharf, driving down Lombard Street, and touring Alcatraz. We even walked across the Golden Gate Bridge. I thought the strong winds might blow us away, but you couldn't beat the view. It was a nice last-minute vacation, and I was more than grateful that Alana's department gave her the time off.

I got my cast removed a few days after my return to Maui. My arm still felt weak. I could have sworn it was a bit smaller than the other, but I was glad to have that annoying hunk of plastic removed.

As I was leaving the doctor's office, I got a call from Mara Winters, Hani's attorney. She invited me to join her for lunch. Ironically enough, it was the same sushi restaurant in Kahului I ate at with Alana on my last return trip to Maui.

I entered the restaurant and was pleasantly surprised to see Detective Glen Adcock in a direct line between myself and Mara, who was in the back of the room. I approached Adcock as he wolfed down a spicy tuna roll.

"Hello, Detective," I said.

"So what smartass comment do I get to hear today?" he asked.

"No rude comments. Just wanted to say hello."

"I suppose you expect an apology from me or something. Well you're not going to get one," he said.

"You were just doing your job, and we all make mistakes, maybe just not as often and as monumental as you do. Good day, Detective. Enjoy your lunch."

Adcock gave me a two word response that I shall not repeat here so I don't offend those readers who are easily offended. But for those of you who have to know, it started with an *f* and ended with a *u*.

I continued my journey to Mara's table. She stood, and we shook hands. The waitress approached, and Mara ordered first. I then ordered my usual and a glass of water.

"Thank you again for representing Hani," I said.

"I should be thanking you," she said.

"Well, I like to think if she had gone to trial, you would have displayed your talent for the courtroom and gotten her free."

"Thank you," she said. "Alana filled me in on what happened in California. Very impressive."

It was now my turn to say "thank you."

"What did you want to see me about?" I asked.

"Have you heard the phrase 'the poor are crazy, but the rich are eccentric'?"

I nodded.

"My firm represents a wide variety of clients, many of whom are eccentric. Sometimes they have certain issues that need services more than I can currently provide. Many of these services should probably be brought to the attention of the local police, but the department has a few problem officers, like Glen Adcock over there, who love to leak embarrassing details about the rich to the media. I assume jealousy has a lot to do with it. Unfortunately, I can't stop the leaks. I was thinking, though, it would be a good idea if I could offer you as an alternative."

"I'm not sure I'm following you," I said.

"From time to time, I'd like to hire you to investigate certain issues my clients may be having. You would, of course, have to keep everything strictly confidential, but if you did have to go to the police, I like the fact you have an inside source who would respect our request for handling these matters in a delicate fashion."

"You're referring to Alana."

"Of course. I certainly wouldn't expect her to do anything illegal. I just like the fact that you could keep a member of the police informed without the whole department knowing about it."

"Your offer sounds interesting," I admitted.

"Good. We'll take it on a case-by-case basis. You can base your fee on the complexity of the investigation. We'll mark it up and pass the expenses on to the client. I'll let you know when something pops up that could use your expertise. You're free to say no at any time."

A few days after my lunch with Mara, I signed up for sailing lessons. It was an intensive course, but I felt pretty confident by the end, and it gave me the certification I needed to be able to rent a boat from the marina staff.

I invited Alana to sail with me the weekend after I completed the course. She was a bit hesitant, which I can understand, but she agreed in the end. I didn't rent a huge sailboat, but it was big enough for Alana, me and Maui. It also had a motor should I get us in a tough spot.

I didn't tell Alana my planned course, but she laughed when we rounded the coast and came upon the secluded beach Panos had brought us to last time. I dropped the anchor and lowered the ladder over the side.

"Care for a swim?' I asked.

I removed my swimsuit, grabbed Maui the dog, and hopped overboard.

"He doesn't need a life jacket?" she joked.

"I think all dogs just know how to swim," I said.

Maui is small, though, so I helped him get to shore. He took off running up and down the beach the moment his paws hit the sand.

I watched Alana remove her swimsuit and dive overboard. We spent a few hours on the beach, alternating between sunbathing and wading into the water to cool down. Maui found a patch of shade under a palm tree. He spent most of his time sleeping on his back.

Once the sun got lower in the sky, we swam back to the boat and motored back to the marina. It was a glorious afternoon, and I was convinced I'd discovered my next hobby beyond photography. Unfortunately, this was a much more expensive hobby, but I had no plans to purchase a boat. As they say, the two greatest days in a person's life are the day they buy their boat and the day they sell it.

Alana had an early start scheduled for the next morning, so I drove her home from the marina. When I got back to the house, I found Foxx lying on the sofa, watching another one of those murder shows on the Discovery Channel.

"What is it with you and these shows?" I asked.

"They're candy for the brain. You don't have to think that hard," he said.

"Apparently. Where's Michelle?"

"Ah, I don't know. We've been kind of cooling things off," he said.

"Really, why's that?" I asked.

"More me than her. I just don't want to settle down. She was talking about moving in here. I've got you and the dog here. Where was she going to go?"

"Don't let me get in the way. If you want her here, I can easily find another place," I said. "Unless you were just using us as an excuse."

Foxx pointed at me.

"There's my perceptive guy," he said.

"Got it," I said.

"By the way, a letter came for you."

Foxx leaned over and picked up an envelope off the table in front of the sofa. He tossed me the letter. It spun in a circle and landed a few feet from me. Maui the dog raced to it and grabbed it in his mouth. He took off toward the bedroom.

"Come on, dog," I said.

Foxx laughed.

I followed the dog into my bedroom. He ran under the bed, so I couldn't reach him. I left the room and got him a treat to lure him out. It worked, and I was able to retrieve the letter, now torn at the edges, while he chewed on the rawhide bone.

I saw my name and address on the envelope. The return address listed the name of a prison. I opened it and saw it was from Daphne. There was only one sentence handwritten on the paper.

He promised to marry me.

DID YOU LIKE THIS BOOK?
YOU CAN MAKE A DIFFERENCE.

Reviews are the most powerful tools an author can have. As an independent author, I don't have the same financial resources as New York publishers.

Honest reviews of my books help bring them to the attention of other readers, though.

If you've enjoyed this book, I would be grateful if you could write a review.

Thank you.

ACKNOWLEDGMENTS

Thanks to you readers for investing your time in reading my story. I hope you enjoyed it. Poe, Alana, Foxx, and Maui will return.

ABOUT THE AUTHOR

Robert W Stephens is the author of the Murder on Maui series, the Alex Penfield novels, and the standalone thrillers The Drayton Diaries and Nature of Evil.

You can find more about the author at robertwstephens.com.

Visit him on Facebook at facebook.com/robertwaynestephens

ALSO BY ROBERT W. STEPHENS

Murder on Maui Mysteries

Aloha Means Goodbye (Poe Book 1)

A gruesome murder. A friend framed. One detective races to stop another bloody masterpiece.

Edgar Allan "Poe" Rutherford just lost his job, his girl, and his chance at a relaxing island vacation. When the brutal murder of a celebrity artist is pinned on his friend, Poe refuses to lose his best buddy to the Maui penitentiary. As he works his way down the gallery guest list, he navigates through bloated egos, heated rivalries, and more than a few eccentric personalities along the way. But he never expected the hunt for truth to reveal a second chance at love.

Wedding Day Dead (Poe Book 2)

A marital murder. A guest list of suspects. Just another night on Maui. Poe has just started his new life on Maui. He's moved in with his best friend and he's dating the woman of his dreams. But when Detective Alana Hu's ex-boyfriend comes to town, Poe discovers more than a few secrets that rain down on his corner of paradise. It's all he can think about until a member of the wedding party is fatally stabbed.

Blood like the Setting Sun (Poe Book 3)

A death threat. A birthright on reserve. Can Poe stop a wealthy hotel mogul from checking out?

When an elderly hotel mogul claims to have received threatening letters, Poe chalks it up to old age. But as the threats continue to escalate, he investigates the real possibility that one of her adult children heirs wants her dead... but which one?

Hot Sun Cold Killer (Poe Book 4)

An old murder. A new threat. Can Poe find the killer before it's too late? When a client asks Poe to look into a decade-old death on the beach, he can't help but be intrigued. The police ruled it a suicide, but it's up to him to prove otherwise. As soon as Poe takes the case, people related to the victim start turning up dead--a sure sign that he's on the right track. But can Poe identify the killer... before he becomes the next victim?

Choice to Kill (Poe Book 5)

A murder close to home. A case that seems open and shut. Will Poe's rush to judgment make his fiancé the next victim? Poe didn't think twice when he took his fiancé's case. After all, Detective Alana Hu had known the victim since childhood. Besides, the evidence is easy to decode: all signs point to the victim's estranged husband. As Poe works to get the killer behind bars, he can't help but be distracted by his fast-approaching wedding. But Maui beaches have a knack for luring people into a false sense of security, and Poe's error could extract the highest cost imaginable. After all, you can't have a wedding... without the bride.

Sunset Dead (Poe Book 6)

A murdered mistress. A wrongful arrest. Can Poe and Alana take down a killer from both sides of the law? Poe can't stand to take another case after his last one nearly killed his wife. When he's accused of murdering his supposed mistress, he's forced back into a familiar role to prove his innocence. But can he do it from behind bars?

Ocean of Guilt (Poe Book 7)

A murdered bride. A suspicious groom. Can Poe catch the killer before the anchor drops? Poe is ready to dive back into his work as Maui's top private investigator. But before he can unpack his suitcase, his sister-in-law begs him to photograph her client's extravagant nautical wedding. Poe is confident he can handle the wedding party from hell, until he finds the bride's dead body on the top deck.

The Tequila Killings (Poe Book 8)

A deadly fall. A dodgy past. Can Poe uncover the truth before a match made in paradise ends in disaster? Poe has the luxury of picking and choosing the cases that spark his curiosity. So when his love-struck mother-in-law demands he trail her latest squeeze, he thinks he's wasting his time. Until a mysterious woman from the boyfriend's past falls off his balcony to her death.

Wave of Deception (Poe Book 9)

A beach execution. A devastating hurricane. Can Maui's best PI solve the case without his family members becoming the prime suspects? Poe is used to weathering difficult cases. And since the victim is his sister-in-law's abusive ex-boyfriend, Poe hopes nobody looks too hard at his own compelling motive. Ignoring the sound advice to keep his nose out, Poe spars with the island's newest police detective who seems to have her own hidden motivations, especially when she asks Poe to help her with another case. Poe has never taken on two murder investigations at once. But as he gets closer to the truth, will he like the answers he finds?

The Last Kill (Poe Book 10)

Lights. Camera. Murder. When lies become reality, can Poe find the truth before a killer strikes again? As Maui's best private investigator, Edgar Allan "Poe" Rutherford understands the importance of keeping a low profile. That becomes impossible when a new reality TV show comes to the island, which features an eccentric handful of divorcees looking for love. But when one of the women is poisoned to death, the show's production comes to a grinding halt. At the same time, a few miles down the beach, a divorce attorney is stabbed multiple times while she sits on a lounge chair and watches the sun set over the Pacific Ocean. The methods of murder, as well as the victims, couldn't be more different, yet Poe has a sneaking suspicion they're somehow related.

Mountain of Lies (Poe Book 11)

A cold body. A warm paradise. A murder with more than one culprit. Private investigator Edgar Allan "Poe" Rutherford is worried. His latest client may have committed homicide, and sharing his suspicions with his detective wife is an argument he'd rather not have. But when she arrests his new employer, catching the true perpetrator means keeping it in the family. Never one to let loose ends go untied, Poe's off-the-record investigation uncovers another suspect connected to foul play from years before. And now he's not sure if he's solving one lethal crime or two.

Rich and Dead (Poe Book 12)

Texas Hold 'em in paradise. A table full of suspects. The minimum bet could cost him his life. PI Edgar Allan "Poe" Rutherford is tired of taking down murderers. So, when a detective comes to him with a suspicious case of a millionaire who drove off a Maui cliff, he declines her request for help. But when the victim's scorned lover demands money in exchange for information, Poe is pulled back into the game. Demanding answers from the selfish vulture, the relentless private eye uncovers a connection to a high-seas, high-stakes illicit poker ring. And after he discovers the vicious men involved, he's convinced the death was no accident. But to find the murderer, the charming PI needs to get on the yacht and take a seat at the table. Can the sharp-witted investigator flush out a sinister cabal before he's dealt a dead man's hand?

Alex Penfield Novels

Ruckman Road (Penfield Book 1)

To solve an eerie murder, one detective must break a cardinal rule: never let the case get personal. Alex Penfield's gunshot wounds have healed, but the shock remains raw. Working the beat could be just what the detective needs to clear his head. But when a corpse washes up on the Chesapeake Bay, Penfield's first case back could send him spiraling. As Penfield and his partner examine the dead man's fortress of a house, an army of surveillance cameras takes the mystery to another level. When the detective sees gruesome visions that the cameras fail to capture, he begins to wonder if his past has caught up with him. To solve the murder, Penfield makes a call on a psychic who may or may not be out to kill him. His desperate attempt to catch a killer may solve the case, but will he lose his sanity in the process?

Dead Rise (Penfield Book 2)

Detective Alex Penfield has to solve a murder case before it happens. His own. Retirement never suited Penfield, but there's nothing like a death omen to get you back in the saddle. A psychic colleague warns the detective that his own murder is coming. When a local death bears an eerie resemblance to the psychic's vision, he can't help but get involved. As the body count rises, the case only gets more unfathomable. Witnesses report ghastly encounters with a man sporting half a face. And the only living survivor from a deadly boat ride claims he knows who's to blame. There's only one problem: the suspect's been dead for 20 years.

The Eternal (Penfield Book 3)

Detective Alex Penfield has put away plenty of serial killers. He never expected to protect one.

Detective Alex Penfield is no stranger to crime scenes. But when he tracks down a killer, he discovers she's in a whole different league. And this assassin is far from alone. It turns out that Penfield's detective skills have uncovered a secret government program that's better left buried. And the men and women of that program have put a target on his back. To survive the day, Penfield's only chance is to trust a ruthless killer. He hopes his risky choice won't be the last one he ever makes.

Standalone Dark Thrillers

Nature of Evil

Rome, 1948. Italy reels in the aftermath of World War II. Twenty women are brutally murdered, their throats slit and their faces removed with surgical precision. Then the murders stop as abruptly as they started, and the horrifying crimes and their victims are lost to history. Now over sixty years later, the killings have begun again. This time in America. It's up to homicide detectives Marcus Carter and Angela Darden to stop the crimes, but how can they catch a serial killer who leaves no traces of evidence and no apparent motive other than the unquenchable thirst for murder?

The Drayton Diaries

He can heal people with the touch of his hand, so why does a mysterious group want Jon Drayton dead? A voice from the past sends Drayton on a desperate journey to the ruins of King's Shadow, a 17th century plantation house in Virginia that was once the home of Henry King, the wealthiest and most powerful man in North America and who has now been lost to time.

There, Drayton meets the beautiful archaeologist Laura Girard, who has discovered a 400-year-old manuscript in the ruins. For Drayton, this partial journal written by a slave may somehow hold the answers to his life's mysteries.

Made in the USA
Middletown, DE
03 May 2022

65208682R00146